Kyana h̶e̶ relationship with Ryker was over.

Their little practice hunt last night was meant to be the last before she set off to find Haven. Instead, he was standing in front of her, packed and ready to go and sexy as hell—freshly showered with his hair slightly damp and curling against the collar of his linen button-up, beach-bum shirt.

She couldn't figure out if she was annoyed that he'd be coming with her, or relieved. Both maybe. With Ryker, it was always that way. A jumble of contradictions that played havoc with her insides until she was confused by her own wants and fears.

She wasn't stupid. She knew why the gods were placing him with her again. He was his father's right-hand man, and Ares would have made certain Ryker knew his duty.

"So you're just my bodyguard? You don't have orders to kill Haven if I can't subdue her?"

That he wouldn't meet her gaze was enough for Kyana.

By Sable Grace

BEDEVILED
ASCENSION

BEDEVILED

A DARK BREED NOVEL

SABLE GRACE

A V O N

An Imprint of HarperCollinsPublishers

This is a work of fiction. Names, characters, places, and incidents are products of the author's imagination or are used fictitiously and are not to be construed as real. Any resemblance to actual events, locales, organizations, or persons, living or dead, is entirely coincidental.

AVON BOOKS
An Imprint of HarperCollins*Publishers*
10 East 53rd Street
New York, New York 10022-5299

Copyright © 2012 by Heather Waters and Laura Barone
ISBN 978-0-06-196441-1
www.avonromance.com

First Avon Books mass market printing: January 2012

Printed in the U.S.A.

10 9 8 7 6 5 4 3 2 1

To the first hero I ever met, my daddy. Thank you for loving me even though I'm a dreamer!
And, of course, to Kyle. As always.
—Heather

To Heather, who knows why. You're the greatest!
And to Carmine, for knowing all my faults and loving me in spite of them.
—Laura

Acknowledgments

A special thank you to our husbands for never reading what we write and, therefore, assuring we stay happily married.

We'd like to thank our agent, Roberta Brown, for her unrivaled support, and our editor, Erika Tsang, for liking Kyana enough to let her return to the page.

Brandy, Jess, and Kat—for always being there. Love you, Mom.

And Sydney and Hunter—for growing up so beautifully. Mom.

BEDEVILED

Prologue

aven Monroe's legs trembled as she looked over the black waters of the Atlantic. She couldn't remember coming here. Couldn't remember how her clothes had gotten soaked, or why her hair and skin felt sticky with salt water. But what worried her most was the three-pointed weapon in her hand, and why it was covered in blood.

She wasn't bleeding. It wasn't *her* blood.

This wasn't the first time something like this had happened. Over the last couple of days, her lapses in memory had grown more and more frequent.

Each time she'd tried to remember how she ended up in the strange places, she'd blacked out and had awakened somewhere new. And when she *was* aware of what was happening to her, her mind kept pulling forth images of a small trailer and the scent of beer and cigarettes, and the possibilities that her new strength could bring her.

*Go. Do what you've longed to do for twenty-seven
years!*

But she couldn't. A small piece of Haven clung
to the knowledge that, should she listen to that evil,
masculine voice that had been taunting her for
days, there would be no coming back to humanity.
Ever.

The thirst for revenge was so strong, she couldn't
shake free of it. Revenge on her father whose own
out-of-control rage had murdered her sister so
many years ago. Revenge on the world for giving
up on Haven when she'd tried so hard to keep it
safe.

And at the top of Haven's list, Kyana. No longer
just her closest friend, but her Sire. Kyana, a Half-
Breed Vampyre/Lychen with balls of steel and a
heart of concrete, had made her what she was now.
Had created the beast inside her in a misplaced at-
tempt to save her life, and Haven hated her for it.
She held on to the anger that had kept her com-
pany when the voices in her head left her alone.
She would rather have died than become what
Kyana had made her, and yet right now, Kyana was
Haven's only hope.

She closed her eyes, wishing the smell of blood
wasn't so strong. Wishing she could block out the
horrible feeling that came with the weapon in her
hand. She shouldn't even be able to touch it. But
there was a god inside her. An angry, hate-filled
god who wanted revenge of his own. She wanted
him out of her. Now. Wanted to lose the pain of her

skin stretching to encompass him, of her own soul shifting to make room.

If she could link to Kyana . . . Maybe it wasn't too late. Maybe revenge wouldn't need to be found on anyone . . .

They'd linked once before, and she had known the moment Kyana stepped into her head. But that had been days ago. She tried it now but nothing came. Kyana wasn't there when she needed her. Revenge sounded better and better.

"No! I am not this person!"

You are whoever I say you are.

The low, masculine baritone was a quiet scream.

"I am not your toy!"

You are whatever I say you are.

She again felt the floating sensation that had become as familiar as her breath. That blackness. The reason for her gaps in memory. She knew if she couldn't find a way to fight him, he'd consume her. Make her do things she couldn't remember.

How did one fight back when the darkest god ever to have lived had taken up residence in one's soul? If she'd ever suspected her powers as a Witch might leave her susceptible to this—gods save her . . . How could she have known?

He was speaking to her now, a cold whisper on the breeze lifting from the ocean. She nodded her compliance, told him she understood his commands though all she wanted was to scream that she wouldn't obey. She knew she would. She had no control anymore.

He was inside her, forcing her to smile, to caress the sharp points of the bloody weapon like a lover's body.

Poseidon's trident. She remembered.

And she couldn't push past his influence long enough to embrace the horror of what she'd done.

Of what she was about to do.

Chapter One

Kyana Aslan shook off the exhilaration shivering under her skin and tossed a grin at Ryker. The demigod smiled back, his teeth blindingly white in the shadows of Matanzas State Forest.

Becoming a goddess certainly had its perks. Like running fifty miles in under five minutes without the smallest hint of exhaustion. She'd only been the new Goddess of the Hunt for a day, and while she didn't yet have most of Artemis's powers, the little she did have made her old pacing look like . . . well, it was like trying to compare a wild Mustang to a sleek, gorgeous black Arabian. Both got you where you wanted to go quickly, but the Arabian got you there in style.

"Ky? You ready? We'll have to take them by surprise."

Ryker looked so incredibly yummy in his camos, it was difficult to concentrate. Wind-tousled blond hair fell over his silver eyes, casting a shadow across his well-sculpted profile making him look more like a statue of his father, Ares, than the half human he was.

This was only a scouting mission, an exercise to practice the few skills Kyana had inherited from Artemis. And she was loving every minute of it. Being allowed off Olympus for the first time in days was like being let out of a cage. Flying off with Ryker, whom she was coming to like more than she should, was just icing on the cake. That he was wearing those yummy camos was the creamy filling.

Ryker's expression of concentration was broken by the tiny smile teasing the corner of his full lips, the small fangs bestowed on all demigods glistening in the moonlight. He obviously knew what she was thinking, knew she was probably remembering what he looked like *out* of those camos, but he was gentleman enough not to mention it. Instead, he pointed to the meeting they'd come to intercept. She studied the clearing as he spoke instructions into her ear, though in all honesty, her blood was pounding too loudly to hear anything else.

If the informant who'd come to Artemis was right, this meeting was being held by those who supported the resurrection of Cronos, an ancient god who'd committed the ultimate sin of trying to off his sons, Zeus, Poseidon, and Hades. If they could catch one of these bastards and bring it in alive, maybe they'd be able to find and stop the person who was trying to bring Cronos back to life.

That person happened to be Kyana's closest friend in the world, which made this *practice* mission even more important.

Her determination settled more firmly in her gut as she peered into the darkness. There was enough of her old Vampyric blood in her to make scanning the trees effortless. Her gaze fell upon rising smoke half a football field away, and while she couldn't see the bodies, the tracer in her could sense them, feel them. She wanted to hunt them.

But the goddess in her wanted answers more than bloodshed.

She wiggled her toes inside her boots. "I'm ready. But I want to listen before we jump in. See if they mention Haven."

She didn't wait for Ryker's protest. A hundred-foot pine fell into her line of sight, almost exactly where she wanted to be. She didn't think her feet ever touched the forest floor as she sprinted the fifty yards, looked up at her branch, and sprang from her toes. When she landed in a crouch on top of the thick limb overhead, she wasn't even winded.

Pressing her belly to the rough branch, she slithered to the end where she could hang her head over, unseen. Pine needles poked through her leather vest and stabbed at her armpits, but she didn't stop to scratch. Soon, Ryker was there, lying flat on top of her as he too pressed himself low to watch.

"This wasn't the plan," he grumbled, his breath fanning her hair.

"Hush."

He'd wanted to strike immediately, to attack before the ceremony had even begun. Surprisingly, she'd been more patient. It went against her normal instincts to wait it out, but she was pretty sure listening and gathering more intel before rushing in was the smarter thing to do. Practice or not, she wanted something to take back to Olympus with her. Something that would help her prevent Haven from doing something too stupid to forgive.

Besides, the gods and goddesses were losing more of their powers every day. Anything Kyana could find out to stop their Chosen replacements from being picked off by Cronos's followers would be a boon.

She wiggled to get more comfortable. Big mistake. Ryker's groin stabbed against the backs of her thighs, and if he hadn't been plastering her to the tree, she probably would have been distracted enough to roll right off the branch and into the middle of the coven below.

His fingers bit into the back of her leg, pinning her in place. "Stop moving."

As a pair, they, apparently, were not built for a stakeout.

"From the fires of the Underworld, I offer you my wings!" The mutterings of the group grew louder and more coherent as a Hatchling lowered its black cloak to the ground and spread its wings to the skies. Thin, golden scales stretched out over spidery veins and bones, and his reptilian face glistened eerily in the shadowed light of the moon.

"I didn't know Hatchlings could speak," Kyana mumbled. "Did you know they could speak?"

Ryker nudged her and she shut up, watching as the being beside the Hatchling also lowered its cloak.

"My loyal offering . . . Take my sight!"

"What are they doing?" she whispered.

"Offering their strongest assets to aid in Cronos's return."

The creature tilted its long neck toward the treetops, its face contorted with agony as blood streamed from its black eyes.

"What the hell is that?"

"Damn it, Kyana, if they hear you . . ." He sighed and pressed his lips to her ear. "It's a Dark Seer. Now please shut up."

Kyana sucked in a gasp before it could escape. Seers weren't demons. They were humans born with the ability to see into the future—the equivalent of Oracles on Olympus but to a lesser, more mortal degree. But this thing didn't appear human. It had black, shriveled skin and looked more like a mummy than anything she had ever seen. Except, of course, for actual mummies.

As the nine others in the circle dropped their cloaks and offered their strengths to the god they prayed would return to them, Kyana listened, waiting to make her move. A hush fell over the group below and the fire blazing in their center danced as though they'd been heard by someone other than her and Ryker.

Cronos hadn't risen, and if she could do anything about it, he never would. But that didn't stop her from worrying. He was dead, yet he'd managed to find a way to circumvent that minor inconvenience and plan his own resurrection. She wasn't dumb enough to underestimate what he was capable of.

Even from the grave, he'd managed to turn Haven, the sweetest, most gentle Witch she had ever met, into a maniacal puppet. The pain of that crime was still so fresh and raw, Kyana wore it like lotion all over. Dead or alive, Cronos was a psychotic, dangerous mother trucker.

Haven was her best friend. That she'd kinda sorta turned Haven into a mix of Vampyre and Lychen to save her life hadn't changed that. Neither had the fact that her blood had driven Haven slightly cuckoo and now she was hell-bent on destroying the world on behalf of the dead-but-still-deadly god Cronos.

It was Kyana's job to hunt her down and bring her back to sanity before she accomplished that goal.

Maybe they *should* have stopped this meeting before it started as Ryker had wanted to. Maybe it *wasn't* wise to give them a chance to make progress toward Cronos's plan to come back.

"Can Cronos really accept what these things are offering?"

Ryker adjusted himself and leaned over her other ear. "They're not offering them to Cronos."

"Then who—" Kyana's blood went colder than usual. She didn't need him to answer. "Haven."

As he nodded, his chin rubbed against her hair, making her shiver. He groaned and tightened his hands on her hips to hold her still.

"But I don't think they have a clue what they're doing," he said. "Haven's not a god. She can't accept gifts like this."

Thank Zeus.

Kyana didn't need these buffoons making her job harder. She had only seven days before she'd lose her Vamp/Lychen abilities in exchange for full goddess-ship. Learning to become the new Goddess of the Hunt while trying to bring down the only real family she had was going to suck. Majorly.

Not willing to consider what would happen if she didn't meet her deadline, she focused on the group below her. One of the creatures down there had the information she needed, and she was determined to get it.

"Ready?" she asked, thrusting her butt in the air to buck Ryker off her back. When his weight disappeared, she pushed herself back into a crouch position and leaned her upper body over the limb. The branch was strong, but with both of them standing on it, their weight unevenly distributed, it cracked under their feet. If they weren't ready, the tree was.

"Give me a minute." He pointed down at the

circle of Cronos groupies. "They're about to start their closing chant. When you hear the final hum, go. I'll be right there with you."

Before she could ask where the hell he thought he was going, he was gone. She caught a flash of blond hair from the corner of her eye, and watched its trail swing through the tree branches to the opposite side of the clearing.

Tarzan. *Me likey.*

The branch crackled again. She sucked in her breath and focused on the chanting, waiting for the hum Ryker seemed to think she'd recognize. But then the bottom fell out from under her feet. Instinct brought her hands straight up, and she clawed at the branch hanging overhead just before the broken limb beneath her tumbled into darkness, crashing smack in the center of the coven.

"Shit shit shit."

She swung herself up to a sturdier branch and swore she heard Ryker mimic her curses. There was no more waiting. She dropped, catching another branch in her hands, and swung out and over the coven, swooping down upon their group to land gracefully on her feet. They closed in just as Ryker landed behind her.

Kyana was pissed. Not that her branch had given way, but that they were going to have to kill these traitors before they could force any useful information out of them.

"Can't leave you for a minute," he muttered, pressing his back to hers.

Furious that their ceremony had been interrupted, all eleven Dark Breed drooled and sputtered, practically frothing at the mouth in outrage. Two human-looking cowards fled, disappearing into the darkness, but the other nine stayed put. She tried to take them all in, to see what breeds they were to better prepare for their strengths and weaknesses, but other than the Dark Seer and the Hatchling, they all wore hoods that covered their features.

She hated fighting blind, but she had no choice.

A few of them flew backward as Ryker tapped into his telekinesis. She hadn't had time to learn such a thing and didn't even know if she ever could. It was going to have to be all sweat and fists for her.

She kicked out, catching one under the chin. Its hood fell off, revealing the face of another Hatchling. Black blood spewed from his mouth and his jaw to make a horrific crunching noise before falling open at a disjointed angle. He came at her, his orangey wings open and his claws outstretched like an eagle dipping in for its prey.

She ducked. The Hatchling tumbled over her and as it landed on its back, she slid her dagger from her boot and shoved it between the beast's ribs. It released a long, soft sigh before it stopped breathing altogether.

Ryker sent two more crashing into each other, bashing them together so hard, one's skull split in two before it crumpled to the ground. She glanced at it long enough to see it had been a Lychen, killed mid-transformation with its wolf's muzzle protruding from a human face.

She turned back to her own fight as a dark, Mediterranean-looking man lunged at her. Instinctively, she brought her fist up and it lodged inside the man's throat. As he slumped to the ground, she jerked her hand free and stared in fascination at the sparkling orangish blood coating her hand.

"I think I just killed a Genie!"

Her momentary shock was broken as, from the corner of her eye, she saw the Dark Seer slip around one of his companions.

"Grab him!" she screamed. If they were going to let any of this coven live, the Dark Seer was their best choice. If they were lucky, he'd peek into the future and point them toward Haven, and if nothing else, he had the capacity to answer questions.

The Seer was smart, however, and braver than she'd given him credit for. As Ryker lunged to carry out her request, the Seer whipped a long sword from the pile of cloaks at his feet.

"I will die before betraying my god!" And with that, he shoved the blade into his heart and fell onto the dead Hatchling beside him.

Great.

They were down to three survivors. All of them looked nasty and incapable of speech, let alone conversation. One morphed into a human-looking male, naked and hairy from head to toe. A Shyfter.

Kyana grabbed his nape and shoved him to his knees. He smiled up at her, his yellow teeth bared, then shifted into an adder and slithered from her hold. He disappeared into the forest before she could react.

Two Dark Breed left: another Hatchling and an impure demon. A Half-Breed of some kind that didn't look as though he even possessed a tongue, his mouth nothing more than a tiny hole in his face.

Maybe the Hatchling could— Ryker twisted the Hatchling's head right off its shoulders.

"Damn it." She thrust her dagger into the remaining Half-Breed's throat and whipped around to face Ryker. "Did you have to kill them all?"

She was so damned angry, she wanted to find something else to kill. They were no closer to finding Haven than they'd been when Artemis's snitch had tipped them off about this ceremony.

"Me?" He pointed at the body that Kyana had just let fall to her feet. "You weren't exactly playing nice."

She scowled, kicked the dead body, and stepped over it. "He wasn't useful. *You* killed all the useful ones."

Ryker rolled his eyes at her. "Really? We're *really* going to debate this now?"

She sighed and pointed to the trees. "Let's go. Maybe I can still track the ones who escaped."

Ryker stooped and wiped his bloody hands on the grass. "No, you can't. You're out of ambrosia, and I'd give you maybe . . . ten more minutes before you're out of fuel."

He motioned in the direction of the camp they'd set up at dusk where they'd waited for night to fully envelop the forest. "Wait for me. I'll bring back whatever I can find."

"You're great in a fight, but you suck at tracking and we both know it. I'm not full goddess yet. I'm still eighty percent tracer."

"More like seventy percent," he muttered, gripping her arm and preventing her from marching off in search of the traitors they'd come for.

She snatched her arm away, frustration making her antsy as hell.

"Fine. Then let's go back to Artie's and see what other tip-offs she might have been given," Kyana said, picking a leaf from her hair.

"The Vamp?" Ryker asked, referring to the weaselly Dark Breed who'd come to Artemis yesterday with promises of information regarding Cronos's disciples in exchange for sanctuary. Kyana didn't trust traitors of any kind. If they could turn once, they could do it again, but right now, he was all they had.

"Yeah. Him. If there's going to be another circle like this one, he'll know about it."

"Then let's port out of here."

Kyana groaned. "Can't I just run back with my goddess mojo?"

"Your speed only lasts as long as your ambrosia does. And while you can get from point A to point

B quickly, you're still running. You can't just jump from point A to point Z."

"Whatever," she grumbled. "Let's just go."

She waited for him to draw his circle and grabbed hold of his sleeve. She barely had time to brace herself before she was sucked into his wormhole and blinded by white light.

Chapter Two

Kyana's hopes for a new lead had proved fruitless. The traitorous informant had been set loose to find another gathering of Cronos disciples in case tonight's stakeout went astray, which it obviously had. When he didn't return, Artemis's tracers had hunted him down and found him murdered, his insides no longer aptly named.

Frustration sat like spoiled cream in her belly as she tossed and turned in the bed Artemis insisted now belonged to her. The only thing new she'd learned tonight was that Genies really did exist. While interesting, that little tidbit wasn't going to do a damned thing to get her closer to Haven.

She couldn't quiet her mind long enough to focus on dreaming and perhaps linking with Haven again. There was too much to think about. Too much to strategize, contemplate, figure out.

She rolled onto her side, still nauseous from Ryker's port. Outside her suites, the rhythmic sounds of sentinels patrolling the halls clip-clopped their way past her door . . . disappeared . . . returned again. Everyone on Olympus was uneasy. It was the realm of Beyond, and yet no one here seemed to be any more capable of preventing the chaos in the world than the less powerful beings of Below, where the magical conducted daily life, and Above, where the humans resided.

While everyone here, Beyond, was eager to see Cronos defeated again, they were distracted with the task of trying to replace the weakened gods. Those who'd already been replaced were powerless to do much at all, like Artemis and Hades, who'd been replaced by one of Kyana's closest friends, Geoffrey. They spent their days tending the more mundane tasks and left their recruits to the hunt on their own. Soon, they'd be all but useless, destined to spend the rest of their eternity in some version of a retirement home for gods.

Kyana shuddered at the unpleasant thought. When it was her turn to pass on the powers of the Goddess of the Hunt in ten thousand years, would she be able to go gracefully into the night? Not likely.

So instead of having a realm full of powerful gods and goddesses focused on stopping Cronos, they had a weak group who was split between protecting humans, guarding the portals that allowed travel between realms, finding Chosen, and hunting Cronos.

None of this boded well for humans, nor for Kyana's ability to rest.

She should have asked Ryker to stay, but her pride had kept her quiet when he'd returned Below to his little beachside bungalow.

Now, as morning crept through her shuttered windows, she swung her legs off the bed and stood, drowsy and disoriented—still unused to needing so much sleep in the first place. As Vampyre, she'd needed a few hours' sleep a week. Now, she needed a few hours each day. It seemed stupid that any part of her would be weakened as a goddess, but that was the way it worked. She was going to have to get used to it and find her new strengths elsewhere.

Digging through her well-worn backpack, she sorted through the odds and ends Artemis had decided Kyana couldn't hunt without. She paused to wrap her blanket around her shoulders, still not used to the stark chill that seemed to hover in the temple's marble walls. Her real room was Above in St. Augustine, Florida. A little restored bed-and-breakfast she'd shared with Haven that oozed charm and personality.

That it had been a funeral parlor before being turned into a bed-and-breakfast in the last century had helped her consider it home. She had always favored the eccentric.

She sighed and eyed the array of items tumbling from the bag. There was definitely an arsenal here, but Kyana didn't know how to use much of it. It was all still so new to her—the need for ambrosia, the charms, baubles, powders, and potions. As a new day of tracking Haven loomed ahead, it was difficult to prepare when she didn't have the comfort of her own things.

Although she shouldn't complain. A few pieces of the leather attire she preferred had found their way into her new closet. As had a pair of new boots—the old ones lost to the ocean several days ago and still horribly missed.

She smiled despite the heaviness in her chest. That day hadn't been a total loss. Just before she'd discovered the disappearance of her boots, Ryker had screwed her senseless on the beach—a memory she was looking forward to repeating if they ever found another free moment to call their own.

Her smile wiped away as she stared at the gold-hilted dirks protruding from her bag. Her favorite weapons, a pair of handcrafted, silver-plated daggers that had been confiscated by Ares the night she'd been arrested for turning Haven, had yet to be returned. While she was skilled with any blade handy, her own were sorely missed. She knew the weight of them as well as she knew the scent of her own breath. They were as much a part of her as her fingers and toes.

Growing more depressed by the moment, she dutifully repacked all the items into her duffel. She had seven days and seven hours—make that five days and several hours now thanks to a wasted day spying on Cronos's disciples—before her Vampyre/Lychen skills would fade and she would become a full-blown goddess. She'd have to figure out how to use the tools given to her before then.

If Haven's life wasn't on the line—not to mention the fate of the world—Kyana would have enjoyed the challenge. But as it stood, she'd have to find Haven before that time elapsed. Otherwise, she'd have to fight as an untrained goddess, and that could get a bit sticky. Haven had been an amazing fighter when the only breed inside her had been Witch. Now that she was Witch, Lychen, and Vamp, there was no telling what sort of skills she'd picked up, or which breed would dominate and come out to play.

Artemis entered the room, pulling Kyana out of her thoughts. "You're up early."

"Couldn't sleep."

Artemis's smile warmed the cool room. "Me either. This burden I've placed on your shoulders isn't a light one. Do you regret accepting it?"

Kyana shoved a rogue bottle of ambrosia into her bag. "No."

"Good." She glanced at the backpack. "You'll be leaving soon, I take it?"

Seeing that Artemis wasn't going to take the hint that Kyana wanted to be left to her thoughts, she plopped onto her bed and sighed. "Until I have Haven safely back where she belongs, I can't rest. You have to know that."

"I do. But I worry I haven't taught you enough."

"I could sit here with you for a year and still not know all you can teach me." And as daunting as that was, it was the truth. There was so much magic within Artemis that Kyana hadn't even yet glimpsed within herself. She had no knowledge of what to do when that magic began to seep into her blood, and as much as she liked power, the thought of having so much of it pumping inside her was kind of intimidating.

Artemis was annoyingly apologetic about Kyana's lack of training. But there'd been no time. After her trial, she'd had only one day to adjust to her new fate before Artemis had requested she and Ryker visit the ceremony in the forest.

Besides, they both knew she'd been a last resort as a Chosen. Haven had been meant to be Artemis's Chosen. Then Kyana had gone and made Haven all wolfy and Vampy, and Artemis decided she would take Haven's place as the Goddess of the Hunt's successor. Artie always seemed to believe in her, even when Kyana herself didn't.

Artemis pointed to the bag. "Have you thrown in plenty of ambrosia? The last thing we need is for you to be caught without it. But stop and check every now and then. Make certain none of the vials have broken in your bag."

"I know," she muttered.

Each vial was wrapped in layers of soft cloth to assure none of the liquid spilled on her belongings. Undiluted ambrosia was deadly to gods. It had to be consumed with food. Any other contact was painful at best, fatal at worst.

Kyana shifted another wrapped vial in her bag. It rolled out of the cloth and she started the whole process of securing it all over again. Holding the pink tube in her hand, she held it up to the light.

"If this stuff is so powerful, why can't the gods just keep drinking it and forget about finding replacements?"

"Because the power within us that feeds off the ambrosia is fading. Our vessels—our bodies—are no longer young enough or strong enough to harbor what we were given at birth. Without that power, ambrosia has nothing to feed off of." Tears welled in the goddess's eyes as she continued. "There is so much you need to know if we hope for this hunt to be a success."

Kyana hated being a constant reminder to all that Artemis was giving up. Not that she wasn't going to enjoy the hell out of being the recipient of all that power, but she didn't like leaving Artemis so empty.

She was one of the few Ancients Kyana actually respected.

"I think I've got it. Dig into my gut for determination to use your—*my*—speed and tracking abilities, eat ambrosia—always diluted with food of course—find Haven, save the world. No problem."

Artemis's eyes narrowed and she pulled herself to her full height. "Don't go off half-cocked, Kyana. Or full of your usual pride. Even with the power of a goddess flowing through your veins, your challenges are great. And stupidity can still get you killed."

Her scolding over, she linked her arm with Kyana's. "Come. I have one last gift for you."

"Please tell me it's a naked man wrapped in a bow. I could really use one of those."

Not that she had time to properly enjoy any man—and certainly not the one she wanted—but it didn't hurt to wish.

"A naked man?" Artemis laughed as they descended the marble steps to stop in the massive entry hall. "This is even better."

"Right," Kyana muttered.

"Ah! There they are!"

Artemis's hounds dashed to her feet, but rather than pounce on her, they sat and beat their tails on the marble floor like they were playing the bongos.

Her fantasies of a naked Ryker went up in a puff of smoke as she frowned. "Uh, you can keep them."

Artemis knelt and took the biggest oaf's head in her hands, scratching beneath his chin as he stared adoringly into her eyes. "Firstly, there is no power in this world great enough to separate me from these babies. Secondly, you'll require your own babies—bonded solely to you in order to be efficient. Now . . ."

She stood again and took Kyana's arm, leading her to a bejeweled box where slightly smaller versions of Dumb, Dumber, and Dumbest blinked up at her. Dumbest stuck his head into the box, gave a low bark, then sat on his haunches and looked up at her as if offering an apology for the crappy gift his master had chosen for her.

"You've got to be kidding. What the hell am I going to do with three dogs?"

"These are not ordinary dogs." Artemis handed her a small velvet bag and a golden whistle. "They know over a hundred commands, the most handy of which is *follow*. If you have an item from the person you are tracking, they will target your prey for you."

She pointed to the velvet bag. "With the help of an herb called eyebright, you can keep them in sight when it is inconvenient for you to follow. I wish I had time to show you a few other commands, but you'll have to learn them as you go."

The dogs in the box sniffed Kyana's fingers, which were still curled around the lip of their container. The smallest one let out a howl.

She'd been part Lychen for more than two hundred years. Owning a pup felt like some form of slavery. "Tugging around these three on leashes is going to slow me down."

Artemis smiled. "They don't travel on leashes. Here, let me show you."

She took the whistle from Kyana's hand, blew into it twice, then set it on the ground between them. The enormous box wobbled, then toppled over, spilling the dogs onto the floor. As soon as they found the traction required to stand on marble, all three dogs charged straight at Kyana, but as she took a step of self-preservation backward, they halted in front of the whistle and . . .

Disappeared.

"Wear it around your neck. When you need the dogs, summon them with one blow. If you need to call them back, two blows. They'll reenter their home if you set it within reach as you just saw me do."

Okay, that was way cooler than she'd expected. Kyana couldn't help but be pleased with her new little toy.

"Name them whatever you wish." Artemis rose. "But do remember they are not normal pets and deserve the respect of good names."

In other words, don't name them Stupid, Stanky, and Slobber. Whatever. Kyana kinda liked Nifty, Spiffy, and Peachy right about now, anyway.

"Got it."

She slid the chain around her neck. The weight of the whistle bounced between her breasts. That was going to get annoying. She didn't wear jewelry as a rule. It tended to get in her way. She'd learned that lesson a hundred years ago when a sadistic Witch had yanked her hoop earrings from her lobes. Funny how such a minor wound could cause so much freaking pain.

"Kyana, please." Artemis met her gaze with worried eyes. "Keep your head on this hunt and remember everything I've told you. In just over five days my blood completely overtakes yours. Since I haven't trained you properly, I advise you to find Haven before that time runs out . . ."

"I'll have Haven safely in bad-girl rehab before five days come and go."

As she made her way to the enormous door, Artie called out again. "Wait."

She moved with a grace Kyana couldn't imagine possessing in a week's time and placed her long fingers around the doorknob.

"You must take one more thing with you. A precaution in case it does take you longer to bring Haven back to me."

"Another pet?"

"In a sense. But you won't have to carry this one around your neck." Artemis smiled, but it didn't reach her eyes. "He can walk on his own two feet and will be your companion until this hunt is complete."

Before Kyana could ask any questions, Artemis swung open the door to reveal Ryker standing on the other side.

To her dismay, he was neither naked nor wearing a bow.

Chapter Three

Kyana had assumed her working relationship with Ryker was over. Their little practice hunt last night was meant to be the last before she set off to find Haven. Instead, he was standing in front of her, packed and ready to go and sexy as hell—freshly showered with his hair slightly damp and curling against the collar of his linen button-up, beach-bum shirt.

She couldn't figure out if she was annoyed that he'd be coming with her, or relieved. Both maybe. With Ryker, it was always that way. A jumble of contradictions that played havoc with her insides until she was confused by her own wants and fears.

She wasn't stupid. She knew why the gods were placing him with her again. He was his father's right-hand man, and Ares would have made certain Ryker knew his duty.

"So you're just my bodyguard? You don't have orders to kill Haven if I can't subdue her?"

That he wouldn't meet her gaze was enough for Kyana. The Order of Ancients was made up of gods and Oracles, and a slew of magical beings, who were the only bodies standing between the human race and the devastation Cronos was threatening to bring down upon them if he was raised. They upheld the world's order and kept mischief to a minimum, and since Haven was trying to resurrect Cronos, they wanted her dead—even if she *was* one of their own. That was something Kyana wouldn't allow. Not unless she knew without a doubt that the monster she'd created couldn't be tamed.

And she was nowhere near that conclusion.

Kyana turned her focus back to Artemis. "I know how important this mission is. Haven has to be found and stopped. I can do that, but you have to trust me."

"Can you bring yourself to kill your best friend?" Ryker asked.

She refused to acknowledge him, but he already knew the answer anyway. As much as it killed her to admit it, she didn't think she *would* be able to take Haven's life. And unless she was sure she couldn't reach Haven's human side and get her to willingly return to the Order, no one else was going to kill her either.

"I'm sorry, Kyana, but this isn't a request," Artemis said, her voice stern though regret filled her gaze. "Ryker will join you."

"Then he doesn't touch her without my permission." Kyana faced Ryker, though her question was put to Artemis. "But those aren't his orders, are they?"

"My orders are to protect the Goddess of the Hunt."

"By killing Haven?"

Ryker held her gaze. "If that turns out to be necessary."

She grabbed her bag from the back of one of the tall, gold-gilded chairs and turned to the door. "It won't be." She was willing to stake her life on it.

"You are free to take a different guard if you truly wish to." Artie held up her hand to ward off Kyana's interruption. "But will you trust a stranger to fight with you as easily as you already trust Ryker? I believe that together, you stand a chance of success. If you refuse his help and fail to stop Cronos, then you've sentenced all of us to a fate much worse than death."

Kyana hadn't intended to put up any more argument anyway, but when she put it like that, Artemis had pretty much made saying no impossible. It was Kyana's responsibility to find Haven. To stop her. Otherwise, all the deaths Artie predicted would be Kyana's fault.

She might not care much for the human race, but she didn't want to be the one responsible for them being wiped off the planet either.

"So much for free will." Reminded of a pair of beings who'd lost their own free will long ago, she straightened to her full height. "Artemis, I can be compliant, and I hope you can return the favor."

"What is it you want?"

"Bring Farrel and Crag here," she said, referring to the minions who'd served her when she'd been a tracer.

They were bound to her, forced to endure a hundred years of service in exchange for their release from the Fields of Punishment in the Underworld. If they completed their hundred years, Hades would lift them from their binds and they'd be allowed entrance into the Elysian Fields. Because Kyana was technically no longer their master, they'd be forced to begin their hundred years all over again. Since they were already thirty years into their servitude, the unfairness of that twisted her heart. They might have been pretty awful in their human existence to wind up in the Fields of Punishment with other sinners who weren't quite bad enough to go to Tartarus, but as her minions, they'd redeemed themselves.

"You have your precious Nymphs," she pressed on. "I'd like Farrel and Crag to continue their service to me so they aren't forced to start all over again with someone else."

Artemis smiled, and Kyana could all but read the thoughts bouncing in her pretty head. Kyana had a heart. Who knew? When the goddess nodded her consent, Kyana started down the temple steps.

"It was nice of you to think of Farrel and Crag," Ryker said, catching up to her.

She ignored him.

When she reached the portal that would take them directly Above to the humans' world, he grabbed her arm to prevent her from stepping through. "This is your hunt, Kyana. I won't interfere unless I have no choice."

Somewhat placated, she nodded. "Good."

His fingers warmed her skin. It felt good. Too good. She pulled away and slipped through the portal.

On the other side, the Castillo de San Marcos was in chaos. Kyana was nearly jostled back through the portal as guards rushed by her, knocking her into Ryker, who had to find a hold on the wall to keep himself upright. She dodged her way to the door, her eyes wide and unblinking as she took in the confusion of what was normally a pretty tranquil fort.

Sentinels ran from every direction, their shouts and pounding footsteps obscuring all sound. Set against the backdrop of a glorious sunrise, panic spread like the plague among those stationed in the old fort, which had become the South Eastern United States' headquarters for the Order of Ancients when Tartarus had opened up over two weeks ago and released Hell on Earth.

A second group of sentinels rushed from the portal room and into the plaza courtyard. She craned her neck, casting her gaze over the tall heads around her to peer up at the sun with a smidgeon of self-pity. It had been more than two hundred years since she'd been able to glimpse a sunrise without fear of being turned into charbroiled Vamp, and now that the sun wasn't her enemy, she still hadn't found a peaceful morning to appreciate it.

Her pity party was crashed by a noxious odor that forced a brutal cough from her lungs.

Ryker stopped walking. "What the—"

"—hell is that smell?" Kyana finished for him, bracing her hands against his back to avoid another collision.

Together, they maneuvered their way into the courtyard and up the stairs to stand on the edge of the bastion overlooking Matanzas Bay. While the sky was gloriously alive, the bay itself looked as though it had died. The stench of dead fish turned her stomach as she looked down to find the surface shadowed by bloated carcasses.

"What the hell caused that?"

Ryker stepped away from the edge. He shoved his way down the stairs through the guards running up them and disappeared out of the fort, leaving Kyana to follow after him. As she moved toward what had once been the fort's pay station, the overpowering stench of dead fish in the air nearly smothered Ryker's scent as she struggled to follow him. He glanced back at her, held out his hand which she took, and yanked her beside him.

Together they ran in a whirl of speed that made their surroundings blur. She had no idea where they were or where they were headed, but she clung to Ryker's hand for dear life.

The sound of distant waves crashing against

the sand tunneled toward her. Minutes later, they slowed and stepped onto the sands of St. Augustine beach. Standing at Ryker's side, she looked into the distance. For what, she didn't know, but figured when he found it, he'd say so.

"Something's wrong."

"I gathered that with the Matanzas Chain Saw Massacre back there. But what?"

His gaze on the darkened waters, he moved his lips, but his words didn't carry on the wind. Kyana frowned, fascinated and puzzled at the same time. She'd seen his ability to speak without being overheard firsthand, but there'd always been someone in the room, someone he'd been talking to.

The small conch shell at his throat glowed red.

"What are you doing?" she asked.

"Trying to get someone to contact Poseidon."

"Can't you just contact him directly? And why didn't I know you could call people with those things?"

The day Tartarus had broken its bounds, they'd all been given Beacons. A way for the gods to contact them when they were needed. Kyana hadn't known *they* could call *the gods* with it.

"Not everyone can," Ryker finally answered, his focus still on the waters. "The tides are all wrong."

She looked at the crashing waves. The tides seemed fine. Okay, so there were lifeless lumps clumped along the waterline that she guessed were dead sea creatures, but nothing like what had happened to the bay.

"How do you know there's something wrong with the tides? Other than the dead fish, I mean."

"The tide should have rolled to where we're standing, yet the sand is bone dry. All the dead fish . . . the tides . . . something's definitely wrong."

Ryker wore a dire look on his face that did nothing to calm her ever rising panic. Maybe he was wrong. Maybe whatever he *thought* was happening wasn't.

"How do you know where the water should be?"

"Surfer Boy, remember?" he said, referring to the nickname she'd given him when they'd first started working together to bring the Chosen replacements safely into the Order of Ancients. "I know the tides. It affects the waves and we can't surf without waves."

Something big at the water's edge caught her eye. Kyana made her way closer to the surf for a better look. Squinting against the sun, she tried to convince herself it was a dolphin or a small whale maybe, but her keen eyesight wouldn't let her fool herself into believing it.

Man, I am out of my element with this one.

"Let's go, Ky. I have to go back to Olympus and check in with Ares, then we can—"

"Ryker?" she interrupted, turning to cast a wary glance at him. "Look."

"What?"

"I can't be certain since I've never met him." She eyed the naked man at her feet. "But I think we just found Poseidon."

Chapter Four

L et the Healers tend Poseidon and I'll send word when we learn what happened."

Kyana couldn't acknowledge Artie's request. She was too busy gawking at Zeus. He loomed tall and broad next to his brother Hades as well as Hades's replacement, Geoffrey. Even Ryker, who stood at six foot seven, was dwarfed by the god of gods.

For the first time in a long time, Kyana was in awe of another being.

It was the first time since her relocation to Beyond that Zeus had made an appearance, and he wasn't at all what she'd expected. He wasn't old or draped in long white hair. He didn't even have a beard. He looked thirty, well built, and had hair the color of Ryker's—sort of dirty blond, sun-kissed around the face. He also had the most stunning ice blue eyes Kyana had ever seen. So blue, in fact, they looked white against his tanned skin.

She shouldn't have been surprised by the god's

appearance, given her first glimpse of Poseidon. He too looked far younger than she'd imagined, even while ghostly pale and nearly dead. Hades, on the other hand, looked like he could croak any minute. Probably that whole lack of sunlight thing. She could only hope her friend Geoffrey would continue to poke his head out of the Underworld on occasion now that he'd taken over the position as God of All Things Shudder-Worthy. He was too beautiful to waste away like his predecessor.

Zeus hovered close to his wounded brother. Worry deepened the lines around his eerie, pale blue eyes. His whispers didn't carry across the massive bedroom–turned–Healing Circle, but the words he spoke caused the gold filament decorating the headboard to quake.

She took it all in. Zeus's temple. *The* temple. While Artemis's temple was floor-to-ceiling marble, Zeus's was molded with gold, silver, bronze. Lots of bronze. Pillars stood one behind the other, spaced ten feet or so apart, and between each, gold and jeweled tapestries hung from the ceiling, lending a richness to the interior that made Kyana feel tiny and insignificant. It was a cold home, one she wouldn't like to live in, but it was stunning all the same.

"Kyana." Artemis's grip tightened and Kyana was forced to look at her. "They need to be alone with their brother."

In case he doesn't make it.

Her gaze strayed to Poseidon. He lay on his belly,

a golden blanket with Zeus's lightning crest covering him from hip to toe. His back was left bare so the Healers could tend the three punctures the size of grapefruits that formed a morbid pattern beneath each shoulder bone, a third in the center of his back.

"What are those marks and why are they killing him?"

The fear in Artie's eyes didn't sit well. "Those are the marks of Poseidon."

"You mean the trident?"

Artemis nodded. "He was coherent enough when Ryker brought him in. He said . . . He said he saw who did this to him."

She didn't want to hear any more. Didn't want to know what had the goddess so worried. But Artemis pressed on. "It was Haven. He saw her, Kyana. She's crossed a line I don't think she can be saved from—"

"No!" Like a child being told there was no Santa Claus, Kyana cupped her hands over her ears and fell onto the last step of the massive staircase behind her. She moved her hands to her face and blocked out the sight of Artemis's sandals. "No. I don't believe that. People have delusions when they're hurt—"

"Poseidon's not a person, he's a god!" Anger shook Artemis's words. She heaved a sigh and sat beside Kyana. "There was no delusion. She is guilty. Above that, she has the trident. If she gets her hands on the other Eyes of Power . . ."

Kyana didn't need her to finish. Poseidon's trident, Zeus's staff, Hades's amulet, and Cronos's own ring all comprised the Eyes of Power. Haven already had one. If she got her hands on the others, she was a talented enough Witch to perform the ceremony that would bring him back. Mix that with the new Vampyre and Lychen blood swirling around inside her to make her loony tunes, and she was way more than capable.

It had to be Cronos pushing her to accomplish his goals. Kyana knew that. He'd come for Haven days ago when she'd been recovering in the Healing Circle where Mystics had been attempting to purge Kyana's Half-Breed blood from her veins. But Cronos had gotten to her first. The result had been the murder of Mystics and Haven's escape.

She had lived with Haven for almost five years. They were each the better half of the other—Haven rational, sweet, and emotional. Kyana rash, temperamental, and strong. They'd fought alongside each other. Laughed. Cried. Loved.

For two hundred years, she hadn't allowed herself to give a damn about anyone or anything. But then Haven had become Kyana's sister in every way that mattered, and had opened Kyana's heart enough to embrace Geoffrey as family too.

And one day, maybe even Ryker.

Now Haven was out there, controlled by a mad god. Knowing what Haven had already done didn't stop Kyana from defending her.

"If she did this, it wasn't her, Artemis. He's controlling her, making her do things. She's served this Order for over a decade. How can you give up on her so easily?"

Artemis squeezed Kyana's knee. "I haven't, which is why I want you out there hunting her before Ares's tracers can find her. They won't be as merciful as mine."

They rose to their feet together, Kyana more determined than ever to get off the mountain and do her job. She let Artemis guide her down the stairs leading to the ground floor of Zeus's temple. When they stood outside surrounded by bronze statuettes and hardy oaks, she ignored the goddess's pooches who nudged her hand in a plea for attention and turned to face Artemis.

"Do you think Poseidon will live?"

"I do. But his powers will not recover. We found his Chosen, but lost him again before we could bring him Below. We must find him a temporary Vessel until we can locate a permanent replacement."

Kyana nodded. If Poseidon died, so would the world's waters. Which would bring a drought the human race wouldn't survive. Extinction would come, and at the hands of Haven and Cronos. *Lovely.*

"So you find a Vessel for Poseidon and I get my hands on Haven before she finds a way to get hers on the other Eyes of Power." She rolled her eyes. "Piece of cake."

"Find Haven, return her to us, and bury Cronos

once and for all. The Ancients will find another Chosen in time."

Making sure no one was within hearing distance, Kyana admitted, "How can one tracer and three dogs stop what Cronos is trying to do?"

"You add one demigod to even out the odds and stir," Ryker said, joining them on the steps of Zeus's temple.

That he'd heard her confess her fears made Kyana want to deck him. That he didn't comment saved him from the punishing blow.

Chapter Five

As Kyana and Ryker made their way through the streets of St. Augustine, he divided his attention between surveying their surroundings and watching Kyana. The changes in her amazed him. It wasn't just that she was taking on Artemis's attributes, like the auburn streaks that now lightened her jet black hair, or even the amber around her dark eyes that hadn't been there a few days ago.

What held him mesmerized was the grace in her movements, the confidence in her step that hadn't been there before.

She had always been confident and powerful, helped along by her ability to intimidate people into doing things her way. But the way she carried herself now demanded respect that had little to do with fear and everything to do with the goddess growing inside her.

He still couldn't believe the turn of events that had taken her from the brink of execution to the next Goddess of the Hunt. He'd tried to bargain with each of the gods to save her life after she'd turned Haven, but he'd failed. She was alive because of her own strength, and because of the belief others had in her abilities to right the wrongs she'd done.

He wasn't sure if she knew it, but she had it within her to save not only the human race, but the Order's world too.

He'd been drawn to her Lychen half when he'd met her ten years ago. Lychen mated for life, and when Kyana had offered him sex, he'd refused, knowing it had been the Vampyric half of her who'd tried to seduce him.

Yes, he'd given in a few days ago and finally made love to her, but he still wanted all of her, not just that promiscuous Vampyric side. He wanted the faithful Lychen side, the powerful goddess side, the fiercely passionate womanly side.

He wanted it all.

He wanted her to look at him with the same softness in her eyes that flickered when she spoke of Haven or Geoffrey. But getting her to offer that to him was proving to be impossible, and it certainly didn't help that his job was to stand between her and Haven if things got ugly. If he had to harm Haven to save Kyana, he damned sure would, but it would cost him any chance he had with Kyana.

His job sucked.

But like it or not, he was here to make sure she didn't let her emotions get in her way, which was the grandest of ironies given how badly he'd been hoping she'd tap deeper into her emotions since they'd met ten years ago. Now she was going to need that stoniness, that coldness that he resented if she was going to stop Cronos from rising.

He studied her profile as they turned onto her street. She looked calm, determined. That pleased him. If she became too stressed by what she was being asked to do, she'd become irrational, and he really didn't like dealing with Irrational Ky.

The small cemetery near her home was full of unearthed graves. Some had been freshly dug for new bodies after the breakout, others had been destroyed by the beings buried beneath the headstones. Leeches. Ghouls. Spirits. They were free now—at least the ones that hadn't been caught and imprisoned already. It was a disturbing thought.

Kyana led him past the cemetery as they followed a waist-high brick wall toward her corner home. The yellow two-story looked odd among the surrounding buildings. It was the only residence that sat untouched, probably thanks to sharing the dwelling with a Witch. They had more bells and whistles preventing break-ins than Alcatraz had for preventing break*outs*.

He'd been here before, and that circumstance had been no more pleasant than this one. He'd allowed himself to get drunk, and gods and demigods weren't exactly known for holding their liquor. One shot of JD and he'd been a mess. Kyana had brought him here to sober up, and they'd been ambushed by a group of Leeches, a.k.a. Zombies, who'd been attracted to his godly aura and had come to feed from it. Kyana had fought them, but she'd been caught in the morning sun.

He'd had to feed her from his own blood to keep her alive, bonding them together for a very uncomfortable day. He'd seen more of her past that day when he'd linked inside her dreams than she'd ever spoken about. She still didn't know how much he knew about her human life . . . and he planned to keep it that way.

While he tried like hell to get that memory off his face, he stepped back and waited for Kyana to open the door. She was getting better and better at reading him lately. Too much time spent together perhaps, and he didn't want her asking about anything he might be thinking.

But instead of entering her house, Kyana stood on the steps, her hands stuffed into the pockets of her leather jacket, her gaze locked on the door.

"It feels wrong. She should be in there cooking those disgusting-looking egg white omelets full of alfalfa sprouts and mushrooms, and I know she won't be."

The anguish in her eyes lulled him closer to her. *This* was why he was falling for her despite his better judgment. She wasn't all cold-blooded. When she cared about someone, she cared with everything she had. And right now, she was aching for the friend, the sister, she'd lost.

She leaned into him, and he tucked his arms

around her waist and breathed in the flowery scent of her shampoo.

"We'll get her back, Ky."

As quickly as he said the words, she pulled away from him. With a trembling hand, she opened the door. "Let's just get what I need and get out of here."

She marched toward a bedroom behind the kitchen that he didn't recognize. "I thought your room was upstairs?"

Judging by the way her eyes went all soft as her gaze locked with his, her mind had wandered to the same day that had filled Ryker's. She cleared her throat and swept her hand to the small room they stood in now.

"This is a guest room where Haven and I share closet space. Anything in here, we're free to borrow."

She disappeared inside the closet, and when she stepped back out, she'd changed into fresh leather pants and a vest that hugged her breasts, leaving enough cleavage visible to make him uncomfortable.

As she dug through a case of weapons at the foot of the bed, Ryker quietly slipped a pouch from the waistband of his pants and held it out to her.

"I was going to give this to you earlier, but with everything that happened . . ."

"What is it?" She took the bundle and set it on the bed.

"Open it."

She unrolled it, and two handcrafted silver daggers fell onto the mattress. "My daggers!"

Ryker couldn't stop the grin from spreading across his face at her excitement. "I convinced Ares it was time to give them back."

Kyana tucked the weapons into her holsters before stretching onto her toes to place a kiss on his cheek. When she moved away again, it took all his willpower not to reach out and pull her back.

"Thank you," she said, turning back to the weapon case to retrieve the flare gun she'd once used to gain entrance into the fort. He wondered if she knew she didn't need it anymore. As a goddess, she'd be allowed entrance without question.

Leaning against the doorjamb, he asked, "Anything you want me to grab?"

She shook her head, zipping up a duffel she'd filled with clothes and spare daggers.

Without a word, she made her way back to the hall and stopped outside another room. *Haven's* room. She pushed open the door. Ryker stood in the doorway feeling useless as he waited, watching her, giving her the space he sensed she needed.

It must be hard for her. To be here amid all these reminders of the devastation that had rocked her world. Of the friendship she'd lost.

He tried to relate, but friends for him were few and far between.

Kyana turned in a full circle, sniffing the air. "She's been here," she whispered. "Recently."

"You could be picking up on an old scent."

"This is the same one I smelled at the Healing Circle. It wouldn't be here unless *she'd* been here since then," Kyana said, closing her eyes, her nostrils flaring just a tad as she drank in the room through her nose. "She smells different now."

He closed his eyes and took a deep breath. "All I smell is perfume and flowers."

She shook her head. "That's not her anymore."

"Why would she come here knowing you could show up at any moment?"

Her gaze narrowed and she worked her bottom lip between her teeth before dropping to her knees. "Move the vanity."

He did as she asked, then watched her dig her fingernails into the loose planks and toss away the boards. Kneeling beside her, Ryker glanced into the hole. A lone silk pouch lay deflated inside.

"She's already begun," Kyana said, falling back on her rear and scrubbing her eyes with her palms. She looked so tired, so defeated, Ryker wanted to wrap his arms around her and soak up some of her doubt.

"Ky—"

"She took everything, even her mother's book of shadows. She's going to try to do this, Ryker. If she's taken that book and her mother's most powerful spells, there's no doubt left that she's really going to try and do this."

"We'll find her, Ky. *You'll* find her."

Kyana wanted to believe him, but with her Vampyric and Lychen senses already fading, she didn't have the first clue as to where to look for Haven.

She plucked the empty pouch from the hole and made her way clumsily to her feet, pressing the pouch to her nose. It carried Haven's scent. Strong and tainted with what she was becoming.

She carried it into the kitchen, where she dropped it into a plastic bag to protect the scent before tucking it into her duffel. "Let's go."

Together, they followed the faint trail back through Old St. Augustine a fair way before she stopped again. Frustration oozed through her pores like earthworms breaking surface after a hard rain. Haven's scent was gone.

The breeze had turned biting, breaking through her skin to rattle her bones. She tied her hair back with a band of elastic and pulled on her leather jacket as they approached the Bridge of Lions. They stopped beside the giant lion sculptures at the foot of the bridge, and she inhaled deeply, hoping against hope that some bit of Haven would be swept up by the bay.

Nothing but rotting fish greeted her, reminding her that time was a scarce commodity just now. The water around them was black and foul, and it wouldn't be long before every body of water across the world mirrored what they saw here.

"I knew it was a bad idea to let Artemis give me her blood so soon. If I was doing this whole, there'd be no question that I could follow her. How am I supposed to trace something I can't smell, short of kidnapping an Oracle to point us in the right direction?"

Ryker raised a cautionary brow. "We are *not* kidnapping an Oracle, so get that look off your face."

"We don't have to actually *kidnap* one. But we could convince one to help us out. Or a Witch maybe. Haven was always scrying when she'd lost her keys or favorite lipstick. Couldn't a Witch help us locate the trident?"

He shrugged. "Getting to the Oracles isn't easy. We could try a Witch, but there aren't a whole lot left in the area. Besides, finding one with the power to tap into something as magical as an Eye of Power? I'm not sure there is such a Witch."

Kyana chewed her lip, thinking. She knew of one Witch who might have that kind of mojo. An image of bedroom eyes and shaggy hair popped into her brain. Eight generations of Witchcraft in his blood. If anyone could do it . . .

"I know a Witch," she said, unable to stop smiling. "A really, *really* good one. I can summon him."

Kyana tossed her duffel over her shoulder, rejuvenated at the thought of using the Beacon Wall Artemis had shown her the day before.

Ryker froze. "*Him?*"

Her smile melted into a scowl. "Yeah. We're, uh . . ." *Booty call buds, old lovers.* ". . . friends."

Kyana dashed toward the fort to save herself from Ryker's look of suspicion. This might get really uncomfortable, but while she hadn't seen Silas Godiva in many months, he was trustworthy *and* talented. She'd just have to deal with the discomfort of having both him and Ryker around for this.

Haven was important.

Kyana's pitiful sexcapades were not.

Chapter Six

It was just approaching noon when Kyana and Ryker made their way down the main corridor of Artemis's temple . . . and to another room down another hall . . . past another set of stairs. This place was bigger than the Castillo de San Marcos. Hell, it was bigger than the Biltmore.

She hadn't had access to the temple long, certainly not long enough to learn the many rooms and paths, but she did remember how to get to the Beacon Wall, simply because it had been the highlight of Artemis's tour two days ago.

"Whoa," Ryker said, his reaction to the enormous wall pretty damned similar to the one she had expressed when she'd first seen it.

The wall was roughly the size of a two-story building, with small grooves separating rows of Beacons, and ladders separating each column. At least a thousand Beacons decorated the wall like necklaces, each one underlined with a golden plaque with the owner's name. They were arranged by "class" of

Order members and then alphabetically, making it easy for her to find WITCH / SILAS GODIVA.

Her gaze drifted briefly over her own plaque, but instead of a Beacon, there was now a golden bow and arrow. She should have felt triumphant over seeing her promotion literally written in stone. Instead, a sad ache of longing knotted up her throat. Her past as she knew it was gone forever. This was the final bit of proof she'd needed to truly realize she was no longer Vampyre. No longer Lychen. No longer a tracer or an average member of the Order of Ancients.

She was becoming Kyana, Goddess of the Hunt, and she was smart enough to be scared out of her ever-loving mind at what that meant for her future.

With a sigh, she stretched onto the ladder and forced her attention back to the Beacon that mattered. Silas's golden bauble fell just out of reach, and she had to make a short leap to catch it in her palm. She landed beside Ryker, held up the Beacon, and grinned. She'd truly hated being summoned like a dog by these things, but now that she was on the other side of this wall, she couldn't wait to make it sparkle.

As soon as she closed her fist around it, the Beacon warmed against her skin. She placed it back on its hook, then led the way out of the room. According to Artemis, that was all that needed to be done. When Silas received the call, it would automatically lead him to where she was, and since she didn't think Artemis would appreciate a Witch

showing up at her temple, it was best to venture
Below to hold this meeting.

She chose a spot right outside the portal alcove
Below where they'd be able to spot Silas coming
right away. She had no idea where he was travel-
ing from, but this was the region he worked for the
Order, just as it had been Kyana's. He would never
stray too far, would never leave his borders when
he was on duty.

"So, who is this guy?" Ryker asked. "A friend
like Geoffrey, or more?"

Kyana bit back a smile. "A friend."

She didn't *want* to make Ryker jealous, but maybe
having Silas around would be good for whatever
this thing between them was. Maybe it would pro-
voke him into realizing the one night they'd spent
together could lead to a few more before either had
to move on again.

Doubtful, but maybe.

Artemis might have been a virginal goddess, but
Kyana sure as hell didn't plan to be. If her nights
were filled with Ryker beside and inside her before
they both got bored and went their separate ways,
so much the better.

While Ryker's shrug was one of nonchalance,
his tense face was anything but. "Of course. He's
a Witch." He smiled. "Male Witches aren't really
your type, are they?"

"Not really, no."

The majority of the male Witch population were
skinny, nerdy, and whiny as all hell. She wasn't

going to tell him now that Silas didn't exactly fit that mold. He'd find out soon enough.

"Ah, Kyana, you wound me."

She jumped at the sound of Silas's familiar baritone and nearly kneed him in surprise when he leaned over her shoulder to kiss her cheek.

"Silas, thanks for coming." He looked good. Damned good. Even in baggy jeans and a ripped T-shirt, Silas Godiva was seriously drool-worthy.

Kyana squirmed, remembering the last time she'd seen him many, many months ago. Naked. Sweaty. And on top of her. He was too arrogant for anything serious to have ever developed, even if she was the sort who wanted that kind of thing—which she wasn't.

"Heard you went and turned all goddessy on me," he said, throwing a possessive arm around her. "Didn't expect a summons from you unless it was our usual kind, though."

Kyana ducked out of his hold, suddenly more concerned than she should be with whatever was going through Ryker's head.

"Silas, you're a rude ass. Hi, I'm Sixx."

Kyana swung around to find a leather-clad blond standing behind Silas, her bloodred lips turned into a pout as she held out black-tipped fingers in Kyana's direction.

Who the hell was she and why was Silas looking at her as though he wanted to get her naked and do very naughty things to her?

And for that matter, why was Ryker? He was

practically panting. She shot her palm up, slapping his mouth closed. He bit his tongue.

"Ow! What was that for?"

Kyana glowered at him before turning back to the sleazy blond, making no move to take the woman's outstretched hand.

"This is Sixx," Silas said, as though the woman hadn't just introduced herself.

Kyana took in Sixx's black-tipped silvery white hair, her bloodred bustier and torn leather pants. She radiated sex, and Kyana suddenly felt old and matronly in her intact leather pants and plain vest and jacket.

"Sister?" she asked, already knowing the answer. Silas had no siblings, and if he did, he'd be a sick bastard for looking at one the way he was looking at Sixx.

"Jealous?"

"Can we get back to business?" Ryker asked, leaning against the wall behind him.

"Right. Yes." She jutted her chin in Sixx's direction. "In private."

Silas whispered something in Sixx's ear, earning him a pathetic pout. She stalked off, muttering something about meeting him at Spirits, glancing back at him every so often to toss him a glare. Ryker and Silas silently watched her go, their gaze settled somewhere around her ass area.

"Nice," she heard Ryker whisper.

"She's a beaut, right?" Silas's grin was wickedly cocky.

Kyana's hopes to make Ryker jealous were sadly backfiring.

She growled and stepped in front of them, blocking their view. "She'll be waiting awhile. You're going to be rather busy for the next few days."

Silas raised his black brows. "This about Haven?"

She nodded. "She's in trouble."

"I heard she went rogue." Silas scratched his stubbled jaw. He knew Haven almost as well as he knew Kyana. Though, as far as she knew, their relationship hadn't turned as biblical. "How'd it happen?"

Unable to voice the story that cast her as the villain, Kyana gave Ryker a pleading glance. Thankfully, he seemed to understand. His fingers played with the small of her back as he recounted the past week to Silas.

"Haven was dying. The traitors tried to kill her when they found out she was meant to be Artemis's Chosen. Kyana turned her to save her. She had no choice."

"Hell, Kyana. *You* did this? And they still made you a goddess? You're one lucky Half-Breed."

She glared at Silas. "Don't call me that again."

Silas grinned, studying her. "I like the red in your hair. Artemis's trait?"

She nodded, self-consciously touching a lock of red dangling over her shoulder amid the cloud of black curls. Ryker hadn't mentioned her physical changes so she'd hoped they weren't so obvious. Apparently, he was just unobservant.

"So, what do you need me for?"

"Right now, scrying. See if you can locate Haven. We'll figure out how to use you from there."

The wind kicked up, tossing Silas's dark hair around his eyes. "Give me an hour? All I brought with me were the few things I could fit in my saddlebag."

Kyana couldn't help but smile. "You still have your bike?"

"Would I travel any other way?"

She could almost feel the heavy metal of his Harley between her legs. The last time she'd seen Silas, she'd had about three orgasms on that bike. He'd tried to get her to take a ride on it, but because of her issue with motion sickness, she'd persuaded him to just let her ride *him* on it instead. She was glad he still had the bike, even though she was pretty sure she wouldn't be finding it as useful this go-round.

Ryker was too imbedded in her head.

It was a struggle to keep her gaze off Ryker as she watched him side by side with Silas. Whatever hold he had over her, it was stronger than her desire to replay old nasty bits on a bike.

"Ky?"

"Huh? What?"

Ryker was staring down at her, his brows pulled together in question. "I asked where you wanted to meet Silas in an hour."

She snapped herself together and prayed her face hadn't flushed with her train of thought. "The fort. Get everything you need and meet us at the drawbridge."

She scooped up her duffel and slid it over her shoulder.

"And what are we going to do in the meantime?" Ryker asked as Silas strode off toward the market strip.

"I'm going to try to tap into Haven again. I want to know where she's taking Poseidon's conduit."

Kyana lay on the warm sands of the beach Below, her arms resting on her belly, her head on Ryker's thigh. Linking to Haven in hopes of finding a hint to their next destination had seemed like a good idea a bit ago, but now she was realizing she didn't know how to sleep on command.

"You need to stop thinking so hard." Ryker rubbed his hand over her eyes. "Just relax, let your mind wander."

She sighed. Instead of concentrating on an image of Haven, she lost herself in Ryker's voice. The low rumbling baritone drifted into her ears and spread a cozy blanket over her mind as the rhythm of his words vibrated from his chest against the crown of her head.

She'd seen Ryker angry, but for the most part, his total calmness was what she liked most about him. And right now, that calm echoed through his throat and out his mouth, shielding her from the stress that had been slicing through her brain.

She seemed to float off the sand and drift toward the clouds. She would have fought it, but that would have meant breaking the focus on the sound of Ryker's voice. The backs of his fingers brushing her face. It wasn't often that she was caressed so tenderly—touched so humanly.

She simply allowed herself to float. Up, up, up. Higher and higher until she realized the reason she felt like she was flying wasn't because of Ryker's touch or voice. He must have used some demigod mojo to make her sleep. Forcing her eyes open, she took in her surroundings.

Sure enough, she wasn't nestled on some cloud. She stood, instead, near the Bridge of Lions where they'd lost Haven's scent earlier.

A searing pain splintered her brain. She couldn't see anything for a moment, and in the next, she found herself blinking into the blazing, hot sun. The gleam of Poseidon's trident glared at her from the corner of a dark room. There was no sign of Haven, and when Kyana reached out to seize the trident, her hand slipped through it like air.

"Haven?" Would she be able to hear her? She racked her brain, trying to remember whether she'd ever heard her Sire, Henry, speak to her in such a state. She'd occasionally been aware of his presence, but she couldn't remember ever hearing his voice.

She sniffed the air, filling her lungs with Haven's perfume. She must have bathed since Kyana had last seen her. The sour, foul scent was barely noticeable now.

She pried her gaze from the trident and drank in every detail of the room. It looked like a shack, or a mobile home. She moved to the window. Outside, all she could see was a three-story brick wall. She wasn't sure how far she could venture from this spot without breaking the fragile link, and was afraid to try.

"I feel you."

The hissed words spun Kyana in a circle like a dog chasing its tail. She could see no one. Nothing other than the yellowed walls and ragged carpet under her boots.

"Haven?"

"I know you're here, Kyana," Haven said in a voice so cold and empty it held no part of the woman she'd once been.

Was she using a Cloaking Charm? Artemis had said her goddess juice would allow Kyana to see through such things. But maybe it didn't work in this state. More than likely, that power, like several others, wouldn't set in until she became a full goddess.

Shit.

"I can't let you find me." Haven's image flashed before her eyes and disappeared again like a candle flickering in the wind.

And just like that, the scent of Haven vanished as though it had never been there at all. Her heart in her throat, Kyana turned and found the trident gone as well.

Haven was on the move again, but wherever she was going, Kyana was more sure than ever that with every hour that passed, Haven was turning darker. If her soul became black, not even the gods of Olympus would be able to save her.

Chapter Seven

Contemporary transportation in all forms made Kyana sick to her stomach. Motorcycles, cars, trains, boats, planes . . . they all made her toss her cookies.

Whatever happened to the good ole days when people rode horses to get from point A to point B? Sure, they were continent bound, but did people *really* need to travel overseas anyway? You'd think the gods would have something a little less vomit-inducing up their sleeves, but *nooooo*. Their transportation revolved around bouncy chariots and the oh-so-pleasant portals and ports. Portals sapped the hell out of her energy, and ports . . . the few times Ryker had physically ported her to a location, she'd gone temporarily blind and a little bit stupid.

But it was the quickest way to get them to Panama City, Florida, which was where Silas's scrying had pointed them to. Actually, it had been pointing to either Panama City or Tallahassee, but Haven had no link to Tallahassee that Kyana knew of. However, she *had* spent the first week of the breakout in Panama City. She'd been ring shopping with her almost-fiancé, a rat bastard traitor who was partly responsible for killing Haven and making Kyana turn her into a Dark Breed. It made sense that she'd return to that place where her world was normal for the last time before turning to shit. More sense than Tallahassee anyway.

After a short jaunt through the blindingly white wormholes, Ryker, Silas, and Kyana landed with a trio of groans on pavement hot enough to fry the skin from their bones. Kyana's elbows skidded across gravel and she heard the light rip of leather across her knees.

"You owe me a pair of pants," she gasped, waiting for Ryker to say the words that would return her sight.

"Libero," he said, and in the next instant, she saw a blurry version of Silas sprawled out in front of her. His cheek was pressed to pavement, his eyes squeezed shut. It helped her ego to know she wasn't the only one with a weak stomach.

"That"—Silas flopped over onto his back—"sucked. I'm going to French kiss the hell out of my bike when we get back."

"I'm sure the two of you will make very pretty Tonka Toys together." She rolled over and pressed her hand to her belly. She hoped like hell Haven was here, or that trip had been for nothing.

From her position on the ground, she could see the glare of a blinking caution light overhead. The streets here were as eerily quiet as they were in St. Augustine, but far less chilling since she didn't know the soundtrack to Panama City as she knew her home's.

She worked her way to her feet, drinking in the sights around her. Abandoned buildings, check. Overturned cars, check. The stench of blood and death, check. Yep, normal town, all right. She was pretty sure that if they ducked into one of the boarded-up buildings, they'd find either a group of humans huddled together, or the evidence that they hadn't been very successful at staying alive.

"So how do we find the mall?" Kyana hadn't really expected an answer. Was there more than one around here that Haven might have visited?

"Ten years ago you could have found a phone booth and ripped the address out of the yellow pages. Now, if you don't carry a smart phone, you're screwed. I hate progress," Silas said, dusting off his jeans.

"Taking it you don't carry one?" Ryker said.

"Nope."

Kyana wasn't surprised. Silas hated the gods' Beacons as much as she had. He didn't like to be tied down to anything, and carrying a cell phone around would have made him too easy to get ahold of. Not to mention, it would have stolen some of the mystery he worked so hard to develop around himself.

"There are a lot of malls in Panama City," he said. "Lucky for you, I think I remember where several are from my spring break partying days a few years ago. But how are you going to know which one she might have gone to?"

"We don't," Kyana muttered. "Take us to the ones you remember and we'll just hope we get lucky."

Turned out, they weren't. Panama City Mall was the first one they stumbled upon, and so far, as they walked the echoey halls, they'd found it empty, save for a few families hiding out in Aéropostale and Best Buy. Ryker used his Beacon to signal help for the humans, but other than that, they'd left the groups alone.

Hopefully, someone would arrive and get the humans safely Below where the other refugees were camped. Regardless, Kyana wasn't overly worried. The malls had been one of the first places cleaned out by Dark Breeds. Lots of succulent young girls there to feed off. The real threat had probably moved on a long time ago.

But as their heels clicked on the tile floors of the empty halls, Kyana noted that, along with the absence of Dark Breed stink, Haven's scent was nowhere to be found either.

"Where's another mall?" she asked Silas.

"There are a lot of town square–type shopping centers. Did Haven give you any idea of a particular store?"

"Dillard's," she said, surprising even herself at how quickly the recollection came to her. "She and Drake were ring shopping when Tartarus broke out, and I remember her saying she'd slept in Dillard's."

"There's one here." Ryker stretched his arm over his head, pointing to the navigational signs. "Should we check it out first?"

Kyana shook her head. "I'm telling you, she's never stepped foot here. Her human-based scent would still be here and there's enough Lychen left in me that I'd be able to pick it up. It's not her style anyway. I should have realized that sooner. Haven's a mall rat, but she likes quirky mall strips, antique shops, boutiques. She's never been into the sterile shopping experience."

"I might know the place you're looking for," Silas said. "It's quirky and I *think* it has a Dillard's."

The jog to the ocean took three times as long with Silas trailing behind. Though she set a slow, steady pace, he was almost gasping for breath by the time the tall palms came into sight.

Kyana slowed to a walk. "Which way?"

Silas pointed to the left and they cut across the parking lot past colorful bookstores, clothing boutiques, and eateries. Most had broken windows, their goods scattered across the floors. Usually, in a disaster, it was looters who caused the destruction. In this case, the red smears along the pastel buildings told a different story.

Ryker moved toward the sidewalk, but Kyana motioned him back into the open. She didn't smell Dark Breeds, but that didn't mean they weren't hiding behind the stench of death carried by the sea breeze.

They stopped near the front doors. Silas knelt to

catch his breath while Ryker and Kyana scanned the large building. There were chains on the inside of the doors and furniture covering the glass. Humans, either trapped or long since something's dinner, had tried to barricade themselves from the danger.

Whether they'd been successful remained to be seen.

She closed her eyes and drank in a gulp of pheromone-laced air. There were definitely humans inside, and they smelled alive. But more importantly, Haven's scent was among them.

"Wait here while I find a way in."

"Break . . . the . . . glass." Silas was still winded from their jog. "Between the three of us . . . the debris will barely slow us down."

"And what if there are people still inside?" Ryker scanned the building.

"There are," she said.

Ryker frowned and pointed skyward. "There may be an opening on the roof. A ventilation shaft we can use. It's not that high."

"Not all of us can do the Spider-Man thing." Silas stood to his full height and glared at Ryker. "Besides, if they blocked the doors, I'm sure they thought about the roof. Otherwise, there wouldn't be any humans left to worry about."

"And there won't be when we're gone if we breach their defenses and leave them wide open to attack," Ryker said. "It will take until dawn at the earliest before help arrives. We can't leave them on their own, and we sure as hell can't take them with us. We have to find another way in. Unless *you* want to stay with them."

Feeling a full-blown battle of wills coming on, Kyana stepped between them before they brought any and every creature that went bump in the night down on their asses. She didn't mind a good fight. Actually, it always made her feel better. But now wasn't the time.

"I'm going to find another way in. You two wait here. I won't be long."

"You can't go in there by yourself," both men demanded at once.

She glared from one to the other, her gaze finally coming to rest on Silas. "I'm not going to risk killing the humans. This is the right place and if Haven came back, there's something important in there. I intend to find it."

"This doesn't look like the place you described from your vision," Ryker said. "You sure this is right?"

"No, I'm not sure, but it's all we have right now," she said, slinging her pack over her shoulder. "I won't be long. Try not to kill each other while I'm gone, okay?"

Before they could offer more objections, Kyana turned and sprinted into the shadows. Jumping to the low roof wasn't even a good workout. Neither was removing the ventilation fan's cover.

She knelt before the opening, easing her head inside the dark hole. She didn't have a problem with small spaces. However, the loud whir of the fan was proof that the mall was still hooked up with electricity, and she didn't much like the thought of falling the wrong way and ending up as a pile of ground beef.

With a deep breath, she eased into the tight shaft and slowly made her way away from the noise. After several false starts that led to dead ends, she finally found a path that opened into a maintenance area.

The minute she eased the heavy door open, Haven's light scent became stronger . . . as did the humans' fear.

She inhaled deeply. The humans' numbers weren't large, but their need for self-preservation was strong. She could sense their determination to survive. It was probably the only thing that had kept them alive all this time. She ran her tongue over her fangs, noted begrudgingly how much they'd shrunk since absorbing Artemis's blood. It didn't matter how small the fangs were, or that she didn't intend to use them, these humans would never believe she was one of the good guys.

Just a few days ago, she would have gleefully walked into their midst, dominating and intimidating them and feeding off their fears. Today, however, that didn't fill her with the joy it once had.

There was no *maybe* about it. She was definitely changing.

Instead of fighting against this new side of herself, Kyana pulled the whistle from beneath her shirt and fingered the gold cylinder. Somewhere in this building was the lead they needed to find Haven—the reason Haven might have returned. If she'd come back here for a sense of the familiar, then there'd have to be a recent scent strong enough to follow.

It would make her search faster if she could be in more than one place at a time, and thanks to Artemis's present, she could do exactly that.

She blew once, then set the whistle at her feet and stepped back. As if nothing more than an illusion, the whistle shimmered, its golden glow warm and inviting. One at a time, the pups stepped from the light to sit at her feet, their tails thumping the dusty floor, their heads turned up anxiously awaiting orders.

With a grin, Kyana knelt before the lead pup and scratched her behind the ears. "Ready to get to work?"

She gave a soft bark and nudged Kyana's hand. Reaching into her pack, Kyana grabbed the velvet pouch she'd taken from Haven's room and slipped it out of the protective plastic baggie. Careful not to leave too much of her own scent on it, she held it to each pup's nose. Hopefully, it would offer something more substantial for them to track.

When the tail thumping became almost deafening in the small maintenance room, Kyana slipped a leaf of eyebright from her duffel and sniffed. The strong anise fragrance reminded her of the raki she enjoyed with a splash of blood. Definitely an improvement over most of the vile substances she was forced to consume when attempting magic.

Slipping the leaf onto her tongue, she sputtered. Instantly, her mouth went numb. The tingling spread throughout her body until she could no longer support her own weight. Dropping to her knees, she placed her hand over her racing heart and willed herself to calm down and let the effects of the herb take control.

Her vision blurred and narrowed into the worst case of tunnel vision she'd ever experienced. The drab, dusty colors slowly faded until all real color vanished completely.

It took her a moment to realize that she was seeing through the eyes of the lead bitch, which might have been pretty cool if it wasn't accompanied by blazing heat that seemed to be devouring her from the inside out. Sweat beaded on her temple, slickened her palms, and dampened her back. She was suddenly so thirsty, she couldn't think straight.

The pups watched her expectantly, their tails throwing up enough dust that it nearly strangled her already parched throat. The smallest of the three licked her chin and whimpered softly. The lead female took a step to the door, then turned back to look at Kyana, her head tilted in question.

Kyana opened the door and pointed. "Locate, find, fetch."

She didn't know the command, but one of them seemed to be right. She received three soft, throaty woofs before they disappeared into the mall.

Pushing the door closed, she leaned against it, rested her head on her knees and closed her eyes. Gradually, she adjusted to the dog's movements, and her body began to cool. Forcing herself to concentrate on the animal's progress and not her own misery, she checked out their surroundings.

They moved with ease, following Haven's trail as they picked their way around scattered displays and broken shelving. The scent filled Kyana with such longing for her friend that it would have brought her to her knees if she wasn't already sitting. Sisters. They'd been closer than any siblings, bonded by trust and faith—things that came too rarely in Kyana's life.

Now, they were enemies.

Days of borrowing clothes and exchanging stories about good-looking men were gone, and acknowledging that seared a burning path from her belly to her throat. The first time she and Haven had met, all Kyana had seen was how opposite they had been. But fighting side by side, she'd come to respect the Barbie doll's ability to kick ass. And right now, she wanted nothing more than to have Haven watching her back again.

She swallowed and tried to focus on the task at hand. She took in the gray images of the discarded bedding and food containers. The pups took turns pawing at the items, then lifted their heads, sniffing the air. As one, they turned and exited Dillard's, then split off. Kyana's vision shifted from the lead bitch's to the other two's surroundings.

She was tied to them all, and she supposed it was kind of like watching a split-screen TV.

They searched several clothing stores, food shops, and jewelry stores, occasionally drifting back to one another for a brief inspection before splitting up again. It amazed her how the pups stayed to the shadows, avoiding detection as they worked to complete the mission she'd given them.

After what felt like mind-numbing hours, the dogs circled back around separately, coming together as though simultaneously finding the trail they'd been seeking. Back to Dillard's, though they'd been there once, and as Kyana watched, they dashed through the jewelry section, busting glass cases as they leaped with excitement over counters and displays . . . and crashed through the glass doors and into the parking lot.

Holy shit. They were on the move.

Without her.

They'd definitely caught something strong. Kyana rubbed her eyes, desperately trying to clear her head, and ran after them. She could only see what the dogs showed her, and as she ran, she stumbled over every damned thing in her path.

"Halt!" she screamed, her voice carrying through the empty halls.

The trio of pooches skidded to a stop in the middle of the parking lot, hearing her as clearly as if she'd been standing beside them. They waited, panting, and Kyana took a deep breath as she waited for her vision to clear. It did so slowly, enough so she could make her way through the mall and department store without killing herself. By the time she reached the dogs, her vision was once again her own and she bellowed for Ryker, afraid to move the dogs lest they lose their precious trace.

The minute Ryker and Silas appeared around the corner, Kyana set the dogs off again. As she followed, she called over her shoulder, "Get help here for the humans now! My dogs just busted their barricade!"

Chapter Eight

Kyana followed at a goddess's pace behind her dogs. Over walls and fences, through unkempt yards and vacant neighborhoods. One barbed-wire fence cost her her backpack, but she was forced to leave it behind or risk losing the trail her dogs were leaving her. This meant her last change of clothes, all the goodies Artemis had given her, and her supply of ambrosia were no longer available.

Lovely.

The only clear images in the blur of colors produced by her speed were the dogs running a dozen yards in front of her. Gradually, their pace slowed. Instead of leaping over obstacles, they picked their way around them until they reached a run-down part of town that, even before the destruction of the breakout, had seen better days.

The pack led her into a trailer park and to a driveway possessing a mailbox label "The Monroes." Her heart dipped into her toes and stayed there, anchored by realization and the hurt over being lied to. This place belonged to Haven's family. Kyana recognized it immediately from Haven's scrapbook. An old photo of Haven and her twin, Hope, had been the cover page, and the backdrop had been this same, dismal trailer.

Kyana truly thought Haven had never lied to her about anything. She'd told Kyana she'd grown up in the Smoky Mountains, in a small Tennessee town where all the kids in the county went to the same school and her father had been the local youth minister. Turned out, she'd grown up in a small town about fifteen miles outside Panama City. Once Kyana was able to gather herself, she inhaled deeply. The double-wide reeked of Haven.

Haven's lie disturbed Kyana as she drank in the dingy aluminum siding and the weed-filled driveway. Cast in the gray halo of night, there wasn't even any sun to cheer the dump up. Why had she lied? Kyana didn't care where Haven had come from. Hell, Kyana knew firsthand that the crap you lived through—or didn't as had been the case with her—didn't necessarily have anything to do with who you became. A trailer park in Tennessee or a trailer park in Florida, what did it matter?

Knowing the truth wouldn't have changed her love for Haven or made Kyana think less of her because she hadn't had the perfect childhood. If she hadn't wanted to talk about it, fine, then avoid the subject the way Kyana did. But why the lies?

"Why'd they bring us to this place?" Ryker's voice took her by surprise. She hadn't realized he'd been following so closely. "Why are we here?"

She ignored his question and looked around for Silas. He could defend himself should something attack, but he didn't have the ability to find her that Ryker seemed to.

"You left him alone?"

Ryker pointed over his shoulder where Silas was just making his way slowly down the street toward them. "Is this the place you saw in your vision?"

She took in the sight of the factory looming in the distance just outside the run-down trailer park. Three stories high and covered in red brick, the factory released plumes of gray smoke into the air and stank to high heaven.

"Yes. She came home."

Feeling the bitterness of Haven's lie creeping back into her throat, Kyana blew into her whistle twice and set it on the ground, then stepped back to let the dogs return home to rest. They disappeared as one slobbering bundle and she slipped the chain back around her neck.

"This isn't her home," Silas said as he joined them. "She's shown me pictures of where she grew up, and trust me, this isn't it."

Knowing she wasn't the only one Haven had lied to didn't ease the hurt. However, the sound of glass crashing inside put a stop to the speculation. The trio glanced at one another before breaking into a sprint.

They dashed up the rickety metal steps and ripped open the squeaky screen door just as a full-grown man flew across the room and collided with the wall. He lay slumped there as they pushed their way inside, his eyes wide, his mouth hanging open. Confusion and fear had turned his features into that of an old hound dog's. Nothing but wrinkles and worry.

"Help me," he said, raising his arms to protect his face.

Kyana followed his horrified gaze to the small, puke-green kitchen, and her heart tumbled somewhere around her knees. Haven glared at her from behind long, knotted hair—her chest heaving, her nails raking into the cabinets over her head. Small splinters of wood rained down on her, coating her head with chips of pea green.

"Haven." The name fell in a whisper from Kyana's lips as she moved forward.

This most certainly was not the same Haven Kyana knew. It wasn't smiling Haven, offering a friendship Kyana hadn't wanted ten years ago. Wasn't the Haven who laughed and flirted with Geoffrey, who wanted that relationship to go further and was too afraid to make it happen. Wasn't the same Haven who sat cross-legged in front of the fire at Solstice, sipping cider wine and wrapping presents she'd been shopping weeks for.

No. This Haven was possessed—a glimmer of evil in her eye that stole Kyana's breath as Haven leaped with ease behind a folding card table. Her mouth spread into a grin Kyana had never seen before. The grin of a madwoman.

"Going to take me home, Kyana?" Her blue eyes were blackened with malice and as she spoke, her eerily long fangs caressed her bottom lip. "And to think I was just about to say good-bye to Daddy."

She couldn't pull her gaze away from Haven to look at the man who had, apparently, sired her before Kyana. As she moved toward the table, Ryker's hand held steady on the small of her back. Unwilling to risk him restraining her when she found her moment to pounce, she brushed his touch away.

"Why would you hurt your father, Haven? You don't want to do this. This isn't you." She held out her hand. "Come with me, please. I can help you."

Haven cracked her knuckles and licked her lips. "Why would I want to hurt him? Do you want to tell them, Dad?"

When the man did nothing but whimper, she continued. "He beat me every day until my mother finally got me out of here. His perversion took my innocence and stole Hope's life. He killed her, and I'm not leaving till I taste his heart beating in my throat."

She glared down at her father. "It's okay, Kyana. He'd like to see Mama and Hope again before the shadows drag his sorry ass to Hell, wouldn't you, Daddy?"

No, no, no. If Haven acted on her impulses right now, she'd never be able to live with herself once she'd been purged and made right again.

Retribution made some stronger, gave them purpose and direction, but for someone kind and compassionate like Haven, it would slowly eat away at her soul until there was nothing left. It would steal the last of her humanity, and Kyana would lose her forever to Cronos.

"Haven, you don't want to do this," she repeated. "Where's the trident?"

She'd hoped the reminder of her bigger task might pull Haven from the intent to kill. She was wrong. Haven ignored her and dove over the table, rolling across the floor and popping back onto her feet just inches away from her semiconscious father.

"Get him out of here," she growled at Silas before diving over the counter and knocking Haven off her feet.

Haven crouched on the floor and hissed. "When I've given him a taste of what it's like to be beaten until you can't think without hurting, I'll finish him off. Then it's your turn."

"I can't let you do this, Haven."

She threw back her head and laughed. "You don't get a say. Because of you, I'm not bound by honor anymore."

Haven's gaze shifted. Kyana didn't need to look to know Ryker had moved behind her. That likely he was standing guard to allow Silas to get the human out of the trailer.

Haven bared her teeth. "Don't push your luck, Ryker. I don't give a shit what you are. You try to stand in my way and I'll kill you too."

"You can try," Ryker said, his voice so low and deadly that it caused the fine hairs on Kyana's neck to stand up.

For an instant, she wondered if Haven was out of control enough to attack Ryker. Haven knew what he was capable of, had to know that attacking him would be suicide. Kyana didn't have to wait long to find out. When he stepped around her, Haven's roar of outrage rattled the dirty windows and she threw herself at him. Ryker's eyes swirled bloodred.

He was going to kill her.

"No!" Kyana roared, launching herself at her best friend. Her sister.

They crashed to the floor. Haven wiggled out from under her and charged again, but Kyana caught her ankle and pulled. Haven hit the floor with a bone-rattling thud.

Behind them, she heard Silas shuffling Haven's father out the door, and glanced up to see Ryker watching intently, his body tense and ready to join the fray. But he stood steadily in the doorway, obviously aware that she needed to be the one who finished this.

She quickly flipped Haven over, straddled her waist, and pinned her shoulders to the filthy, threadbare shag carpet. "Damn it, Haven. I don't want to hurt you."

Haven, apparently, didn't have the same issues. Her fist connected with Kyana's jaw, knocking her off balance long enough for Haven to shimmy to her feet. "You want to stop me?"

Prepared to strike if Haven moved toward her father, Kyana nodded. "You know I have no choice."

Eerie blackish eyes that shifted to yellow locked on Kyana. "Then you'll have to hurt me, because I have to finish this."

"You don't want to do this."

"Oh yes, I do. I want to kill that bastard. Then I'll finish my task and bring Cronos back from the grave."

They circled each other. "You know I can't let you do that either."

"I know. When the time's right, I'll have to kill you too."

The hard, lifeless look Haven directed at her wasn't bluffing.

"What are you waiting for?" she goaded. "Come on, Haven. Show me what you can do."

With a chilling laugh, Haven nodded. "Okay, we can play. It's about time someone knocked the mighty Kyana on her ass."

In a blink, Haven was on her—fangs bared and claws surprisingly accurate. They raked across her cheek, spilling blood that only seemed to inspire the lunatic inside Haven.

She tried to dodge her attacks, to let Haven wear herself out so she could bring her in safely, but Haven moved so quickly she could only duck every other swing. The cat-and-mouse tactic wasn't working anymore. She smashed the hilt of her dagger into Haven's jaw. The sharp crack of bones snapping sent Haven to her knees, her hands cupping her face.

Taking advantage of Haven's moment of weakness, Kyana let loose a roar and gripped the front of Haven's shirt. The instinct to drive her fangs into Haven's exposed throat made her stomach cramp. Afraid she might act on the lingering Vampyric impulse, she slung Haven into the kitchen. She landed on the table, but was on her feet again before the broken furniture hit the floor.

She lost track of who hit whom and whose roars of rage echoed louder. However, soon Haven's swings became slower, more off balance. Seizing the advantage, Kyana gripped Haven's throat and dangled her in the air.

"This ends now." She squeezed lightly. Even though Haven didn't need to breathe anymore, the constriction would cut off the blood flow, but it would be a fine line between killing Haven and knocking her unconscious. "When you wake up, you'll be on the road to finding yourself again. I'll be there with you. You won't have to face this alone."

Haven's laughter came out in gasps. "You don't get to win."

Her smile was sly and chilling, her eyes shifted from eerie yellow to lifeless black, glassy and narrowed with venom. "I know where Zeus keeps his staff. Amazing what a father knows about his sons . . ."

Before Kyana realized Haven's intentions, she shifted to Lychen. Her fur-covered body slipped from Kyana's grasp as Haven shot across the room and out one of the grimy windows.

Chapter Nine

N o!"

Kyana's scream was echoed by Ryker's curses. He leaped out the front door and onto the pavement, where he attempted to use his telekinetic powers to restrain the wolf and failed.

"I need ambrosia," he yelled, running back to her. "Where's your bag? I can't chase after her—"

"Gone," Kyana whispered. She had no idea where the barbed-wire fence that had stolen it was or how far away it might be.

He cursed and kicked the skirting. She guessed he was trying to summon the same godly speed that she was attempting to conjure, but they were both out of juice.

Kneeling, she attempted to shift to Lychen and give chase that way, but nothing happened. Cursing hotly, she pulled the chain from her neck, blew into the golden whistle, and placed it on the ground at her feet. Instantly, the hounds looked up at her, waiting for instruction.

"Follow," she said, her voice weak and barely above a whisper. With a trio of barks, the three golden pups disappeared to do her bidding.

Fatigue overwhelmed her and she dropped to the metal step and rested her hands on her knees. She wanted so badly to slide into her own wolf body and follow the pack, but she was at a disadvantage without a dose of ambrosia. She'd be no match for Haven in this state. Hell, without her eyebright, she couldn't even see through the dogs' eyes now. If there was any leftover store of energy inside her, she was too defeated to find it.

"I underestimated her," she admitted, swearing to herself that she would never make that mistake again.

"We both did," he said, sitting beside her and resting his hand on her shoulder. "Ky, where is she going?"

She wiped the blood from her mouth and nose. "How would I know? I can't shift," she whispered, appalled at how much her body hurt. As Vampyre, she could tolerate a high amount of pain before giving in to the need to rest and heal. Shouldn't a goddess have an even higher threshold? "I can't go after her. I had to send the mutts in my place. That's bullshit."

"You did the right thing. The smart thing. Without ambrosia you're—"

She shoved to her feet. To hell with this. She hadn't yet lost all the powers that made her a tracer. It might take the last of her reserves, but damn it, she wasn't sending a trio of puppies to do a bitch's job.

Squeezing her eyes shut, she let her determination to follow Haven coax her into a near trance until she felt the slight tug in her abdomen and a surge of adrenaline in her veins. When she next opened her eyes, the world had become black and white. Her fur-covered skin rippled as she leaped over the driveway, following Haven's scent as quickly as her four feet allowed.

She ran, but the continual flicker of energy nearly cost her the hold on the form over and over, and it took all her concentration to maintain it, making holding on to Haven's scent all the more difficult. She tried instead for the scent of her dogs, and followed as best as she could in her half-handicapped state.

She wound around a Dumpster and squeezed under a fence leading into the factory behind the park. This must have been where Haven had been hiding out until the sun had set and it had become safe for her to come out and visit her father. Or maybe not. Maybe she'd adjusted to the Turning faster than anyone had considered.

She'd definitely been stronger than Kyana had expected, so maybe Haven could hold to Lychen form long enough to roam a couple of hours of daylight. Regardless, she couldn't hold it as long as Kyana could. Drained or not, Kyana wasn't going to lose her form unless she keeled over and died right there on the street.

If she could just follow Haven's trail long enough for her to weaken and shift back, she could catch up to her and take her in.

But no sooner had the thought occurred to her than Haven's scent vanished like a puff of smoke. Its disappearance was so sudden, it made Kyana's head spin. She rocked back on her haunches, afraid to move.

She looked up. She was yards away from any building. The factory entrance was half a football field away. She shouldn't have lost the trail here, in the middle of a street with nowhere to hide.

What kind of magic was Haven using to elude her? Charms? Potions? Both?

Silently chastising herself for not paying more attention to Haven's spell crafting when they were living under the same roof, Kyana made her way sluggishly back to the trailer. They were going into that factory, but she wanted her opposable thumbs back when they did.

Her ears flattened to her head at the sight of her tattered leather pants and boots lying in ribbons on the driveway. Her tank top was unsalvageable, and she'd lost her change of clothes to barbed wire.

Lovely.

Ryker held out a wad of fabric so she could see it, then tossed it inside the open door of the trailer. "It's all I could find inside, but I figured anything was better than nothing."

Grateful for his thoughtfulness, she made her way back inside the metal heap, snatched the bundle of clothing between her teeth, and dragged it into the kitchen where she could shift and maintain a tiny bit of dignity.

She waited for her bones to adjust to her two-legged body, then unrolled the bundle of clothing and groaned. Men's sneakers. Men's jeans. A size XXL flannel shirt with two missing buttons near the collar. The only good thing was her daggers lying on the plaid, making the fabric look dingy.

"You've got to be kidding me." She couldn't intimidate a puppy in this getup.

Regardless, she dutifully put them on and half tripped her way to the bedroom behind her in search of a belt. The jeans slipped past her ass with every step, and the long fabric wrapped under each foot making grace an impossibility.

She dug through the drawers as quickly as she could manage and found a wide leather belt. Rolling her eyes at the horrible, rusted belt buckle that weighed more than she did, she slipped it into her belt loops. She had to puncture another hole to make it fit and then wrap the belt around her waist twice, but it would hold her pants up and secure her weapons, so it would work for now.

She rolled up the jean cuffs and slipped back outside, deciding to forgo the shoes. The damned things were about four sizes too big.

"Let's go."

Silas looked up from where he crouched beside Haven's father. "What about him?"

Kyana shrugged. "He'll live."

She was only half hoping she was right. If he was really the reason Hope had died, if he'd really beaten Haven's childhood out of her, he deserved whatever fate awaited him after they left.

Part of her wished they'd come five minutes later so Haven could have finished him off.

Kyana knew all too well about abusive fathers. It was a shame she'd never known they'd shared that particular bond. She couldn't really fault Haven for not sharing her past. She'd never told Haven about hers either.

"Ky?" Ryker rested his hand on her shoulder and shook her lightly. "Silas asked where we were going and if you needed him to scry for Haven again."

"We're going to check out that factory where I lost her scent." She looked up at the starless night sky. "Hope you brought a flashlight."

Not that Ryker or she would have any trouble seeing in the dark, but Silas would be an accident waiting to happen. Maybe bringing him hadn't been the smartest idea.

"You're going to get my ass kicked aren't you?" Silas complained as he helped Haven's dad stand. "We should wait till the sun comes up when she's weaker."

"Are you turning into a wuss?" she asked, glaring at Silas. She turned her attention to Haven's dad. She wasn't sure if she'd kill him as a favor to Haven, or if she could force herself to go against her instincts to use him as bait to get Haven to come after him again. "It's not safe for him to come with us."

Silas raised an eyebrow. "Thought we were all protect-the-humans now."

"For him I'll make an exception. Besides, he's been fine here for two weeks. Dark Breeds don't seem to want him either. Take him inside and let's go."

Silas glanced at the man barely standing beside him. "How did you avoid the Dark Breeds, anyway?"

Blood oozed from the older man's lip as he cracked them open to speak. "The factory . . . I was hiding . . . there. Haven. Haven brought me here."

So *that's* what she had been doing when they'd linked. Damn. Maybe she hadn't gone back there after all. Maybe since she'd gotten what she'd wanted from the place, she had no further use for it.

No. Haven would have to go back there. The trident had been in Kyana's vision, and Haven hadn't had it here. She had to have left it in the factory.

Ignoring Ryker's intense stare, Kyana moved around the back of the lot to study the tall brick building. She should've known he wouldn't take the hint to stay put. He had something he wanted to say and he wouldn't rest until he'd spoken his mind.

"What?"

"Are you okay?" he asked.

"Dandy."

He stiffened at the sarcastic sting of her words. "I don't mean physically, Ky. I wouldn't have let—"

She spun on him and thumped her fist in the middle of his chest. "You take your orders from *me*. I thought I made that clear before we left Olympus. You will do *nothing* where Haven is concerned. Do you understand me? You're not a tracer. Your job is to bring her in after *I* subdue her."

"I'm not to interfere unless your life is at risk." Ryker held up his hands, but a flicker of cold steel flashed in his eyes. "I know you think you are, but you're not completely in charge yet, Ky. Artemis and Ares are still my bosses."

"Fuck that," she spat, loathing that he was right and that, technically, there wasn't a damned thing she could do to stop him from taking Haven down without her say-so.

He reached for her, but wisely dropped his hand before she had to remove it at the wrist. "You're more important than Haven. Protecting you, keeping you alive, is my priority."

Because she was a Chosen.

Bullshit.

"So if she'd had the trident with her, you would have killed her tonight?"

"I don't know, but I'm almost certain you wouldn't have."

So much for their truce. Whatever soft, gooey emotions might have been growing inside her these last weeks hardened to bitterness. *This* was why things would never work out between them.

Ryker had the ability to dig so deeply into what made her tick that at times like this, she hated him for it. How was she supposed to give herself completely to someone who could piss her off so easily?

And if he dug far enough, he'd see she wasn't as strong as she claimed to be, see what she'd come from to get where she was. What then? Would he look at her the way he'd looked at Haven today?

No. This was never going to work. Once this job was over, so were she and Ryker.

"You think you could have stopped her from shifting and getting away?" she asked, knowing she was taking more of her anger out of him than he deserved.

Ryker was duty-bound. His place in the Order came before everything else. She'd known that from the moment she met him. So why was it bothering her so much now?

She plowed on, preferring the anger to the gnaw of guilt and frustration. "I seem to remember you trying to blast her with your Jedi mind power and it didn't work either. If you have all the answers, then what's our next step? How do we find her? The trident?"

The compassion in his eyes settled a bit of the ire boiling in her gut, and that pissed her off even more. She wanted to be angry right now, damn it. She wanted this to be as personal for him as it was for her.

"I don't know," he admitted, his voice low and steady.

They'd come to a crossroads.

There was nothing else to say except "Give me your word that you won't kill her."

She didn't know how long they stood matching each other glare for glare. Neither was willing to back down or to admit the other just might be right in his views . . . or at least have a right to them.

"You know I'll have to stop you if you go after her," she said. "Whatever it takes."

"If it comes to it, I hope your judgment will be sound enough that I won't have to do anything."

This time when he reached for her she didn't glare him down, but when he put his hand on her waist, she pushed him away. As much as she wanted to lean on him, she couldn't. It was only going to be worse if she kept letting herself daydream about what could happen if she believed the way he seemed to that they were supposed to be together.

When Ryker didn't make another move to soothe her, she knew the argument was over. He wasn't going to give in and neither would she. Still, she believed he wouldn't step in unless he saw absolutely no other way to prevent her death.

He'd kill Haven before he stood by and let her kill the new goddess, but otherwise, he wouldn't interfere.

He lowered his head and looped his thumb in her belt loops, drawing her into him again. She stepped back, but when he tangled his fingers in her hair, she wanted nothing more than for him to kiss her. Her pride wouldn't allow it, however, and she lowered her face, forcing him to press his lips to her head instead.

Later, she would tell him whatever this was between them was over. Right now, she didn't have the strength for it.

As Ryker slipped his fingers from Kyana's hair to under her chin, he wished that he wasn't one of Ares's sentinels. That he was just a normal man who could comfort this woman who'd pricked her way beneath his skin. The fact that she wouldn't even look him in the eye right now told him she was sorry she'd ever let him get as close as he'd gotten, and that pissed him off more than anything she could have said directly to him.

He pulled her closer, burying her face in his neck, and winced as he felt her hands push against his chest. With a sigh, he dropped his arms and released her.

Their jobs always seemed to be in the way of their future—whether she acknowledged that future or not.

Silas stepped around the side of the trailer and Ryker waited for him to make a smart-ass comment, but the Witch wisely restrained himself.

"You sure I can't talk you out of going into the big, dark, scary building at night?" Silas asked.

Kyana smoothed her hair over her shoulder and jostled herself back into business mode. "I think you've been hanging out with your pouty girlfriend for too long. You've become as pansy-assed as she is."

Silas laughed. "I'm just a realist. I've discovered that fighting is more fun if you actually see your opponent's face when you ram your fist into it. And Sixx isn't pouty *or* a pansy. You'd be surprised how well her body—"

Kyana elbowed him in the stomach and shut him up.

Silas slipped his arm lightly around her shoulder, and the searing sensation of jealousy ripped through Ryker's stomach.

When Silas glimpsed his face, he shrugged. "Lots of debris in this field." He pointed at Kyana's bare toes. "Thought she might want a piggyback ride."

"If anyone's giving her a piggyback ride, it's me," Ryker grumbled.

"I don't take piggybacks from *anyone*."

Silas laughed. "Someone really needs to teach you that you're a woman and showing those attributes outside of the bedro—"

Kyana shot the Witch a deadly stare that silenced him as quickly as her elbow had, but Ryker could finish Silas's statement for him. Surely he was kidding, though. The bedroom? There was definitely a flirtatious relationship here, but Ryker couldn't see Kyana hooking up with someone like Silas.

Why? Because he's nothing like you?

He scowled. Kyana wasn't exactly his type, and he was willing to bet he wasn't hers. If they weren't being forced to work together, would the constant need for her have subsided by now?

He considered that for a moment and decided that the answer was undoubtedly no. The effort she put into fighting for her friends was exactly what he wanted in a woman. The compassion she displayed for Haven today, even if it was buried under an exterior of steel, proved she wasn't the hard-ass everyone else saw her for.

She was exactly his type in exactly the right package. Strong, independent, with a creamy soft center you had to dig deep to taste. His type, indeed.

He pressed on behind Silas and Kyana. None of that mattered now. When this job was done, then maybe he could think about what should and should not be between him and Ky. But right now, he had to make sure she did *her* job, so he wouldn't be forced to do his.

He'd still give Kyana the space and time she needed to try and subdue her friend, but if it looked like she couldn't complete her task, or if Haven attempted to flee again, he'd have to step in.

That thought soured his mood even more. If he was forced to step in, it wouldn't matter what fate had decided for their future. There would be nothing left between them if he was forced to kill Haven.

"You know we can't just leave her dad here to die," he grumbled, forcing himself to stop mooning over what might or might not happen. "We have to get him help just like we get everyone else."

Kyana shrugged. "We'll come back when we're done in the factory. If he's still there, maybe I'll think about saving him. It would be a pity for a Dark Breed other than Haven to sink its teeth into that ass—"

She stopped abruptly and Ryker knew she'd caught a scent as she lifted her head and sniffed the wind. Ryker smelled it too.

Silas's face lost all traces of humor. "Dark Breeds?"

"Yeah, and something a hell of a lot worse," Ryker muttered.

If Haven was still here, she wasn't alone anymore.

Chapter Ten

The door to the abandoned factory hung by one rusty hinge. It was a relief to find a place they could easily access, though as they stood on the steps, Kyana was pretty sure Ryker and Silas didn't want to go inside any more than she did.

"Dear God, what *is* that smell?"

Finally, Silas was able to detect the stench Ryker and Kyana had picked up halfway across the debris-littered field. It was familiar, sulfuric, and as nasty as unclean ass. Kyana had smelled it on the key to Tartarus when she'd been assigned to lock Hell back up, as well as in the room at the Healing Circle from which Haven had escaped after Kyana had turned her.

Given those two associations, that sulfuric stink was putting a knot in Kyana's stomach now.

"I'm not sure," she said, taking her first tentative step inside. "But I'm starting to think it might be Cronos."

The sulfuric stench was overpowering enough

to hide the real scents of the factory, which Kyana was beginning to suspect would have been foul with or without Cronos's presence. Already she could see the hooks hanging from the ceiling, the dried blood, the carcasses left to rot weeks ago when the world had gone topsy-turvy. "Think it's a meatpacking plant. But that stink isn't from this place, it's from the people in it."

"Well, it can't be Cronos. He's still dead," Ryker said, stepping beside her. His eyes swirled red as he honed in on his ability to penetrate the darkness.

"Haven's seeing him, remember? Now they have the trident too. I'm guessing Cronos is more than just bones now. A spirit maybe."

She studied the large, nasty room. That piggy-back ride Silas had offered wasn't looking too bad right about now. She looked at Ryker. "I still have my natural immunity to disease and infection, right?"

He nodded.

Kyana sighed and began the tedious chore of picking her way to the stairs without losing a toe.

"Hello. I don't have any such built-in defenses," Silas grumbled. Ryker and Kyana ignored his complaints and he finally followed behind them, muttering under his breath.

Thanks to the open slaughter area, there weren't many hiding places on this level. Only pride kept Kyana from moaning or cursing out loud as the debris cut into her bare feet. By the time they'd cleared the second floor, finding nothing more than what were most likely Haven's father's meager belongings and empty booze bottles, she was beginning to wonder if anything they might find was worth the pain of retrieving it.

The stairway was blocked by a large door with a sign declaring EMPLOYEES ONLY.

Slowly, she eased open the door. The stench nearly knocked her backward. Ryker caught her around the waist and hissed. Silas cursed. Weren't they a sorry bunch? They made enough noise that deaf humans could've heard them coming from a mile away.

"I'm not sure I want to know what was living in there." Silas's voice was muffled. He'd pulled the neck of his T-shirt over his nose. "At this point, I don't even want to fight it. Just tell me it's gone and we can get out of here."

"It's not gone," Ryker and Kyana said together.

Proof lay in the violent whispers of an all-too-familiar voice. Haven. She was arguing with herself, frantically gesturing at the brick wall in front of her.

Kyana drew her daggers and looked at Silas, who held his long, lethal-looking blade in his fist, then to Ryker, who simply stared at her. "When are you going to learn that it's important to pack a weapon?"

His lips curved in a slight smile. "About the time you learn I don't need one."

She rolled her eyes. Okay, so she'd seen him take on an army solo, but it would have made her feel better knowing he was armed with *something*.

She pulled a spare blade from her belt and forced it into his hand before slipping through the partially opened door. Haven turned as though she were ankle-deep in syrup. Slow, smooth. As her gaze fell on Kyana, her eyes narrowed to black slits that looked capable of shooting venom.

"Mm mm mm . . ." The noise originated low in Haven's throat, releasing in a rumble of mockery rather than a threatening taunt. "That nose of yours. I have to admit, I was hoping it wouldn't be so sharp since you stole my destiny."

She smiled, flashing a glimpse of bloodied teeth. "Tell me, Kyana. How does it feel to be a goddess? To know you are now becoming what by all rights should have been mine?"

The accusation stung, but Kyana wasn't taking the bait. "You would have been dead if I hadn't turned you. Hard to become a goddess when you're six feet under."

Behind her, she could feel Silas and Ryker edging closer. She stepped sideways to block their path. Her own instinct to lunge immediately was making her toes tingle, but she kept her feet firmly to the floor and stood as still as possible while Haven scrutinized her.

Haven certainly wasn't herself at the moment, but neither did she have that gleam of craziness in her eyes. If she could talk coherently, maybe they could find out what Cronos was planning.

"My hair," Haven said, shaking her head. "My powers. My *fucking destiny*." Spit flung from her mouth as her fangs tore into her bottom lip. She still wasn't used to them, unskilled in keeping her mouth safe from their deadliness. The blood oozed from the center of her lip and she licked it clean. "You stole it all."

Kyana's fingers were wrapped around the hilt of her dagger so tightly, her knuckles throbbed. "Fine. Come with me, Haven. I'll tell Artemis I don't want it. We'll convince her to give it all to you. It's not too late . . . yet. But if you keep at this, if you keep listening to Cronos, I *won't* be able to save you."

Haven's laughter contained a sadness that didn't live up to the blackness glimmering in her eyes.

"I can help you, Haven. You don't have to listen to him anymore."

"Help me? There's no *me* to help anymore!" Haven backed away, her lip curling with disgust. "You think I care that you're the new Goddess of the Hunt? That will be puny in comparison to what *he* is. What he'll be. When I'm finished, whatever fancy skills Artemis is teaching you will look like nothing more than a useless fly swatter. So many holes for me to fly through, Kyana. So many ways around what you've become. You have nothing to offer me. *Nothing!*"

Kyana winced, forcing herself to cling to the tiny trace of fear lacing Haven's words. She refused to believe Haven meant everything she said. She was a fighter. There was no way in hell she was going to let Cronos win without resistance. He was in her now, Kyana was sure of it. The blackness in Haven's eyes didn't belong to her any more than the deep, husky voice did.

"Just come with us. We can fight this. Together. Me, you, and Geoffrey."

Her head jerked as though she'd been slapped. "Geoff?"

She grabbed hold of the hope in Haven's voice and nodded. "He misses you. And he's worried about you. He wants you to come home."

A glazed sheen fell over Haven's dark eyes as she stepped away. "Fuck you."

Kyana took a step forward, unwilling to allow Haven even an inch of retreat.

"You're our family. We'll always love you." She took another step closer. "Just come back with me. Let us take care of you."

She reached for Haven's arm, and just as her fingers were about to close over her wrist, she jerked out of Kyana's grasp.

Haven convulsed, her head jerking wildly from side to side until an eerie calm settled around her and the eyes staring back at Kyana once again belonged to a stranger. "You had your chance. You refused. She's mine now."

Kyana lunged for Haven. As her hand circled Haven's wrist, a flurry of dust kicked up and slowly grew near the window. Ryker and Silas were at Kyana's side and together they watched the dust storm, their breaths puffing white as the temperature dropped enough to form ice crystals on the ceiling. Haven didn't so much as wiggle to break free.

Instead, her hair blew behind her and her eyes flashed with menace. "What you've started can't be stopped."

Kyana could have sworn she saw a flicker of fear pop from somewhere in those black depths that had once been Haven's eyes. Cronos was working her like a puppet.

She intended to make sure his bones were turned into dust and his sorry ass was scattered to the four corners of the Earth.

"Leave her alone."

The pink tongue that flicked out to dampen Haven's lips looked eerily human in such a demonic face. "My new friend here is very powerful, or she soon will be. Scatter my bones if you like. She will raise me, regardless."

He was in Kyana's head, hearing her thoughts. She concentrated so hard on not thinking, her eyes began to burn.

"I trust you'll let my sons know that their time is short."

Haven spun in a dizzying speed that forced Kyana to release her. Something gold appeared in her hand, and Kyana heard herself gasp when the dust swirl revealed the trident. But before she could reach for it, Haven pulled a small pouch from the pocket of her dirty jeans and threw a handful of greenish powder at her feet.

"Grab her!" Silas shot around Kyana, throwing himself at Haven.

"*Devito!*" Haven screamed. A white light engulfed every inch of the foul-smelling room. When Kyana could see again, Silas lay in a heap on the floor and Haven was gone.

And so was the trident.

Kyana ran to the window, looking out into the darkness. Haven was nowhere to be seen. Her scent, the stench of Cronos, and the smell of death that had filled the factory only seconds ago were gone. She'd simply vanished.

"Sonofabitch!" Kyana spun on Silas. "What was that?"

Rubbing his shoulder, he struggled to his feet. "It's a powerful, ancient spell. I've read up on it, but have never seen anyone actually attempt it."

The awe in his voice didn't ease her frustration. "You can be impressed later. Right now, I just want to know what it was so I can figure out how to keep her from doing it again."

"The spell allows her to maneuver her way out of sticky situations."

"Like astral projection?" She'd tried that once. Wasn't fun.

"Not exactly. It's like suspended animation. Or maybe the slowing of time would be a better explanation." Silas wiped his hands on his jeans. "Either way, she's casting the spell that binds us and allows her the freedom to slip away. It covers her scent. Leaves no markers. It's damned hard to track and even harder to prevent."

So that was how she'd been evading Kyana's tracking skills. She was exhausted, and being outsmarted by a dead god wasn't exactly rejuvenating. She sighed and grudgingly followed as Ryker and Silas led the way out of the factory.

"I need food. And ambrosia. I'm running on empty but we don't have time for more than a quick snack. I won't lose her this time."

She saw Ryker nod from the corner of her eye, but kept her focus on Silas. "Can you create a counter spell so she can't leave me in the dust like this again?"

"Doubt it, but I'll start working on it the minute we return Below."

"The trident's gone," she said, "and we've seen for ourselves that Cronos is able to take over Haven's body. Guess we know now how she's able to touch the Eyes of Power without dying."

"Yeah," Ryker said. "Because *she's* not technically touching it. *He* is."

Yes. Cronos was living and breathing inside her best friend, and she was beginning to fear that the only way to get him out was to wreck the vehicle he was driving. If she couldn't get through to Haven soon, Kyana was going to have no choice but to kill her.

Chapter Eleven

When they finally stumbled their way out of the meatpacking plant, the sky had lit up with oranges and pinks, offering Kyana only her third experience with a real sunrise in two hundred years. She'd seen the black and white version while in Lychen form and she'd seen sunrises Below, where the sun wasn't actually real, but neither was comparable to seeing the beauty of an authentic sunrise.

Unlike the previous two mornings, however, this time, she could drink it all in while Ryker shared the last of his ambrosia and bread with her. She sat on the edge of Haven's father's cracked, grease-stained driveway, waiting for Silas to return with a car that would get them back to St. Augustine. They couldn't wait the hours it would take for Ryker's port to be usable again.

She closed her eyes and reluctantly reopened them to finally look at him.

"Tell me that I won't be knocked out of commission every time I face a fight," she said.

"When you learn to balance the ambrosia it'll get less debilitating. Remember, your transformation isn't complete. You're only half you and half what you'll become."

She didn't want to think about being only half as good as she was used to being. She was facing enough of a challenge as it was. A cloud rolled over the bright sun, casting shadows over the trailer park before the sun popped out once again and coated her skin like a fleece blanket. She wished she could sit here and do nothing but drink in the day, but sadly for her, the agenda wasn't going to be that pleasant.

Haven's father tripped his way down the trailer's steps, stinking up the moment with B.O. and stale cigarettes. She glared over her shoulder at him, pissed that, not only was he ruining her sunrise, but that she'd also been talked into returning to pick him up in the first place.

Ryker and Silas had insisted that it would go against the Order of Ancients if they left the man to die. They'd sent for help for the people huddled in the malls; it was only fair to help Haven's bastard daddy as well.

As he made his way toward them, she squinted, scrutinizing his face for some resemblance to Haven. She found it buried beneath thick gray eyebrows that covered the familiar blue eyes staring back at her with apprehension. This man had fathered her best friend, had given Haven to the world, and yet even that acknowledgment didn't soften her toward him.

As far as she was concerned, there wasn't a Dark Breed ever created that could equal the evil of an abusive parent.

Pushing herself to her feet, she finished chewing the last bite of her bread and looked to Ryker, who was leaning on the lamppost beside her. "You know what pisses me off the most? I know what it means to be a monster. I don't want to believe I've given that fate to my best friend."

"She's only a monster when you've given up and left her to whatever fate Cronos is trying to hand her."

Kyana tried to read him, but his face was a blank page. She knew he didn't think Haven was worth her time, but something in his voice told her he *wanted* to think she might be. That because Kyana believed it, maybe he'd try as well.

"I could try to link with her again," she heard herself say, though it was the last thing she wanted to do. So far, each time she'd reached out to Haven, what she'd seen had grown darker and more frightening.

Ryker gave a faint smile and turned his attention back to the road, probably wishing Silas would hurry the hell up so they could be on their way. "We have a long drive. A nap might not be a bad idea. If you sleep, maybe you can reach her."

Nodding, she looked around at the mobile home

and tried to envision her friend growing up here. It was hard. Haven was so bright and bubbly, so sunny. How did someone grow up in this environment and turn out so damned happy and eager to help people?

The same way someone born of privilege ends up cynical and bitter like I did.

Kyana knew better than anyone that one's material environment meant nothing. She'd been born with a silver spoon in her mouth. Wanted for nothing as the daughter of a very wealthy businessman. She'd married a prince, lived in a palace, and yet the royalty and nobility that had surrounded her had been no better than the scum Haven had been brought up with.

The only difference was, Kyana had cleaned up her blood with silk and Haven had dabbed hers with toilet paper.

"You're shivering," Ryker said, pulling Kyana from her funk. "It's like eighty degrees and you have warm blood now, so what's making you shiver?"

"Just thinking."

"About?"

"Family."

The sigh she released was filled with weariness as she shut her eyes against the sun. "It takes strength to care, I think. Haven was way stronger than I ever was."

"Just because you care about different things doesn't make you weak, Ky."

She felt him watching her, but she refused to look up at him. "What if she *is* stronger than me, in every way that counts?"

"She's not Haven right now, which means all those attributes you're envying don't exist. *You* have the advantage."

Kyana dug the heels of her hands into her eyes. "And how's that?"

"This time, you're the one who cares."

His faith in her was generous, and it gave her the courage to meet his gaze. "So love conquers all, huh?"

"In this case, yeah, I think it might." He stepped toward her but stopped when a small red car spun into the tiny driveway, braking a mere foot away from them. Silas was back. It was time to hit the road. Time to admit she didn't have the first clue where to go from here.

She tossed a glare at Haven's dad. "What's your name, anyway?"

He blinked. "K-K-Kevin."

"Well, K-K-Kevin, if you have anything you want to bring, grab it now. Unless you want to be stranded alone when your daughter decides to come back and finish what we interrupted, you're coming with us."

His throat rose and fell in a deep swallow before he turned and stumbled into his home.

"We give him five minutes," she muttered. "Then we leave him to whatever fate he deserves."

She waited six. Then, with an irritated huff, she

snatched up her baggy jeans, hoisting them so she wouldn't make an ass of herself by tripping, and went in after him while Ryker and Silas fussed with the car's radio.

She heard Kevin rustling around his bedroom and waited by the door, half tempted to stomp in there and drag him out by the scruff of his neck. That would require physical contact, however, and she'd already met her quota of filth today.

While she waited, her gaze skimmed the dusty shelves behind the television, the yellowed family portraits lining the walls. This was all a tiny piece of Haven. Her childhood. Her past. This was where she'd come from, and it was absolutely amazing that she'd managed to become such a phenomenal woman despite it. Even evil, Haven was a force to be reckoned with.

Kyana traced her fingers over the grimy pane of glass covering a collage of snapshots hanging above the kitchen bar. Her fingertips came away black, and as she brushed her hand on her flannel shirt, her gaze froze on a photo of identical twins, grinning ear to ear.

She felt as though she should have been able to tell which child was Haven, but the girls were so alike, Kyana couldn't make out a single attribute that was distinctive to one but not the other. She squinted, leaning in closer. Still nothing.

They even wore matching bruises over their left eyes.

Bastard.

The girls wore pink dresses and stood in front of a road sign. She tried to make out the grainy words, and when they finally became clear, she chuckled.

CAUTION: SPIRITS CROSSING

It looked exactly like a deer crossing sign, but clearly had to be a joke. Behind the twins, a bright pink building looked like it had been painted with Pepto-Bismol. The sign on the lawn read:

AURA READINGS $10.00
TAROT READINGS $25.00
PAST LIFE REGRESSION—PLEASE INQUIRE

"I know this place," she muttered aloud. But for the life of her, she couldn't place it.

"Cassadaga." Kevin's voice boomed behind her. "It's a spiritual camp down South."

Kyana made the connection in her head. "Where the psychics go to retire."

Haven had made Kyana go there with her once at the beginning of their friendship.

She swallowed. If Haven was scared, if she felt at all inadequate in what Cronos was making her do, she'd have her nose in a book committing new spells to memory. And if there were any rare spells, charms, or potions to be learned, she'd likely find them in a place like Cassadaga.

She'll return to the familiar.

It was why Panama City had made sense. If

Haven was returning to places that held some trace of her humanity, why not Cassadaga? Why not a place where she might find answers that could possibly help free her of Cronos?

Or even help her give him what he wanted?

Her heart began to race. "Did she go there often?" she asked.

Kevin stuffed a jacket into a beat-up duffel bag. "Her mother took her there all the time before . . . before our family fell apart."

Before you murdered your daughter, you prick.

Leaving Kevin standing between his kitchen and bedroom, Kyana jogged out of the trailer and leaped down the stairs, landing on the pavement with a smack to her bare feet.

Ryker and Silas looked at her with curious expressions.

"You said Cronos might be telling her things she can't possibly know," she managed, excitement making it hard to be coherent.

It was Ryker who answered. "Yeah. Haven knew how to get to the trident and claims to know where the other Eyes of Power are hidden. She can't possibly know without a psychic connection."

Kevin loped down the steps to join them and she gave him a rough shove toward the vehicle. "Get in the car."

"Where are we going?" Silas asked.

"Where the psychics go to retire."

Chapter Twelve

Even without traffic as a hindrance, the trip from Panama City to Cassadaga was tort-uously slow. Silas drove, Ryker navigated, and Kyana tried to lie in what some might call a backseat of the little red car. But lying down was impossible given the size of the seat and the bulk of Haven's dad wasting space beside her. She'd considered stuffing him in the trunk, but was pretty sure he wouldn't fit.

He let out a rumbling snore and Kyana elbowed him in the ribs. She might have to put up with his presence but she didn't have to put up with his obnoxious breathing patterns.

"Sonofabitch." Silas brought the vehicle to an abrupt stop. "Another barricade."

Haven's father sputtered, knocking Kyana in the chin with his big ogre-sized palm as he flailed back to life. "Whasgoinon?"

"Go back to sleep."

His eyes darted nervously around the car interior before focusing on the roadblock illuminated in the bright orb of headlights. "Another one?"

The GPS chirped as Ryker punched buttons searching for another route. The damned thing had already given Kyana a headache. She didn't do any better around electronics than she did automotives. It was the Lychen in her. She had hoped Artemis's blood might quiet the static technology caused in her head, but that probably wouldn't happen until her other breeds completely faded into the background.

Her patience worn completely thin, she struggled to separate herself from Kevin's bulky mass. "I swear I can walk faster than you two can drive. Let me out."

She wanted to get to Cassadaga and find out if her hunches were right. If someone there was peering into the unknown on Haven's behalf, she wanted to find them and cut that connection off pronto. She didn't want to leave Haven even more lost and alone, but evening the playing field meant not being two steps behind all the time.

With a heavy sigh, Ryker exited the car, flipped his seat forward, then offered his hand to assist Kyana. She didn't need a hand, she needed a bloody *shoehorn*. It took Kevin another five minutes to unfold himself from the tuna can on wheels, his joints snap, crackle, and popping as he tried and tried again.

Finally Ryker reached in, grabbed the man by his collar, and lifted him out of the open convertible top as though he weighed no more than Kyana.

Leaving their tagalong to Silas and Ryker, she stood in the middle of the interstate and took in their surroundings. The green highway marker declared they were just outside Tallahassee. At this rate, Ryker's porting powers would be ready again before they even reached the halfway point.

"This is ridiculous," she snapped at Ryker. "If you don't know how to read the bloody map, why don't you let someone else navigate?"

Ryker raised his eyebrows, but remained quiet. Silas wasn't so polite. He climbed from the car and tossed the keys at her. She managed to catch them before they hit her in the nose.

"If you think you can do better, you drive."

She felt a little guilty. It wasn't their fault. Unfortunately, GPS didn't mark Dark Breed destruction or military barricades. They were doing the best they could with what they had to work with. However, knowing that did nothing to cool Kyana's frustration or motion sickness.

She chucked the keys back at Silas. He wasn't as quick on the draw and they caught him on the chin.

"If you hadn't gone for cute and sporty and had gotten us something useful, we could push our way through this mess." She pointed to the wide patch of wet winter grass not yet fully greened by the approaching spring. "Or at least go around it."

"We'll backtrack to the last exit and find a way around this," Ryker said.

"Fine, you two have fun. When you get back to the interstate, look for me." She didn't make it two feet before Ryker had her arm and Silas blocked her path.

She snatched her hand away, knowing what they were going to say and not wanting to hear it. "I can take care of myself. And trust me, I'd rather take my chances on the road than in that contraption with the two of you."

She wasn't used to needing a nursemaid. She understood their concerns—she wasn't running on all cylinders yet and her role as Goddess of the Hunt was too precious to put in danger. But goddess or not, she wasn't going to be babysat or held against her will. The Lychen and Vamp sides of her might be dying, but the independent woman inside her sure as hell was not.

With one last look that warned them to back off, she vaulted over the first row of barricades. She shuffled her way around the second set of obstacles only to be brought up short by a very young, very nervous soldier and his rifle. Judging from the grunts and muffled expletives behind her, Ryker and Silas were giving pursuit and Kevin was desperately attempting to roly-poly his way over the barricade as well.

She looked around for the soldier's companions as she waited for her own to join her. There didn't seem to be anyone else here. "Put the weapon down. You have nothing to fear from us."

The kid shook his head but did what she asked.

She was surprised and a little put off that he'd given in so easily. She eyed the gun for a moment before swinging her gaze back to the man's face. He was pale, but certainly didn't seem to be in shock.

"You all right?" she asked.

He swallowed, a sheen of perspiration glowing beneath the fine hairs pressed against his forehead. "I'm not allowed to let anyone pass."

It took great effort to keep from snapping him in two for being another obstacle in her path. Instead, she dug deep and found a tiny bit of compassion for the lone soldier.

"Your orders don't include us."

His jaw clenched and he shook his head, but when he opened his mouth, he said, "You may pass."

He looked so startled by his own words, she expected him to pop his hand over his mouth. "You sure you're okay?"

Nodding, he stepped aside, and as Ryker caught up to her, she cast the man one last glance over her shoulder. "What was that all about?"

"I'll explain later," Ryker mumbled, looking back to make sure Silas was following with Kevin.

"Was he under some sort of spell or something?"

The muscle in his jaw ticked, intriguing Kyana even more. "Something like that. Like I said, I'll explain later."

Something had put him on edge, but the hope-on-wheels looming before them shoved Kyana's questions to the back burner. A row of Humvees lined the barricade walls to the left, looking far roomier than the sports car, not to mention a better choice for avoiding obstacles like this.

"Is your troop sleeping in those?" she asked, turning back to the soldier.

"No." He rubbed his temples. "They'll be back at sunset."

"We're going to borrow one. And a list of any roadblocks set up between here and Cassadaga if you have one."

"Ma'am, you're going to get me in a lot of trouble." Once again, he looked like he was going to object, but instead, he walked toward them, pulling a well-worn piece of paper from his pocket and handing it to her. "Blockades are marked in black. Open roads are outlined in green. Try to avoid back roads and smaller towns. They're not guarded."

"We're not the ones who need to be careful," she said, tucking the map in the waistband of her pants. "Whoever left you out here alone should have his ass kicked. Stay hidden from anyone else that comes this way."

Without another word, the soldier turned, opened the door to a nearby armored car, and disappeared inside.

"Well, he was certainly agreeable," Kyana muttered when the door shut behind him. "Think he was on drugs?"

"Didn't expect it so soon."

She snapped her gaze to Ryker. "What? Drugs? I'm sure those who could get them started building a habit the night Hell broke open."

He held a serious gaze on her as he folded his arms across his chest. "He wasn't a pushover, Ky. That was Artemis working through you. Humans have a hard time denying gods' requests. Once we put some distance between you, he'll forget your order and return to guard his post."

Not sure what to make of this revelation, she took a moment before following the men to the lead Humvee. Ryker offered her the front seat, but certain it was better for her stomach if she couldn't see the trees flying by, she refused and climbed into the back.

"So, I have the power of persuasion," she finally said. "Interesting."

"Don't abuse it, Ky."

She glared daggers at the back of his head as he jumped into the shotgun seat. "I wouldn't."

"You drive," Silas said, stepping in front of Ryker's door. "I want to work on something that might help us."

Kyana peered over the shoulder of the car seat as Ryker moved to the driver's side and Silas hopped in front of her. He began pulling items out of his bag and settling them around his legs.

"What's all that?"

"You'll see. *If* I have all the materials I need."

When Kevin crammed himself in the backseat beside Kyana, she tapped Ryker on the shoulder with her newly acquired map. "See if you can get us there without any more delays."

He shut his door and ripped the map from her

hand. "Take a nap, Ky. See if Haven can show you where we go once we get to this place."

In other words, stop bitching and do something useful.

Two hours later, it turned out Haven had nothing to show her but the backs of her eyelids, and they were approaching Cassadaga.

Ryker pulled over next to the SPIRIT CROSSING sign Kyana had seen in the photo of Haven and Hope and turned off the ignition. "What now?"

She eased out of the Humvee and stood in the middle of the road. Closing her eyes, she turned in a slow circle. She didn't know what she hoped to sense, but apparently, all the *spirits* were crossing elsewhere because she didn't detect a single human—or anything else, for that matter—in the entire area.

With a sigh, she looked at Silas and Ryker. "One of you stays with Kevin. The other goes with me to search for Haven."

Chapter Thirteen

It looked like a bomb had gone off in the center of town, destroying everything in its path. Bodies lay strewn in the streets and buildings—dismembered, broken, or disemboweled. While the odor was familiar, she'd not seen destruction like this in any city.

The stench of death, much like what had plagued every city for days after Tartarus broke free, was enough to make Kyana retch. Fresh blood was rather appealing. Old, stale blood revolted even the hungriest of Vampyre. Though she supposed Leeches might be drawn to decay like this.

Why hadn't the psychics seen their own fate and gotten the hell out of here before the Dark Breeds struck?

A shrill scream, much like that of a Banshee, pulled Kyana from her thoughts and stopped her in her tracks. Moving slowly, she unsheathed her daggers from her waistband as she turned in the direction of the screams. Peering through the broken window, she took only a second to spot the source of the noise.

It wasn't Banshee. It was Haven.

"I won't, I won't, I won't," Haven threw her neck back and screamed again, her hands raking her hair, ripping at her scalp. She paced the littered shop, broken glass crunching beneath her bare feet, but she gave no indication of pain.

Kyana watched, trying to form a plan. Making a reckless dive for Haven would be a bad choice. She'd expended all her ambrosia-charged goddess strength at the trailer park and it would be over quickly . . . and painfully for Kyana.

She fingered the small pouch in her pocket. On the drive here, Silas had set to work crafting Binding Charms for all three of them. His hurried explanations on how to use them were barely heard, but she was fairly certain it couldn't be that difficult. She knew Binding Charms could be extremely powerful depending on the Witch who'd created them. Silas *was* such a Witch, but would it work on Haven now that she had Cronos's spirit inside her?

She wasn't letting Haven out of her sight for even a second to find Ryker. He'd taken off to inspect a building two blocks down. There was no time for backup. Her decision made, she pulled the charm from her pocket, hitched up her baggy pants, and stepped silently through the shattered window, avoiding as much of the debris as possible.

Haven stared directly at her, but didn't seem to see her. She was shaking her head violently, her lips pinched so tightly together they'd almost vanished in her milky white face.

Kyana stopped, afraid to so much as breathe as she waited for Haven to move, to say something. Anything. She gripped the charm in her hand. She thought Silas said she had to be within five feet before discharging it. Or was it fifteen? Either way, she was well within that range.

As she eased forward a step, Haven remained frozen in place. But then, her mouth opened and her lips moved as she spoke silent words. Kyana considered calling out to her, but if she was in some sort of trance, best to attack before it broke. Then she could take Haven in without a fight and no one would get hurt.

She took another step, but then Haven's gaze jerked to the corner of the room. Haven began shaking her head again as though violently disagreeing with something Kyana couldn't hear. Everything moved in slow motion as Kyana turned to see what Haven pointed at. Her eyes burned from the golden glow of the object propped against the wall.

Poseidon's trident.

If she bound Haven to her as the charm was meant to do, she'd have to fight Haven and figure out how to carry the trident at the same time. She wanted Haven badly, but the world needed the trident more. No, she'd have to bind Haven to her own body, make it difficult for her to flee until Kyana could get the trident to safety.

The second she decided to be logical, the room suddenly filled with the suffocating odor of sulfur. Not giving herself time to think about her actions, or the consequences they might carry, she shot across the room.

She tossed one end of the Binding Charm at Haven's left foot, and the other around the right. At the same instant, her hand closed over the shaft of the trident, and she silently prayed that there was enough of Artie's blood in her to keep the damned thing from killing her.

When she wasn't immediately stricken by whatever god force was attached to the conduit, Kyana jumped out a busted window, nearly impaling herself on the shattered glass, and took off down the street toward the entrance to town, her bare feet slapping the rough concrete. Her heels were on fire, shards of embedded glass shooting pain up her legs, but she refused to stop even long enough to look back to see if her charm had worked.

She didn't need to. Haven's roar of outrage erupted like an explosion.

"Ky!" Ryker shot out from a large building on her left and she almost sagged with relief.

"What the hell—" His gaze took in the trident. He vaulted over the railing and fell into stride beside her. He grabbed her arm, forcibly pulling her down the street.

The instant Silas saw them coming, he leaped into the Humvee, dragging Kevin inside with him, and started the engine.

"Go, go, go!" Kyana screamed when they were about five feet away. She took a running leap and threw herself and the trident into the backseat, nearly skewering Ryker in the process as he landed beside her.

Twisting in her seat, she watched the sky darken overhead, watched the building they'd been in collapse on itself, and her heart twisted violently. Haven was in there!

"I couldn't get them both! She's restrained in there. She'll die if I don't go back!"

Grief and panic had her ordering Silas to stop the car, but he kept driving. She contemplated jumping out, running back to grab her friend, but Ryker must have sensed her intentions because he snatched the back of her pants and held her in place.

"You can't help her now, Ky."

She glared at him, wanted to hit him and ask him if he would have abandoned her back there too, but she was pretty sure the answer would have just pissed her off even more.

To save the trident, damned right he would have.

She buried her face in her hands, choking on the building need to weep like a baby. If she let loose now, though, she'd never stop. Haven. Her sister. Her closest friend in the entire world.

The woman who'd held Kyana's hair back when a spoiled batch of blood had curdled in her belly and kept her bedridden for three days. The woman who'd asked her to be the maid of honor at a wedding she'd known Kyana had disagreed with. The woman who opened windows to release spiders rather than squash them and purposely left crumbs in the attic for the mice who'd wandered in.

How could all this have happened to someone like that? Certainly this couldn't have been the destiny the Fates had chosen for Haven. So why then was it happening to someone as pure and good as Haven while someone as selfish as Kyana retained her free will? She choked back a sob, praying with everything she had that some miracle might have saved Haven from the explosion.

Then, there was a loud squeal and she was thrown into the back of Silas's seat. The trident fell from her hand, rolled on the floor by her feet. They were spinning. Around and around, until finally, they stopped, facing the direction from which they'd been fleeing.

"Duck!"

Silas's scream was muffled by a loud thwack, and Kyana instinctively grabbed Kevin, shoved his head between his knees, then draped herself over him. Every window imploded, shards of glass erupting in an explosive shower around their heads.

As she carefully lifted her head to see if Ryker and Silas were okay, a momentary calm fell over the Humvee. A slash of blood fell over Silas's right cheekbone, but otherwise, he looked fine. Ryker, on the other hand, was cussing up a storm, brushing glass from his lap even as he was lifting his hands to grip the metal around the broken window and lifting himself through the opening.

"Ryker, stop!"

She didn't know exactly what had prevented their getaway, but she sure as hell didn't want him out there facing it alone. Using Kevin's curved back as a stool, she pressed her knee into him and shoved herself out the window after Ryker.

He didn't acknowledge her, his gaze narrowed on the road. Her breath caught in her throat at the freakish event heading their way. A funnel tore over the streets, roughly six feet tall and four feet wide. Not huge, but sweeping street signs and trash cans out of its path as it hurled itself in their direction.

But what held Kyana's attention was its brightness. Green and gold fireworklike lights spit out from the top, making it look like a sad little birthday cake.

"What the hell is that?"

Ryker folded his arms over his chest, looking less impressed than even Kyana was. "That, I believe, is Cronos."

She sputtered. "You're kidding."

"Well, Cronos through Haven of course. Gods have the ability to screw with weather, and I'm guessing the devastating sort of weather was Cronos's specialty."

Relief kept her rooted in place. If Haven was indeed at the center of that whirlwind, then she'd made it out of that damned explosion.

"I would have thought he'd be bigger," she muttered.

"Size matters?"

Kyana snorted. "Most definitely."

The faint trace of a smile lit up the side of his face she could see. "Not in this case. Get in the car. I don't want to see what that thing turns into when it stops."

Together, she and Ryker jumped back into the Humvee, only to find Silas slumped over the steering wheel.

"Silas!" Kyana dragged him away from the wheel while Ryker scooted over them into the driver's seat.

She glanced at the floorboard in the back and a groan escaped her. The trident was gone. As a sick feeling twisted her gut, she looked at Kevin in the backseat. When she saw his white face and bug eyes, she knew they'd fallen into a trap.

Silas moaned. Taking that as a sign that he'd be fine, she turned her fury onto Kevin.

"What happened!" she screamed.

Kevin said nothing, instead raising his arm to point over her head. She swiveled in her seat to look out the windshield. Haven stood some twenty feet away, and in her hands, all glowy and taunting, was the trident.

"Looking for this?" Haven smirked. Soot covered her from head to toe, making her look like more of a monster than should have been possible. Only the whites of her eyes showed through the blackness, eerie, whitish yellow slits encasing black pupils that flickered with such menace, Kyana actually flinched though an entire vehicle separated them.

She pushed Silas off her, ready to jump from the car and go after that damned conduit again. She'd been so freaking close! But the engine sputtered to life and she was thrown backward as Ryker smashed the gas.

She had an instant of regret when the Humvee sped toward Haven, but she kept her gaze focused on that trident. They plowed into her, but rather than sending her flying, it was the Humvee that lifted into the air and smashed onto its front bumper. Kyana's head cracked against Silas's as the vehicle righted itself. The hood now held a dent the size of Arizona, but Haven was unscathed.

She stood in exactly the same spot, a wicked grin on her face.

"Cronos, you son of a bitch," she muttered.

"What the hell is she made of?" Kevin asked, finally daring to poke his head over their shoulders. "God, please don't let her have me!"

"She doesn't want you right now, ass hat." Kyana's gaze finally moved from the trident in Haven's hand to Ryker's face. "She should be dead or really hurt, but it's like Cronos encased her in steel. How do we get that trident back?"

"You don't." Haven was closer now, her hands on the dented hood as she leaned forward a bit to peer into the broken windshield. She gestured down the length of her body. "He shouldn't be strong enough to do this yet, but you really really pissed him off." She smiled, her fangs flashing over her bottom lip. "Thank you."

The funnel was gone, but there was a heavy wind circling Haven now. Her hair was blowing, her filthy clothes puckering against her body, then out again.

"You think you can stop us from finding the conduits by killing the psychics?" Haven roared. "My friends?"

Kyana blinked, gripping the dashboard until her knuckles cracked. Haven thought *they'd* murdered these people? Had she not seen the gruesome way in which they had been killed? Totally not her style.

"There are others who can show me what I need to see," Haven continued, her black eyes glimmering, looking like tiny obsidian stones. "It will take me no time to return to St. Augustine, Kyana. How long will it take you?"

Thunder crackled overhead, and Haven threw her arms into the air while Kyana and Ryker shimmied back out of the window to grab her. The smell of gasoline smothered the scent of death in the small town, and before she could pull her body free of the vehicle, there were flames. Kyana barely had time to react before the hood of the Humvee shot up in a blaze.

Wild laughter surrounded them from all sides, and then Haven was gone.

Chapter Fourteen

Get the human!" Kyana strained against the Humvee's door in an attempt to get Silas out. The door creaked, but opened only an inch, the side of their vehicle damaged more than she'd realized. She summoned what little remaining Vampyric strength she still possessed and ripped the door from its hinges, sending it sailing overhead to impale the heart of a palm tree.

She reached for Silas, but his body had become wedged when the collision with Haven had shifted the driver's seat, pinning him against the high center console. The denim encasing his bent legs smoldered from the heat of the motor and the ever-growing flames.

If she ripped him out of the vehicle, he'd be torn in two. She could dismantle the metal that had become a cage around him, but that would take care she didn't have time to give. He didn't have the healing powers she and Ryker possessed. If she hauled Silas out of the Humvee too quickly, she'd kill him.

However, if she took the time required, he'd die in the explosion. Already the flames were bubbling the green and yellow paint on the dash. She needed to cool the Humvee off. Needed a hose or . . .

Gods have the ability to screw with the weather.

Ryker's words bounced around Kyana's head as she stepped away from the vehicle and stared at the sky. If gods could screw with the weather, surely that went for goddesses as well.

She imagined a hurricane dropping buckets of rain down upon them. The skies darkened. Thunder rumbled. It started with a light drizzle, but the two drops of rain that splattered against her head gave her enough hope to dig for more.

Her skin zinged and her blood grew hot—a sensation she hadn't felt as a Vamp in centuries and made her feel more alive than she could ever remember. The sky opened up, and a torrential rain exploded down upon them, dousing the flames and filling the air with thick, black smoke.

They weren't in the clear yet, but she was pretty sure the Humvee wouldn't explode. Reaching around Silas, she placed her hands on the console. She tucked her head toward her chest in an effort not to inhale the stench of burning flesh and shoved. The metal and motor refused to budge.

With a curse, she quickly checked to make sure Silas was still breathing before vaulting over the roof. Her bare feet barely found traction on the wet grass before she jerked open the passenger door, leaving it swinging from its hinges.

Placing her foot above the back tire, she wrapped her fingers around the console. It took several attempts before her rain-drenched hands could find the dexterity needed to pull the large chunk of steel away, careful not to let the torn metal slice through Silas's ever-paling skin.

When her hands could easily fit between Silas and the console, Kyana moved back around the Humvee and extracted him from the wreck, setting him carefully on the wet pavement.

Kneeling beside him, she rested her cheek against his chest. The steady beat of his heart calmed the rush of adrenaline warming her blood. Suddenly, she was very cold. Shivering. Icy.

She gently ran her hands over his legs. The warmth coming from beneath the denim caused her hands to quake. Though the thick fabric had protected him some, he'd still been burned.

"I need my bag," Silas groaned, finally coming around. She reached inside and snatched the pack from the floorboard before returning to grab him by the collar. She dragged him across the street where Ryker was propping up a rather stunned-looking Kevin.

"I—don't want to—do this anymore," Kevin said, gripping his chest.

She kinda hoped he was having a heart attack.

She shot her gaze to Ryker. "Can you get us another vehicle?"

"Yeah, you got them?"

She studied the pale-faced duo on the ground

and nodded, her heart finally slowing to a less painful tattoo. "Yeah."

"Back in a minute."

He disappeared around the corner, giving her the chance to catch her breath. When Silas rubbed his head and opened his eyes, she fell onto the ground beside him. He tried to rip the denim away from his calves. Failing, he looked up at Kyana. She sliced his pants with her dagger from hem to knee and carefully separated the edges. His legs were red and covered in nasty bruises, but it didn't appear as though anything was broken or burned too badly.

Once she'd helped him dig through his bag and apply a cooling salve to his wounds, she asked, "What the hell happened back there?"

It took him a minute to look capable of any kind of speech, then he finally said, "Distraction."

Well, that explained everything. "Elaborate."

He pulled himself up to lean against the wall of the brick building behind them. "When you and Ryker left us to confront that funnel, Haven appeared in front of us. She knocked us out. Bait and switch."

"She took the trident," she muttered, feeling like every kind of fool for leaving it in the car in the first place.

"Lovely," Silas rubbed the back of his head. "I think I'm sitting your next adventure out."

Kyana was beginning to wish she could too.

Chapter Fifteen

Cassadaga was as bereft of working vehicles as it was living citizens. Kyana, Silas, Ryker, and Kevin walked the circumference of the entire town twice before finally giving up and settling in to rest in one of the few buildings still intact. A local occult bookstore. They'd agreed that by the time they found a car and drove back to the portals in St. Augustine, Ryker's powers would have returned anyway.

The bookstore contained only three tall shelves of books that looked older than Kyana. Each volume was coated in a fine layer of dust behind glass, locked cabinets, and just at a glance, she could tell they were valuable. She wished the store she'd found Haven in hadn't been demolished in the explosion. At least then maybe they'd be able to look for some clue as to what Haven had been doing there. But here, in this untouched bookshop, there was nothing to do but sit and wait. Wait and sit. It was enough to drive a Lychen, Vampyre, goddess to suicide.

Perched on the edge of a reading table, she stretched her neck, peering over her shoulder at Silas, who'd curled into the corner to sleep on the other side of the room. Haven's dad was finally asleep, his snores a rude reminder that he was here and his daughter wasn't. Ryker had disappeared into the office section of the shop to try and refocus after the chaotic day they'd had. She couldn't blame him. Refocusing sounded like heaven.

Technically alone now, she felt the silence was beautiful and refreshing . . . until Kevin snored again, breaking her moment of calm and rattling the windows.

The hairs on the back of her neck prickled, and she turned to find Ryker standing just outside the office watching her.

"What?" she grumbled.

He gave a one-shouldered shrug. "You're beautiful."

"Oh." That certainly hadn't been what she'd expected him to say. "Thanks?"

Chuckling, he eased onto the table beside her, his hand falling casually on her thigh as though it belonged there.

"So surprised at such a small compliment," he said.

It was her turn to shrug. "Beauty really isn't my priority these days."

As her gaze fell to her torn, baggy jeans and sooty, ripped flannel, she chuckled. "Besides, *beautiful* isn't exactly the word I'd use. Not right now."

He took her chin in his fingers, his touch so soft she would have thought she'd imagined it if not for the momentary feel of the callus on his thumb. "I'm not talking about your clothes. I'm talking about you."

He pressed a light kiss to her nose, making her feel like both a six-year-old child and a sexual woman, and all thoughts of pushing him away were forgotten. She was supposed to be ending this thing between them, and yet, all she wanted to do was curl up against his chest and let him hold her. Let him keep telling her things like this.

"What about me?" she heard herself ask. Her cheeks burned hot as she realized she was fishing for more—a moment of humanity that she so desperately needed after everything inhuman she'd encountered these last few days.

His finger trailed down her neck and rested over her breast. "This."

"My breasts?"

His smile was crooked, his dimples deadly. "Your heart. You're chasing down your best friend in order to save a race you have no use for."

"I don't hate humans," she defended.

"You should. They've never done a damned thing for you."

Kyana forced herself to meet his gaze, afraid that if she didn't, it would tell him too much. "They're no different than Dark Breeds. There are some worth my time. Others don't even deserve my efforts to kill them."

It was true enough. A few weeks ago, she'd pretty much believed all humans were more monstrous than the Dark Breeds they hadn't known existed. But since then, she'd met a few that had gotten under her skin and warmed her toward the race. Like Hank, the retired cop who'd helped them track down the Order members responsible for killing the Chosen. And his adoring wife and their sweet son. *They* deserved saving, and Kyana had to believe there were other humans out there who did as well.

Uncomfortable with the personal direction this conversation had headed, she stood and walked around the table to the bookcases behind them. She could feel Ryker watching her as she studied the titles. *Taming a Demon. The Spirit Inside You. Herbs and How to Use Them.*

"Taming a demon?" She laughed. "That's rich. Do they think you can stick one on a leash and have it do your bidding?"

She took a deep breath and closed her eyes, the musty scent of paper and words swirling up her nose, intoxicating her. "Gods, I love that smell."

"Dust?"

She smiled. "Books. There's nothing like it."

Ryker watched Kyana trace the glass case with her finger, leaving a clear path in the dust. Typical, he thought. Just when the conversation turned personal, she changed it. She wasn't a coward by any means, but when it came to dealing with real issues, she wasn't just yellow, she was freaking neon.

"I wouldn't have taken you for a book lover."

"I told you before I liked to read."

"Yes, but liking to read books and savoring the scent of them are two different rungs on the ladder of book geeks."

"I'm not a geek. But when you can't watch television or mess with a computer or even listen to a radio, you need some sort of entertainment to fill the downtime. Besides, book worlds are the only places I'm guaranteed to find decent human beings, aren't they?"

"Tell me why you hate them." He eased off the table to face her directly, knowing she wasn't going to like his pushiness.

But these days, moments of quiet to talk were scarce, and he was praying for one small morsel of her now. One small truth that would prove she trusted him. He'd felt her pushing away today, and knew she was going to break the connection they were making. So be it. If she felt she needed to run from him, fine. He'd figure out how to deal with that. But first, he wanted to see how far beneath her skin he'd gotten, and if she could admit even one secret of her past, it would tell him a lot.

"I already told you, I don't hate them," she said, her back still turned to the bookcases, where he could see her reflection in the glass. She wasn't really looking at the books anymore, but her pride wouldn't allow her to turn around.

Her gaze met his in the glass and quickly returned to scanning the books.

So that was it. She wasn't going to offer him anything. He was going to have to pry it out of her,
confess that he already knew about her marriage
and the abuse she'd taken as a young girl. And
when he did, she'd hate him as much as she hated
her abusers.

"Kyana—"

"Drop it."

He reached for her, pulled on her shoulder until
she faced him, and regretted it. The anger staring up at him made him rethink confessing he'd
seen her secrets when she'd fed off him. There was
already a wall between them. Why turn it into a
damned fortress?

"Fine," he said, dropping his hand as well as the
subject.

"That was quite the thinking session you had in
that office. Next time, focus your thoughts on you,
not me."

"I said, *fine*. I'll drop it. You'll talk to me when
you trust me. I get it."

Her eyes narrowed and the muscle in her temple
ticked. "Trust you? I do, as much as I can. What about
you? You have your own secrets. Why do you hate
Ares so much? What happened to your mother?"

Ryker stiffened and stepped back.

"Not so easy is it? Tit for tat, Ryker. I'll tell you
mine if you tell me yours."

How much did he want her trust? How much
was he willing to tell her that he'd never told another soul?

The words were on the tip of his tongue, but rather than speak them, he leaned forward and kissed her. For now, this would be enough. She was right. He couldn't expect her to share her secrets when his own were so deeply buried. Sadly, he *would* have told her what she wanted to know. If only she'd given him one thing, one small piece of herself just now.

Since she hadn't, he'd take the only thing she seemed comfortable giving.

Her body.

She moaned into his mouth, her tongue slick and warm as he suckled it, all thoughts of their conversation forgotten. His hands slipped to cup her ass and lifted her body up and against him so they were pressed chest to chest. She smelled like fire and Kyana, and it was delicious.

"Silas," she breathed.

Ryker growled. "I'm not Silas."

She smiled, the remnants of anger flickering out of her eyes. "Trust me. I know that." She nodded toward the corner. "But they're here and could wake up at any—"

He kissed her again, effectively shutting her up, then walked their linked bodies into the office and shut the door. Inside, he pressed her to the wall, pinning her with his hips and lips as he dove into her mouth again and again. She wrapped her legs around him and clung to his neck like a tie.

"You can't do this every time I get mad at you," she said when he moved his mouth to her throat.

He grunted, slipping his hands between them to unbuckle her belt.

"We're not even supposed to be doing this anymore. It's not smart."

He grunted again and tugged the belt free and eased her legs from around his waist. The enormous pants puddled around her feet, leaving her stark naked from the waist down. He found her heat and smiled when she gasped and rocked against him.

"This still doesn't mean . . . anything . . ."

Ryker groaned and eased his hand free. "I don't remember you talking this much."

"Your turn," she whispered.

And when he stripped off his pants and buried himself inside her, she panted his name against his neck, over and over.

This time, he didn't tell her to shut up.

Kyana lay curled against Ryker's naked body, her own slick with sweat and completely sated. She hadn't realized she needed that kind of release, but damned was she glad he'd offered it.

But now that her body was a pile of goo, her mind was the only functioning piece of her. In the quiet, her brain was sprinting a marathon, and she wished it would just relax like the rest of her. She'd never outright asked Ryker about his past before, and his adamant refusal to share it with her today hadn't sat well.

It made her understand that it wasn't really her

secrets Ryker was interested in. Rather, it was the trust that came with telling them. She knew that because the moment she'd asked about his parents, she'd realized that she'd been truly hoping he'd trust her enough to spill his own secrets. She was beginning to want to know more about him than where the scars on his body were hidden. She wanted to know where they were hidden in his heart.

When had she become so damned sappy?

This thing between them might not be forever, but it was for now. She was finally coming to terms with that. One day, one of them would grow bored enough to walk away. But that day wasn't this one.

"Ryker?"

"Hmm?" His voice was drowsy and low in his throat. She curled in closer, wanting some of the peace he seemed to have found.

"I'm not ready to talk about my past."

"I know." He began a slow, rhythmic circle at the base of her neck with his thumb, and she felt her eyes grow heavy.

"But," she continued, stifling a yawn, "soon. Maybe."

His hand stopped moving for a long moment before starting up again. "All right."

"Tit for tat?" she asked.

And as she drifted off to sleep, she heard him faintly clear his throat and say, "Yes, Ky. Tit for tat."

Chapter Sixteen

When Ryker's powers to port returned, they wasted no time getting back to St. Augustine. He'd zapped them just outside the Castillo de San Marcos, and together, all four of them studied the structure in silence. Sex with Ryker hadn't done more than temporarily balm Kyana's worry, and now, it was back full force. Judging by the tense silence hanging between her companions, they were definitely worrying too.

Kevin likely worrying about his fate now that he was so far from home and had a monstrous daughter who wanted his blood.

Silas was likely worrying whether Kyana would request his assistance again, or if he could balm his own stress with a little romp with Sixx. He wasn't limping anymore. At least her guilt over the day's events could be assuaged a bit by that.

Ryker . . . who the hell knew what was worrying him? He was as locked up these days as Kyana.

It was up to her to voice her own worries. Gods knew, she wasn't getting anywhere thinking about them alone.

"Do you think she's going to stay like that?" she asked as they started up the grassy bank toward the fort. "Teflon girl, I mean?"

"I don't see how Cronos could maintain the strength to do it again, much less make it permanent." Ryker's answer was so swift, she knew it had been the same worry plaguing him this morning. Good to know she wasn't completely alone.

And hopefully, he was right. Kyana didn't relish the thought of pounding her fist into pure steel. They headed toward the drawbridge, the grass slick with dew from the chilly morning air, chilling her bare toes. She couldn't wait to get a fresh pair of boots and burn the horrible clothes that were chafing her skin. Soon.

"I still don't know why she threatened to find another psychic. Who? Why warn us? And she can't port, so how, exactly, did she plan on beating us back here?"

Not to mention, how the hell had Haven been getting around so swiftly in the meantime? The disappearance of her scent had been explained by spell crafting, but there were no spells Kyana knew of that would allow Haven to keep zapping herself from place to place.

"Even with Ryker's porting, she always seemed to be beating us to our destinations," she said. "How was that possible?"

All the questions spilled from her mouth the same way they'd entered her brain. She and Ryker had already discussed most of them, but neither had come to any definitive answers that satisfied her. As much as she didn't like admitting it, talking her problems out with Ryker seemed to help her figure things out. If it got on his nerves that she was repeating herself, he'd just have to deal.

"Has to be Cronos," Silas offered. "There's nothing in her breeds that would let her do that."

"Definitely Cronos," Ryker agreed. "It's almost as if he's sucking her into his realm and popping her out in this one. Whatever he's doing, I'm glad we decided not to drive and wait out my port. We're here at least two hours before we would have been otherwise."

He gestured to the calm sentinels patrolling the bastion overhead. "Maybe we beat her. Doesn't look like anything's gone down, and she *did* say St. Augustine."

Kyana nodded and told herself to breathe. He was right. If Haven had planned to return to St. Augustine, it didn't appear she had arrived yet. "Maybe we'll get lucky and she'll need time to recover before doing something big again. Gods know, I could use the time to think this through and take in some ambrosia."

As soon as they reached the fort's entrance, sentinels from the San Pedro Bastion greeted them and the drawbridge lowered. Their first attempt to catch Haven had failed. It was time to return to

Olympus and face the music. Hopefully, they'd get the yelling over with quickly so they could figure out what Haven might be getting ready to pull out of her hat for them next.

Kyana also wanted to find someone who could make her a charm or potion that would allow her to see through Haven's tricks in the first place. Artemis had promised that when she fully became the Goddess of the Hunt, she'd see through spells and magic better than any other god.

She wouldn't be immune to harmful magic, but the Illusion Charms and potions that kept Dark Breeds from being hunted accurately by tracers shouldn't affect her anymore. Of course, that would not happen for a few more days.

They made their way through the plaza courtyard toward the small alcove that held the portal to Below. Ryker and Kyana could've ventured straight from here to Olympus, but that would have left Silas alone with Kevin. Given what they'd put Silas through already, he didn't deserve to be abandoned with their baggage like that.

The minute she stepped through the portal and caught her breath, her instincts came alive. The air Below was charged with electricity. The bellowed orders and the cries of pain drew her to the entrance of the portal alcove where she could look out into the market square streets.

Not a hint of this chaos had been evident in the fort, where the guards had been oblivious to what their brethren faced Below.

"Fuck me," Silas whispered beside her, a moment later followed by Ryker and Kevin.

She drank in the sight before them, her stomach twisting into a painful knot as she followed the trail of bodies.

"She wouldn't dare . . ." she said, her quiet, trembling voice unfamiliar to her own ears.

Haven had threatened to find a new psychic but Kyana hadn't even considered that she'd be brave or stupid enough to try this.

"Why would anyone attack Below?" Silas gently nudged a body by his feet with the toe of his boot. It didn't budge.

She grabbed Kevin roughly by the arm and turned him to face the beach. "Go. Now. You'll find a camp of refugees on the shores. Run."

"Kyana, wha—"

She cut Silas off and didn't bother to make sure Haven's father obeyed. She was already off and running.

"She's trying to break into Olympus!" she called out over her shoulder. "Haven wants an Oracle."

Chapter Seventeen

Kyana sprinted to the alcove housing the gate to Olympus with Ryker and Silas at her heels. From the number of bodies lying about, the attack hadn't been well thought out—nor had it been a solo effort on Haven's part. The attack seemed to have originated from Cronos's supporters—suicidal supporters who'd thought they could actually take on Olympus?

However, the attacking army had been large enough to take many Order members down with them. The corpses of Mystics and Witches were mingled with dead Hatchlings and Lychen. It was disturbing, to say the least, to see a sentinel spread out beside a mound of Leeches, his body half gone from where they'd fed upon him.

Anger, rage, and a tiny bit of fear waged war in Kyana's belly. She didn't doubt for a moment that Cronos was responsible for this through Haven. Those who supported Cronos knew Haven was leading their war. Did they truly expect to get into Olympus without being stopped? To steal an Oracle?

"Stay here. Try to help the injured."

"Like hell I will," Silas tried to shove Ryker aside but, like a stone pillar, Ryker didn't so much as sway. "I'm not a god, but I may be able to help where it really matters."

Not willing to waste valuable time arguing, Kyana grabbed Silas's arm and fell through the portal. Together, they hit the ground with a thud. Ryker caught her gaze over Silas's head. The red swirled in his eyes. Beyond looked much like Below with bodies of the fallen strewn everywhere. Except here, the battle still waged.

She had to pull Silas to his feet when his stunned disbelief seemed to hold him immobile. She pointed him toward Artie's temple. "Find Artemis and stay with her until I come for you."

She didn't wait to see if her order would be obeyed. Pulling out her daggers, she dove into the fray. The road to Zeus's temple was lined on the left with Dark Breeds snarling at Order members on the right. Bodies clashed together, raining blood upon Kyana as she ran by, searching for any sign of Haven, any sign of Artemis. Something slammed into her side and she tumbled toward the ground only to be righted again by a strong hand on her elbow.

Ryker yanked her away from the road, away from the steps leading to Zeus's gardens.

"Take cover, Ky. This isn't your fight."

"The hell it isn't."

She jerked her arm away and pushed off her toes, soaring twenty feet into the air to land on the other side of Zeus's massive gates, where the focus of the fight had centered. Hundreds of beings, Dark Breed and light, spilled blood all around her.

She slit the throat of a Hatchling before sprinting forward, weaving her way between the clashing bodies. Because so many Dark Breeds had joined the Order of Ancients over the years, it was hard to tell friends from enemies at a glance. In order to know who she was killing, she had to look them in the eyes, see if the wildness existed there, then decide what to do. Not her usual style of fighting. Too many of their own were going to be slaughtered by friendly fire.

Better to keep her focus on the top of the mountain where a series of rocky pathways would lead her to Zeus's Oracles. If Haven had stepped onto Beyond, that would be her destination.

Ryker was beside her again. He swung his elbow backward into the gut of a Dark Breed approaching from the rear. "Get safe or I'll *make you*."

"Not until I find Haven."

"I will hurt you if that's what it takes to keep you safe." His eyes swirled bloodred and the bodies blocking the path away from Zeus's temple flew backward.

"Are you trying to save *me*, Ryker, or the Goddess of the Hunt?" It was a question she'd been struggling with since becoming Artie's Chosen.

Which half of her was Ryker drawn to more? Even as she ran, her bare feet being sliced to ribbons on sharp pebbles, she mentally kicked herself for even caring. Here she was ready to fight and spill blood, and she wanted to know if Ryker liked her? What the hell was wrong with her?

Ryker seized her around the throat and dragged her behind a huge willow tree before shoving her to the ground. "Do you see any other damned gods out here? No. They're smart. They know they can't risk—"

She kicked out, catching Ryker in the groin before spinning on her knees and diving back into the fields. She had her answer. He was more concerned about the goddess in her than the woman. Well, he could go be concerned somewhere else. Right now, Haven was here somewhere and Kyana wasn't about to be manhandled into submission.

She had just reached the fork that led to the mountain peak behind Zeus's temple where the Oracles' cave resided when a white light burst overhead. The heat emanating from it lifted her from the ground and tossed her back fifty feet. She rolled down the jagged, stony cliffs, rocks cutting into her shoulders and ripping her baggy jeans. She landed with a skull-rattling thud against the base of an oak tree and saw stars.

Ryker was still standing where she'd left him, unaffected and unharmed.

She gritted her teeth against the throbbing in the back of her head and tried to stand, but her legs wouldn't obey. The light burst again, this time throwing bodies past the gates, near the glowing portal that was beginning to pulse an ominous red. Too many uncleared bodies were passing through now. By all rights, those without permission to pass on to Olympus should have been sent into a void realm. Yet here they were—on forbidden land. How?

There were two portals on Olympus: one that led to the human realm and one that led Below to the magical realm. Why hadn't the attackers used the portal from Above? Why take the risk of having to get through Below unnoticed before attacking Olympus? None of this made any sense.

A screaming howl sounded among those landing near the portal to Below. Kyana flipped onto her belly trying to see what had happened. It was then that she realized that only Dark Breeds—from both the Order and the enemy army—had been thrown.

A pop exploded about five feet away. Ryker appeared out of nowhere and grabbed her under the shoulders and dragged her behind a large oak. As he shoved her between his body and the tree, she couldn't pull her eyes away as one by one, the Dark Breeds popped open, their bellies exploding with clouds of black dust as they disintegrated right before her eyes.

She wiggled against Ryker. She had to get out of here. A panic that was unfamiliar and yet violently urgent was choking her. A tingling had begun in her gut, and she was certain if she stepped even one fraction closer to that damned light, that tingling would become an explosion.

"You still have Dark Breed in you! Stay still!" Ryker jammed Kyana's back so deeply into the bark of the tree that it tore through her flannel shirt and cut into her shoulder blades.

"What is it?" she asked, her eyes burning from all the black dust. Bits of Dark Breeds fell into her hair and coated her throat, making it hard to swallow or even to speak.

"Him."

Taking Ryker's warning more seriously now, Kyana was careful to keep her body safely tucked between him and the tree, but craned her neck to see what held his attention. Zeus, cloaked in white and gold robes, marched between five sentinels down the temple steps. His staff held out in front of him, he thrust it into the air. Another bolt of white shot out, clearing the field of more Dark Breeds.

Even the Dark Breeds of the Order were expendable. Faces she recognized exploded all around her. Kyana tucked her face against Ryker's back, blocking out the vision now seared into her brain.

"Half the Order are Dark Breeds," she managed, unsure now if her throat was constricted from dust or the threat of tears. "What the hell is he doing?"

"Protecting us all."

"At the expense of us who get in his way? Gods, stop him, Ryker!"

"Casualties of war," Ryker muttered.

She looked at him, found him watching her from over his shoulder, his jaw tight and his gaze unapologetic. She opened her mouth to berate him for his casual attitude over the loss of her peers, but another blast of white lightning flew past her head. Suddenly, she was on the ground, gasping for air, Ryker pinning her to the grass with his body sprawled on top of her.

He managed to pull her behind a low wall. "Keep your head down," he shouted, trying to force her to stay on the ground.

Kyana fought to her knees and peered over the wall. Morbid fascination had her watching Zeus continue his slow parade down the road. Bodies soared off the plains and over the cliffs of his mountains. Screams accompanied roars of pain, and Kyana cupped her ears to shut them out. They were unlike anything she'd ever heard before, and Dark Breeds or not, they were puncturing what little soul she had left.

Knowing they were outnumbered and completely beaten by the power of the God of Gods didn't persuade the remaining enemies to turn tail and run. Instead, they pushed forward as one, determined to take as many Order members' lives as possible before they gave their own.

Another bolt flew overhead. More Dark Breeds fell, but still more surged through the portal to take their places. Kyana pulled her gaze away from Zeus to take in the fight still being waged on the bloodied field. Most of Cronos's supporters fought with Order members, but a few, however, were taking to the outer rim where trees, rocks, and protective walls could hide them from Zeus's wrath.

Kyana struggled against Ryker's hold. "Zeus and his sentinels aren't guarding this path anymore. The Oracles are unprotected, and if Haven is going after them—"

Ryker refused to budge. "No. If you die, there's no one left to fight for Haven."

Yes there was. There were Geoffrey and Silas . . . Kyana froze. Ryker believed she could still save Haven? After everything Haven had done, he believed Kyana had that kind of power? She swallowed and fell limp beneath his stony body. His belief in her was overwhelming, but her muscles grew taut again as she pushed those emotions aside and sought out her logic.

If Haven had a chance to get her hands on an Oracle, they'd all be dead. One Oracle could lead Haven to all the Eyes of Power, though with Zeus's show today, they already knew where *his* was. Likely, Geoffrey still had his amulet as well, but the whereabouts of Cronos's ring was still unknown by all except Ryker and whomever he'd given it to. If Haven succeeded in this suicide mission, she could find out. Then she'd be able to retrieve them all and finish raising Cronos.

"We don't have a choice." Kyana wiggled her arm free to point at a group of Dark Breed picking their way around a small outcropping near the edge of the cliffs. "Zeus can't stop them all and his guards won't leave him. It's up to us to make sure those Oracles are protected."

She didn't wait to hear his objection. Bracing her hands against the wall, she shoved backward as hard as she could. Caught off balance, he released his hold and Kyana broke free.

Knowing he'd follow her, and praying she wasn't about to get herself ashed, she ran straight for the path that would take her farther up the mountain above Zeus's temple. From the corner of her eye, she saw Zeus raise his staff again.

Certain she was about to find out how much electricity a body could hold before it popped like an overfilled balloon, she skidded to a halt. The blast soared several feet overhead, clearing a path in front of her, but somehow, she remained on her feet.

Zeus's icy blue eyes locked on Kyana. He gave a slight nod before returning his full attention to the frontal attack. It was all the encouragement she needed. Not willing to risk her remaining strength on a god-speed sprint, she balanced on the balls of her feet, bent her knees, and jumped.

She landed in the middle of the pack of Dark Breeds stealthily making their way toward the Oracles' cave. Kyana swung out with her leg and sent two over the edge into nothingness. Their companions charged forward but then the three closest to her careened backward and disappeared into the mist.

Ryker had joined the fight.

She didn't wait for the remaining Dark Breeds to coordinate an attack or run away. She flew forward, breaking a Lychen's neck before turning on the remaining four. Saliva dripped from their bared teeth, and they lowered their furry bodies toward the ground in preparation to pounce.

Not giving them the chance, her blades quickly sent two to their bellies. The others flew backward, sailing into the boulders, bones snapping upon impact.

Turning slowly, she checked to make sure they hadn't missed anyone. Satisfied that the path to the Oracles was deserted for the moment, she nodded at Ryker. "Let's go."

As they started back up the mountain path, shrieks of pain kept calling Kyana's attention to the temple gates. There had to be hundreds of attackers still spilling from the portal. The Order was fighting a losing battle. For every one that Zeus's bolt turned to dust, two more quickly took his place. Even with every Order member willing to give their lives to protect Olympus, too many were going to die before this battle ended.

Kyana cursed, swinging her head to look up the path toward her destination. This could be her last chance to get her hands on Haven. But if Zeus was overtaken, it wouldn't matter whether Haven figured out where the conduits were or not. Zeus had no Chosen, which meant his powers would cease to exist with his death. As much as it pained her, she grabbed Ryker's hand and began pulling him away from the mountain peak toward the bottom they'd fought so hard to get away from.

"What the hell are you doing?"

"The portal!" she yelled, her voice muffled by all the screams cocooning Olympus. "We have to clear the path so Zeus can shut it down!"

If they could manage *that*, then not only would they prevent more from breaching Olympus, but they'd also have trapped Haven inside. *If* she was here at all.

She summoned what was left of her energy and surged forward, hoping Ryker would trust her instincts and follow. She lost track of the number of Dark Breeds she brought down as she ran, giving herself only a moment with each to check their eyes before delivering their deaths. Her hands and clothes were covered in black blood that smelled so horrendous it was smothering.

Each time Zeus raised his bolt in the air, she took cover behind the nearest wall, tree, or boulder, waited it out, and began the fight through the mobs once again. It was a painfully slow journey, but inch by inch, she made progress, getting closer and closer to that damned portal and the evil continually pouring through it.

"KY-A-NA!"

The familiar voice brought Kyana to a halt, knocking her shoulder into a tree. The pulsing red portal had darkened to near black, but that wasn't what held Kyana so still she couldn't feel the lower half of her body. It was Haven, standing in the center of Zeus's gate, her arms held out wide, the trident gleaming in the late-afternoon sun.

"You lose, Kyana," Haven's laughter carried over the battlefield like broken wind chimes, high pitched and grating. "This is only the beginning. The path to the gods is open now. Cronos will take his rightful place on the throne—"

Zeus's roar stopped all sound, all motion. He held out his staff. The ancient words that flowed forth caused the ground to quake. Lightning flashed overhead. A blinding white-hot flash of light shot from the end of his staff. Order members fell to their knees. Dark Breeds disintegrated in a puff of black smoke carried on the wind toward the portal.

"Non est! Ut igne inferni consumet!" A loud whoosh shook the grounds, and like a vacuum, Dark Breeds were sucked toward the portal and through it.

Knowing she was about to lose her chance, Kyana lunged forward, a scream of protest on her lips as Haven's body soared high into the air. Her torso bent backward as it was propelled through the portal and out of sight. Kyana stumbled, a bright light blinding her as the portal glowed red again . . . then white.

Then, with a deafening boom, it imploded.

Chapter Eighteen

Kyana's gaze held steadfast to the chaos around her, her heart frozen solid in her chest. Tiny quakes shook the ground beneath the crumbled portal. Six or seven small sinkholes spread out ten feet from the spot that had once held so much power, and drank in the red and black pieces of the doorway.

The damned thing had eaten Haven.

She felt Ryker's hand on her back, and try as she might, she couldn't look away from the horror. "Is she dead?" she whispered.

Ryker squeezed her hip. "No. The portal would have sucked her back Below."

Relieved, she stepped aside as Zeus's procession made its way back up the mountain to his temple. Behind him, the cleaning process began. Sentinels bent to lift their dead and wounded allies over their shoulders. They kicked enemy bodies from their paths, bodies likely to get tossed on a burning pyre this evening.

Kyana tried not to drop her gaze to the Mystic's body at her feet. The poor bastard. Mystics lived like monks, believed in peace and simplicity above all else. This one had gotten pulled into a fight that had cost him his life. What a brutal way to go.

"If he could do that," she said, jutting her chin in the direction Zeus had disappeared, "why did he wait until so many were dead?"

"He waited until he had no choice." Ares appeared from around the corner, his tunic and sword stained with blood both black and red. Human and Dark Breed. "Closing that portal sealed out those Below who might require our aid. We've left them defenseless. If you had caught Haven like you were supposed to, all of these deaths could have been prevented, you inept whelp."

"Watch it," Ryker growled, stepping between his father and Kyana. "If Haven was so easy to catch, you and your men would be wearing the glory of her blood on your swords."

She flinched. She wasn't about to let that happen. If it came down to killing Haven, she'd be the one to do it. She'd be the one to make sure it was painless and swift. She stepped around Ryker to stand beside him.

Ares looked her over before returning his attention to his son. "Until a new portal is constructed, no one can enter or leave Olympus. We're shutting down the one to Above as well, so find something useful to do in the meantime."

"How long will that take?" Kyana asked, unsettled at the thought of being trapped here while Haven was still loose.

"Several hours. It will take longer to decide on new precautions than to actually rebuild it."

Sighing, she rotated her shoulder to work out the kink slowly torturing her to death. "I want to see the Oracles. Make sure they're all where they're supposed to be."

She had no intention of explaining to Ares her suspicions that Cronos had maneuvered this attack to get new prophets since the Cassadaga psychics had been killed. Haven didn't need more black marks against her, especially ones based on theory, not fact.

"No one can get to our Oracles—"

"I'll take you," Ryker said, his jaw clenched so tightly, Kyana was afraid it might start to chip away from his face. As he pulled her past Ares, he stopped to face his father. "Just once, would it kill you to be a help rather than be a pain in our asses?"

Ares opened his mouth but Ryker was already pulling Kyana up the path before the God of War could respond.

Twenty minutes later, Ryker was leading her back down the path to Zeus's temple. All Oracles were accounted for. Unharmed. Kyana was relieved. She'd considered the possibility that Haven had been here and taken what she wanted before showing herself at the portal. Apparently, she hadn't gotten any further than where she'd been expelled from.

So why make the empty threat in Cassadaga about finding someone else who could read for her? Why make such a grand appearance rather than try to sneak her way to what she'd wanted?

When they reached the foot of the mountain, Ares was still standing where they'd left him, bellowing orders to his sentinels and yet not lifting a finger to help clear the bodies.

"Well?" Ares barked, giving them a cursory glance.

"They're all safe," she muttered.

Ares's grin was one of triumph. "You see? We are well defended."

Of course he had to say that. It would be his fault if they weren't.

Ass hat.

Ryker ran his hands through his hair and tugged hard before looking at Kyana. "She's obviously sending us on wild-goose chases."

"This attack had to have a purpose other than to kill Order members." But since the Oracles were safe, Kyana couldn't for the life of her think of what that might have been. Without an Oracle, Haven had no way to know where Geoffrey kept his amulet or where Cronos's ring was. Even if she *had* been able to steal Zeus's staff right out of his hands, there would still be pieces of the puzzle missing.

"The Oracles are fine," Ryker said. "She's just messing with us."

"There's one way to find out," Silas said, appearing behind Ryker. Kyana had forgotten he'd been on the mountain at all. She was relieved to see that, other than a scratch below his eye, he was seemingly unharmed.

Silas turned to Ares. "Where are the surviving enemies being held?"

"You're assuming I allowed there to *be* survivors."

"You didn't keep any alive to give you answers?" Silas said. "I don't believe that. If you let me, I can offer some assistance in questioning them."

Ares's glare sharpened. "I trust Witches about as much as I trust Vampyre/Lychen Half-Breeds."

Silas shrugged, unaffected by Ares's intimidating demeanor. "Suit yourself. I'm sure the gods are still powerful enough without my kind of magic to help things along."

When Silas started to walk away, Ryker grabbed his arm and held him in place, his gaze locked on his father. "You know you can use him. You're willing to let your pride stand in the way of getting answers?"

Ares's dark eyes flickered with something Kyana couldn't put her finger on. "Why would you assume his methods would prove more useful than mine?"

As much as he and Ryker didn't get along, she almost pitied Ares when she saw the pair together. There was always a longing, a sadness, that crept over the god when his son spoke to him. It made him seem almost human.

Ryker shrugged. "Because brute force doesn't always ensure compliance."

"You'll vouch for him, then?"

Ryker gave one curt nod, and Ares motioned for a passing guard. "The Witch is going to accompany you. He's not to be left alone with any of the prisoners. When he's done, bring him to me. Understood?"

Silas crossed his arms and glared. "If you really can't trust me, why allow me to assist your men at all?"

Ares's gaze shifted to Kyana, though he still talked to Silas. "Because I want to make sure you report all details to *me*, first."

She rolled her eyes. "A few more days, Ares, and you'll have no authority over me. Becoming a full-blown goddess has never been more appealing."

She pushed past the men and started toward Zeus's gardens. She needed a minute to breathe. To decide what to do next. She was locked here until a new portal was created, which gave her both time to think and time to drive herself nuts with the lack of action. Knowing Haven was somewhere out there and unreachable at the moment was already getting under her skin.

Kyana quickly scanned those roaming Zeus's gardens and spotted Geoffrey. He was holding a frantic conversation with Hermes. Geoffrey, in his Hades garb of black robes, pointed to the east, and Hermes flittered off in that direction, his winged sandals taking him above the arriving chariots on the mountainside.

She glanced behind her to make sure she was

still alone before making her way to Geoffrey's side. She'd rather pick his brain without an audience.

"You all right?" she asked, letting him pull her into a tight hug.

"Ah, my heart is breaking minute by minute, lass."

Kyana nodded against his chest. While she loved Haven like a sister, Geoffrey had been falling in love with Haven for years. He'd never acted on his adoration, though, knowing Haven wanted a family one day. Vampyre were notoriously infertile. Only one in a thousand or so were even capable of producing children, and after what Kyana had seen on the penal isle where Cronos had created the first Vampyre, she now knew why it was so. Vampyric children were horrific monsters. Geoffrey would never act on his desire for Haven because he cared too much for her to let her sacrifice so much.

She led him to a less populated area and cringed when she saw the pain etched in his face. He was still as beautiful as always—his Irish blue eyes dazzling with intensity beneath long black hair that hung loose around his face. But now, there was worry lining those eyes and streaks of silver in his hair—not all of which were attributes inherited from Hades, Kyana suspected.

"Did you see her?" she asked, sitting on a cold stone bench in front of the iron gates sectioning off Zeus's temple from the rest of the mountain.

She watched him swallow, let him take a minute to find his voice. "Aye."

Kyana sighed. "I can't seem to get through to her, Geoff. When we saw her in Cassadaga, it was as though there was no Haven anymore. Cronos is inside her and I'm not sure she's strong enough to kick his ass out."

"She is. Don't give up on our girl." Geoff sat beside her and rested his hand on Kyana's knee. "The rest of the world will want to see her dead, Kyana. It's up to us to make sure that's not how all this gets sorted out."

If she'd restrained Haven in Panama City or even Cassadaga, she might have been able to prevent the deaths of the Order members still being carried away by the sentinels.

"I'm not giving up," she grumbled. "I'm just not sure I'll be able to . . . do what's necessary should my options run out."

"Who else then? Your surfer boy?"

"He could kill her, yes. But I'm talking about reaching through to her. Getting past Cronos and bringing Haven back. I'm not sure I can do it. Ryker certainly can't."

Ryker didn't truly believe in Haven's innocence. Not the way Kyana and Geoffrey did.

"You could try to get through to her," she suggested. "She's always been as close to you as to anyone."

His shoulders sagged. "And if I couldn't? Should it come to having to destroy Haven, I . . . would sooner destroy myself."

Kyana studied him as he dug his palms into his

eyes and ground out his frustrations. How did he do it? He'd been Vampyre too. How had he pushed past their polygamous nature to find himself in love with one person?

She sighed. The situation hadn't changed. She'd still try to find Haven. Still try to bring her back to the world of sanity. And if the time came when she had no choice but to kill her friend . . . if she wasn't strong enough, Ryker would be.

Life sucked.

Her mind flickered to Ryker again, and she remembered him staring at her so thoughtfully in Cassadaga. He'd watched her the way the human cop, Hank, watched his wife. With worry and fondness, and maybe a bit of possessiveness. At the time, it had made her uncomfortable, but when he'd turned that same focus onto her body minutes later, it had made her world right for just a few moments.

What did he see when he caught her looking at *him*? Maybe lust. Maybe wistfulness at what she couldn't see ever happening. But could he see the care for him she was developing? The sincere hope that she could one day go against her instincts and actually commit?

She cleared her throat and changed the subject, her chest suddenly tight with questions she didn't have time for. "Were any of the gods injured?"

"No, thank Zeus."

"Good." She turned and straddled the bench so she could better see Geoffrey. "She can't get to Cronos's body on that island even if she does get her hands on all of the Eyes of Power. She'd have to port there, and there's no one who would do that for her. Right? I mean, she *is* zipping from place to place. Maybe she *can* get to that damned island without Ares or Ryker to port her."

Geoff shook his head. "No. Cronos might be lending her his dormant god-speed, but even he didn't have the power to port. She's faster than you because she has no need for ambrosia. She doesn't need to rest the way we do. But she can't get to that island. I don't believe she can raise Cronos because of that, but that doesn't mean our fate is any brighter if she manages to get her hands on all of the Eyes of Power."

"After Zeus's display today, she knows he still keeps his staff close by. You'll have to make sure your amulet is hidden well, and I have no idea where Ryker put Cronos's ring."

"My amulet is safe. And the ring . . ." he shook his head.

"She's hard as hell to catch, Geoff. We can't risk her taking another conduit."

They had to stop all this before more people were killed, before the gods were any weaker. The more damage that was done, the less likely Haven would find any leniency when Kyana did bring her in.

She sighed and closed her eyes. When she opened them again, her gaze rested on Ryker standing about a hundred yards away, deep in conversation with Artemis. She should head over to them, but her legs weren't cooperating. They seemed to want to sit here until this whole mess was over.

Servants blocked her view, pouring out from the temples, their hands balancing huge trays of food and drink.

"What are they doing?" she asked.

"Making sure all the gods get their strength back in case there's another attack. We should eat too."

As she nodded, Ryker caught her gaze from across the lawn and held it, the silver in his eyes visible even from where she sat. Suddenly, he was too far away. Even amid all this, she still wanted him.

How pathetic was that? She'd hoped once she'd tasted him, that need, that pull would have dissipated. At least a little. It hadn't. Not the first time she'd lain with him, nor the second. Instead, it had only intensified. The ache more intense even than her thirst for blood had once been as a newborn Vampyre.

But now, she didn't just want him inside her, she wanted him *beside* her.

In Panama City, she'd convinced herself that stopping their relationship from going further was the smart thing. Now, she couldn't remember why. Didn't *want* to remember why.

As she watched him now, he smiled a half smile and gave her a nod. His attention sent a bolt of strength up her spine. Whatever might be brewing between them, for this fight, she wouldn't push

him away. She didn't have to be in this alone. She
might not have Geoffrey any longer now that he
was the new Hades, and Zeus knew, she didn't
have Haven on her side either, but she had Ryker.

She was usually a solo artist, but knowing she
had backup made her feel a lot better . . . a lot more
capable of completing the task she'd been given.

When Ryker started across the garden toward
them, she finally convinced her legs to obey and
lift her to her feet. He snagged a plate of food off
a passing servant's tray and continued toward
her and Geoffrey. Artemis followed behind him,
her long amber curls flowing against the breeze,
hiding most of her face from view. Even through
the curtain of hair, Kyana could see her fear. Seeing
Artemis afraid didn't bode well. She was stronger
than Kyana. If she was afraid, Kyana should be ter-
rified.

Ryker approached, the scent of sunshine issu-
ing from his body like a golden cloak that settled
around her shoulders. He handed her an ambrosia-
laced peach, which she greedily bit into. Juice
spilled out of her mouth and ran down her chin.

He gently wiped the mess away. "You okay?"

She nodded and took another bite, turning her
attention to Artie. "Are they working on the portal
yet?"

Artemis's hair settled down around her shoulders to give Kyana a glimpse into her amber eyes.
They were red and puffy, as though she'd been
crying.

"We have Witches conjuring protection and detection spells as we speak. When the Ancients decide where to place this new, hidden portal, it will be useable. But right now, that isn't our priority. Before we can even think about creating a new entrance to Beyond, we must make certain those we protect here are . . . well, that certain precautions have been made against their demise."

"What do you mean?" Kyana asked, finishing off her peach and cupping the sticky pit in her fist.

"We have to make our gods and goddesses strong again. Especially Poseidon and Zeus. Hades"—she gestured to Geoffrey—"has already found a worthy replacement, though I don't believe your beloved Geoffrey has caught on to just how important he is. Zeus is weakening by the day. As it stands, Hades—Geoffrey—is the only one of Cronos's 'sons' with any significantly threatening power. We must fix that at once."

"I'm not his son," Geoffrey grumbled.

"You may as well be." Artemis eased onto the bench beside Geoffrey. "When Cronos comes for his children, it will be their powers he searches for, not their bodies. A third of those powers reside in you."

"What about Zeus's and Poseidon's Chosen? Haven't they been located yet?" Kyana knew they'd been found days ago, but lost again in all the chaos. That they still might not have been tracked by Artemis's tracers was troublesome.

"Zeus's was killed two days ago. We are currently searching for a replacement, and Poseidon's Chosen is still missing. Since Atropos struggles day by day to keep track of those still living, there's no telling when he might be found or even if he's still alive. Poseidon believes that the best possible solution is to locate a temporary Vessel for his powers. Should something happen to him, at least his powers will be stored until they can be placed into the Chosen."

"Where will you find someone strong enough to become Zeus?" Geoffrey asked. "You'll have to take a Chosen from another god to make that possible."

Artemis nodded. "We know. They're debating it now."

Kyana squinted in an attempt to stop the sudden throbbing that had consumed her temples. "Poseidon is willing to give up his powers entirely just to shove them into a container for later use? Doesn't that weaken us a great deal more? Especially since his conduit is already MIA?"

"The Vessel will be trained just as you will be and I have been, lass." Geoffrey stood and took Kyana's hand, earning him a scornful look from Ryker. "A new body containing Poseidon's power will immediately be stronger than he is in his current state. Even untrained and unskilled, he'll be more powerful and better able to aid us than Poseidon is."

"But why Poseidon? His conduit's already gone," Ryker said, stepping between Kyana and

Geoffrey, *accidentally* breaking their hands apart. "The chances of Haven coming after him are slim. The focus should be on finding a new Chosen for Zeus."

"When we finally get our hands on the trident, whoever's in charge of that arena needs to know how to use it," Artemis said. She smiled at Kyana. "And there's still hope you'll bring that trident back to us soon."

"I'm going to," she muttered, and meant it with every fiber of her being. Even if she had no idea where it was or how she'd find it.

Again.

"Not just anyone can carry such power." Ryker folded his arms across his chest. "Temporary or not, it requires a Chosen or someone already touched by magic. How are they going to find someone strong enough to hold enormous powers like Poseidon's?"

"Apparently, they just play a game of eenie meenie minie mo and the loser wins."

As one, the group turned to find Silas walking toward them, his face pinched and possessing a slightly green tint. He was supposed to be questioning any surviving attackers. He couldn't have finished so soon . . .

Kyana didn't like this. Not one bit. "They didn't . . ."

He gave a pathetic nod, looking absolutely horrified and pained. "Didn't have a choice. It's to happen tonight."

"What's he talking about?" Ryker asked. His eyebrows rose so high, they almost floated over his head.

"I think," she started, taking Silas's hand and helping him sit, "that Silas has just been minie mo'd against his will."

Silas swallowed and Kyana watched as the realization struck him that his nomadic, free-man lifestyle had just been temporarily caged.

"Poseidon," he whispered. "They're turning me into Poseidon."

Chapter Nineteen

Kyana stood as close to the altar in Zeus's main entry hall as she'd been permitted. The ceremony to make Silas Poseidon's Vessel was almost complete, but even though they'd spent the last hour watching the sun set over Olympus and talking about what was to come, the worry had yet to leave his face.

She glanced out the window and caught a glimpse of a group gathered so far in the distance they were barely moving specks. A circle of thirteen Witches were toiling away at the foot of the mountain, recreating the portal to the human world that would exit from inside a fountain in St. Augustine, accessible only by those who possessed godly or Oracle blood.

They had to wait for Silas's ceremony to be finished before sealing the magic into the portal, however, because the three Fates, or Moerae sisters, and a group of Healers were required to make the transfer of Poseidon's blood complete.

Once their duty was done, even the Moerae, one of the most powerful trios in the world, would no longer be allowed on Olympus without personal godly escort. At least, not until the threat of Cronos was forever behind them. As for keeping Cronos out—that wouldn't be possible without trapping the other gods on Olympus. If one god could pass, they all could. That was the way it had to be. But at least if he arrived again—through Haven or some other means—he'd have to do so alone. None of his groupies carried his blood. They wouldn't be able to follow him through the portal.

The Moerae ended their chanting, recalling Kyana's attention. In unison, they stepped away from Silas and lowered their heads. Healers quickly moved in to transport Poseidon back to his makeshift hospital room, and Kyana rushed to Silas's side to help him sit.

"How do you feel?"

He leaned heavily against her. "I think I'll have to wait until I get this blood out of me before I'm anywhere near okay again." He sighed. "When does this change happen? I don't feel any different."

"They said you'll know it worked by morning."

She hadn't felt very different after her own blood exchange, either. Granted, turning a Vessel versus turning a Chosen were two different things. A Chosen was given more time to acclimate to the changes, which was why Kyana still had three days before she'd fully become Artemis. Vessels, on the other hand, were emergency transport, and the change was immediate. And, from what she'd picked up from the hushed whispers, much more painful a transition.

She wasn't about to tell Silas that, though.

She rested her hand on his tattooed arm and squeezed. "It's only temporary. The tracers could be bringing in the Chosen now and this could all be over tomorrow."

"Stop, you're exciting me," he mumbled, pushing to his feet. "Can you do me a favor?"

"Sure."

"Could you let Sixx know it'll be a couple days? Tell her to hang around St. Augustine until I've given this power to the next sucker? They're not going to let me out of here while Cronos is after his sons."

Kyana sighed, wishing she'd taken the time to ask what he wanted before agreeing to do it. She didn't know Sixx, but first impressions were everything, and Sixx's had been pretty shitty.

"Fine," she said through a forced smile.

Silas's own smile was a bit stronger this time. "Thanks. We had a room reserved at Spirits. You should be able to leave a note or something for her there." He studied her for a minute before asking, "How 'bout you? You all right?"

"Why shouldn't I be?"

The question sounded pathetic even to her.

He leaned forward and pressed a long kiss to her forehead. "You can find Haven. And you can stop all this. I know you can."

She wished she believed in her own abilities as much as everyone else seemed to. This didn't used to be her problem. A few days ago, she would have thrown on her proverbial cape and set out to prove to everyone that she was the world's answer to salvation. A lot could change in a few days.

"Do you think you can do me a favor in return? Before you become all godlike?"

Silas chuckled. "I'm not going *godlike*. Just a little training until I can give this sorry fate to the person it rightfully belongs to."

"Well, whatever you call it, can you scry for me one more time? I . . . have no idea where Haven's going next. And since she has a head start while I'm trapped here . . ."

"I can try." He looked around the nearly deserted antechamber. Spotting his well-worn pack in the corner, he quickly set out his supplies.

"Have anything that belongs to her?" he asked.

Sure, in her pack . . . back in Panama City. "Can't you scry without it?"

"Yeah, but you're going to have to help me focus. Concentrate on her and don't let anything else intrude on the images in your head. Between the two of us, it should be powerful enough to get a feel on her."

"Shouldn't be hard given she's been the focus of my concentration for days now." She knelt beside Silas, watching the tiny crystal spin over the map, her brain throbbing at the intensity with which she was picturing Haven in her head. When it finally stopped, he nodded and returned to studying the map. Kyana leaned over him and sighed.

"Well that's a big help." The point of the crystal was directly over St. Augustine. They already knew that much. There was no way she'd have had time to escape given that Zeus's mojo had very likely caused her at least a little injury.

"She's still Below."

"How can you be sure?"

She'd figured Haven would have wanted to get out of Below by now where everyone would recognize her and potentially hunt her down. She'd be safer in the human world.

He lifted the crystal from the map and revealed a tiny puncture mark directly on top of the Castillo de San Marcos. "The puncture means she's in the mirror world. Below."

Silas rolled up his map and carefully placed his crystal in a velvet pouch. "What is she after, Ky?"

She rubbed her head, wishing that it was someone else on this hunt. "I don't know. Maybe she's just recovering. Maybe she's after supplies . . ."

"It would be a perfect time to gather some if that's the case. The sentinels Above likely still don't know what's going on, and, given that Below's sentinels were here on Olympus when Zeus closed that portal, he locked them all here with us—"

Kyana cursed. "Which left Below completely unguarded."

Silas nodded.

The headache building behind her eyes was

never going to dissipate at this rate. "I was certain she was going after the Oracles, but I was wrong. I've been wrong about a lot of things, Silas. Pretty sure I have no clue what she'd be after Below."

"Well, you'd better think of one. There's a whole mess of trouble she can cause there."

She paced the small path in front of Silas, her brain moving a mile a minute. "Her *advisors* were killed in Cassadaga, so I'd assumed she'd be after new ones . . . That's why I thought she was coming for the Oracles— Oh hell. Maybe she is."

"What are you thinking?"

Her heart began a rapid tattoo. Half of her prayed she was right, and the other half prayed she was wrong. "Why bother risking your neck for an Oracle when there's easier prey Below?"

Silas's eyes bulged. "Seers."

She nodded, her pulse picking up an even more rapid rhythm. "And there's only one Seer left in this region. I have to go."

As Kyana hurried off in search of Ryker, her head began to swim. Haven had used the fight at the portal to Olympus to throw them off. Another bait and switch. While they were looking left, Haven had taken advantage of the lack of guards patrolling Below. That was why she'd made her presence known on Olympus. She'd *wanted* Zeus to seal off the portals. She'd *wanted* free access to Below. To the Seer.

Kyana's thoughts were a muddled mess as she tried to work through them. So much to do. So little time to do them. In three days, her life was going to change forever. She needed to finish this before then—before she no longer knew her skills and powers as comfortably as she knew her Vampyric and Lychen abilities. They fit her like a second skin, but these goddess powers that were growing inside her felt far too big for her size ten pants.

Her boots slapped on the marble floor as she made her way down the temple steps. It felt good to be in her own leather again. Her feet were burning. They'd been sliced and diced from her sprints. And it had been hard to do anything effectively when the clothes she was wearing felt as though they weighed a ton and her pants slid down her hips every five minutes. Now, dressed completely in the leather she preferred and a brand-new pair of boots, she at least looked like her old self, even if she didn't come close to feeling like it.

Exiting Zeus's temple, she scanned the grounds. Spotting Ryker talking to Ares, she stormed toward them and was nearly on top of them before she realized they were in some kind of heated argument.

"We need to go."

Ryker's eyes locked on her and she took a step back.

Slowly, his tension calmed. The red in his eyes dissipated until only the silver swirled. "We need to talk."

Ares grabbed for Ryker but he easily sidestepped his father's reach.

"You gave me your word. I granted your request. You must pay the price as agreed."

"And I've honored that vow," Ryker said through clenched teeth. "Your payment has been received."

Ryker took Kyana's arm and led her away from the God of War. When they were alone, she pulled to a stop. "What was that all about? What agreement did you make with Ares?"

Ryker shook his head. "It doesn't matter. There's something I need to tell you."

"Yeah, me first, though." She led the way toward the alcove being raised for the new portals. They stopped just outside, out of hearing range from the Witches working there, and leaned close together for privacy. "I had Silas scry for me and I'm pretty sure we have to get to the Seer."

Ryker raised a brow. "You think she wants Nettles to replace the dead psychics in Cassadaga?"

"It makes sense. Nettles is the most prized possession we have Below, and there was no way Haven could have believed she'd really have a shot at an Oracle. Nettles would be far easier to get her hands on. She made a racket here so Below would be left unguarded and the Seer would be easy pickings."

"Okay, I'll play along with that idea. What now?"

"If Haven hasn't gotten to her yet, maybe the Seer can tell us where she is."

"You should definitely check it out."

She didn't like the stress he put on the word *you*. "Yes, *we* should check it out."

"*We're* not going anywhere, Ky. That's what I wanted to talk to you about."

The look on Ryker's face created a dread in her that weakened her knees. Something bad had happened. At least something bad for her. "You're not coming with me?"

He leaned in and pressed his mouth to hers, and before she could lose herself to his kiss, he exhaled a heavy sigh and pulled away.

"I can't," Ryker said, finally.

She looked back to where they'd left Ares. Night was falling over Olympus, a gray mist forming over the massive cliffs to the east. "Does this have anything to do with your argument with your father?"

Ryker cupped her cheek. "I owed Ares a debt."

"Just spit it out, Ryker." She didn't want to know, not really. More than that, she couldn't stand *not* knowing.

"I asked Ares for a favor a few days ago. In return, he requested that I become a Chosen."

She managed to choke down her shock. Of all the things she'd imagined, that hadn't even made the list. "So when we find Haven and stop Cronos you're going to be the next God of War?"

"No." Ryker shook his head. "When we made our bargain, I just promised to become a Chosen. I didn't say anything about becoming *his*. And last night, I volunteered to be Zeus's."

Chapter Twenty

Ryker watched the emotions flickering across Kyana's face. The very air of Olympus seemed to absorb her outrage, and he was pretty sure she didn't realize what she was doing. The sky darkened. The air became thick. The wind shifted from a gentle breeze to a gust that whipped her black and amber curls about her face.

"Ky, you need to calm down before Olympus sees its first lightning storm in centuries."

She blinked.

He pointed skyward where a jet black cloud had gathered directly over their heads. "Your temper. You're doing this."

Lightning danced in her eyes then flashed overhead.

"Let me explain."

"Explain?" She crossed her arms and glared. "By all means, please explain how abandoning me and Haven in order to get some twisted revenge on your father should make me calm down."

Ryker glanced around, wishing for a secluded place for them to talk. He could feel Ares watching them. This wasn't a conversation he wanted to have in front of his father. While this wasn't about revenge as Kyana thought, he'd be lying if he said that Ares's outrage wasn't an added benefit.

But mostly, this had been about *not* having to become Ares, as well as his fierce belief that Zeus needed a replacement pronto. Very few people, even a Chosen, had the ability to contain the power of Zeus. But Ryker was already a demigod. He *could* hold those powers and learn to wield them effectively.

That it was making Ares so mad only made his decision that much more satisfying.

Moving them around the temple to the elaborate labyrinths on the north side, Ryker maneuvered easily through the maze. When they reached the center, he motioned for Kyana to sit, and waited while she contemplated whether she would. He knew his relationship with Ares was driving her nuts, but he wasn't any more ready to explain that catastrophe to her than she was willing to talk about her human life with him. Hell, he didn't even like to think about most of it himself, let alone share the details.

Finally, she placed herself beside him, but the anger in her eyes didn't calm.

"The day of your trial," he started. "When you needed to go to Haven's quarters, I wanted to give you what I thought—what *we all* thought—was your final request. There was only one way I could make that happen for you."

"The deal you made with Ares."

Ryker nodded.

She'd been so devastated that day, knowing she was facing the possibility of death for turning Haven. He'd only wanted to give her peace of mind before her hearing. He'd known that she could never go to trial with enough fight left in her to win unless she knew first that Haven was going to be okay. He would have agreed to anything to grant Kyana that wish. And he had.

"Ares does nothing for free, not even for his son, so I vowed to pay whatever price he demanded to let you go to Haven before your trial."

He knew there was only one thing that Ares wanted and that was for Ryker to acknowledge him as his father before the Ancients. It was a wish Ryker had sworn never to grant. But for Ky, he'd agreed. However, Ares had thrown him a curveball.

"Ares demanded that I become a Chosen."

"Yeah, I gathered that already. What I don't get is how you went from being the next God of War to being the next freakin' God of Gods."

"The price for granting your wish was for me to become *a* Chosen. I knew what he really wanted, but wasn't fool enough to point out that he'd provided me with a loophole. So when I learned of Poseidon's and Zeus's need for hosts, I offered my services."

"But why the hell did you pick Zeus?"

"Your friend beat me out on the duty I wanted."

She flinched, but the tension around her mouth eased. The wind calmed and the clouds lightened. "Oh."

He knew she understood. Her loyalty to the Order was secondary only to her loyalty to Haven and Geoffrey.

"If you'd asked, Silas would've gladly given it to you, Surfer Boy. You might be the only soul in existence who loves his waters as much as Poseidon does."

"Yeah, but that would've left us with another dilemma. Silas isn't strong enough to hold Zeus's power." Ryker knelt in front of her and rested his hands on her knees. "Ky, I had to honor my word to Ares, and Zeus needs a Chosen *now*. This was the only way."

"I can understand why you'd jump at any chance to get one up on Ares, but would it have really made a difference if you'd given me a couple of days?"

He shrugged. "Zeus's power could fade tonight or it could linger for another year. There's no way to tell. I'm the only one strong enough who could step up right away."

"But what about us?" She looked away. "Our mission, I mean."

A tiny part of him had accepted Zeus's request *because* of her. He was becoming too used to being by her side, to being there in case she needed him.

Hoping she might need him. Distance would help them both put things in perspective, and he could still assist her with finding Haven, even if he wasn't working directly with her.

"You don't need anyone else, Ky."

That was half of the problem. She didn't need him and likely never would.

He wanted her to need him, to understand that he didn't look at her and see Dark Breed. He saw a woman who cared so much for her friends that she continually risked her life for them. Saw a woman who could kick ass like a man and kiss like pure woman. Saw a woman he wanted to take care of and have it reciprocated.

"Haven's cloaked and I can't see through her spells until I'm firmly entrenched in Artemis's powers," Kyana said, jolting Ryker's stare to her mouth. He liked the way she suckled her bottom lip when she was worried and the way her eyes were flashing as she recounted all her problems to him now. "I don't know if I can find her before she can complete her mission to raise Cronos. Or if I can do all this before I lose my Vamp/Lychen abilities."

Her voice dropped to a whisper. "Or if I can bring her in before there's no part of Haven worth saving."

"Yes, you can." He sat beside her, but she moved away to pace in front of him.

"Really?" She stopped pacing to stare at him. "I know almost nothing about Artemis's powers or how to use them in a fight. Haven knows how to fight. She's damned good. I told you yesterday that she might be more prepared for our confrontation than I am, and that was when I wasn't flying solo."

She sighed. "Listen to me. A week ago, I was ready to fight for the right to fly solo. I feel weak. Inept. I feel . . . broken. I'm not sure I like what I'm becoming, Ryker."

He swallowed. He sure as hell did. He was falling hard for this softer side of Kyana and it made him uneasy as hell.

He watched her walk away, her shoulders not as high as they usually were. He supposed it was difficult to keep them raised when the weight of the world was constantly pulling them down. He didn't know what else he could say or do to fix things. He'd thought this through. Or so he'd believed.

He hadn't considered what this would do to Ky. He'd been entrusted with protecting her, and he'd walked away from that duty at the first opportunity to get out of his agreement with Ares. So what if his motives had truly been good? What did doing your duty serve when it meant letting down those you were closest to?

She'd have to go it alone. And not just in figuring out what Haven might do next, but in stopping Cronos and protecting the Eyes of Power. In short, she was now alone in her duty to save them all.

Ky was strong and smart. She could handle any-thing Haven threw at her if she believed in herself and her newfound abilities. Kyana, the Goddess of the Hunt, was unstoppable. However, the odds for Kyana, the Half-Breed tracer . . . weren't nearly as good.

Chapter Twenty-One

As Kyana stalked around the back of Nettles's townhouse Below, her gaze swept the dark, quiet streets. There was no one around that she could detect with her nose or eyes, but that didn't mean she wasn't being watched. By Haven? Possibly. The heat on the back of her neck made her shift uneasily where she stood, trying to peer into Nettles's kitchen window. All she could see through the lacy curtains was the dim red light of a coffeepot.

The itchy sensation of being observed nearly had her coming out of her skin. She wasn't worried about a fight. She could handle herself. But it was hard to keep track of all four sides of a building solo. She didn't want to be taken by surprise, and she certainly didn't want Haven to catch her scent before Kyana could catch hers.

She wished she had Geoffrey or Ryker . . . or even Silas.

Silas. Damn. She'd forgotten to deliver his message to his sweet bimbo. Whatever. Helping appease his little girl toy wasn't exactly high on Kyana's priority list. She would deliver the message . . . when she got around to it.

She reached up and dug her fingers between a row of bricks and crawled halfway up the two-story home, peered into an empty bedroom window, then swung her body around to the alley-side of the townhouse. She passed two more windows—a bathroom and another bedroom. Both were empty. If Nettles was here, she was downstairs in the front of the place, the only section Kyana hadn't scoped.

She didn't want to bust out a window around back until she knew for sure whether Haven was inside. She dropped to the ground and inhaled deeply, but there was no scent of Haven. She could smell Nettles, but this was her home. The scent didn't necessarily mean she was still here.

Everything about this place felt off today. There was usually a line of people waiting for readings a mile long around Nettles's home. There were also usually Witchy guards who protected the small Seer. Where was everyone?

Kyana jogged down the alley and stopped at the front stoop where a chalkboard sign had been erected on her little porch, explaining the absence of customers.

CLOSED TILL SATURDAY

Frustrated that she'd hit a dead end already, Kyana thrust her boot against the door and smiled

with satisfaction as the wood splintered and
cracked down the middle. She tore the slabs apart
and stepped inside Nettles's sitting room. Maybe
this was a good thing. Maybe the Seer had boot-
scoot boogied out of town.

Starting with the basement and then working
her way upstairs, there wasn't a single sign that
anything was amiss. She worked her way back
down to stand in the small parlor Nettles used for
her readings. The table was empty. No mirror or
candles or burners.

Her heart sank. Where was she? Surely Haven
hadn't already gotten her hands on her? No. Nettles had placed a sign out front, which meant she
likely had something to do or somewhere to go.

A shuffling sound coming from the front porch
pulled Kyana from her thoughts. Pivoting, she
pressed her back to the wall and vanished into the
shadows, ready, waiting.

Peering around the corner, she watched as a
tiny face appeared in the gaping hole in the front
door. Kyana exhaled and stepped into the hall.
The face jerked back and let out a tiny squeak of
alarm.

"It's all right, Nettles," Kyana said. "It's just me.
Kyana."

The hobbit-looking woman plopped her hands
on her hips and glared at her through the hole
before stepping inside the house. "What took you
so long?"

"What?"

"I've been hiding out at my neighbor's watching for you. I was beginning to think your friend would find me before you did."

"You knew— Never mind. Of course you did." Kyana sighed, grateful to see she didn't appear to be any worse for wear.

"Did you do this to my door?"

"Yeah. Sorry 'bout that."

Nettles shook her head. "Don't fret. I appreciate your concern. That *is* why you're here, isn't it? Finally realize she would come for me?"

Kyana nodded. "I take it you haven't seen her, then?"

"Not yet, but I will soon if you don't get me somewhere safe."

"What exactly have you seen?"

Nettles pinched her small mouth together in a thoughtful pucker. "She wants the location of the other Eyes of Power and she thinks I can show them to her, which I can. Can't say you arrived a minute too soon."

Kyana raised a brow and pulled her away from the broken door. "You know where they all are?"

Nodding, Nettles plopped onto a bench in the entryway and shivered. "Zeus still has his."

That much, she knew.

"Of course, Haven already has the trident, so the only ones to be concerned about are the ring and the amulet. Both of which are in the possession of the new Hades. That handsome Irish Vampyre friend of yours."

"Geoffrey has his amulet. But I don't think you're right about the ring. Ryker had the ring."

And no way in hell would he have given it to Geoffrey. They didn't like each other much at all. Why trust someone you dislike with something so powerful?

Nettles shrugged. "I've seen them both in the Underworld. That is all I know."

Kyana hadn't seen that one coming. It was further proof that Ryker cared more about duty than personal feelings, because he really didn't care for Geoffrey at all. Giving him that ring meant, despite his dislike of the new Hades, he trusted him.

"We'd best be leaving now before Haven gets her chance to snatch me up. She's going to find a way to make me tell her even if it's against my will. Mark my words."

The little woman's face was pale, but she lifted her chin defiantly. Nettles might look like a mouse, but she roared like a lion. The smooth baritone barking from her lips always managed to surprise Kyana. She always expected the woman to squeak.

Nettles stood and sauntered up the stairs. Kyana followed, wrinkling her nose as they stepped into a doily heaven of a bedroom. Haven would have loved it. Or maybe Haven's grandmother would have. It was all too musty and fussy for Kyana, though. Quilts, lace, and the smell of old lady and mints hung in the air like potpourri. Nettles stooped and grabbed at something under the bed.

Kyana leaned in the doorway and watched. "Peek into your crystal ball and tell me where Haven's at now. Maybe I can stop her from coming after you altogether."

Nettles paused in her task of pulling several satchels from beneath the bed to glare up at her. "I'm not all knowing, but I imagine she's about five steps ahead of *you*, so why not predict where you'll be in thirty minutes and I'm sure you'll find her."

This snarky, sarcastic Nettles was about two seconds away from a smack down. Did the little woman even realize she was talking to a new goddess?

Of course she did. She was a bloody Seer.

Nettles tossed two of the bags at her and pulled the third over her own head and one shoulder.

The fear in her eyes reached a soft spot in Kyana's heart. She hadn't actually been aware she *had* any soft spots left. It was rather like finding a bruise on a shiny apple—her first instinct was to carve it out with her dagger before it spoiled the whole fruit.

"I'll get you to a well-guarded place to hide until I either locate Haven or she decides to find her answers elsewhere."

Nettles shook her head, her large eyes filling with tears. "Your friend isn't going to give up."

"I won't let her touch you," she heard herself say, and realized she meant it. She didn't know Nettles well, but the few times she'd come to the Seer for help, she had given it. It was time to return the favor.

Nettles wiped the tears from her eyes and smiled with quivering lips. "Thank you."

The simple acknowledgment of trust was a kick to the gut. There was no way in hell she would let anything happen to Nettles now. It would be worse than kicking a puppy.

"Where will you take me?" Nettles asked as they stepped outside. She cast a long, sorrowful glance at her broken door and let out a heavy sigh.

"I don't know yet." She couldn't take Nettles Beyond now that the portals had been rebuilt to forbid anyone without god or Oracle blood to enter. And everyone in Kyana's circle was there, on Olympus, unable to babysit a Seer while Kyana hunted.

"You must find a place for me before we run into Haven. I do not fight, Kyana. I will be of no assistance."

"I don't need assistance," Kyana mumbled. "I need you to paste yourself to my ass and not stray so much as a foot away from me. Got it?"

Nettles said nothing as Kyana led her down the empty street and past a row of houses where two women were hanging laundry and laughing. They seemed oddly out of place, so normal amid the chaos that had happened today, as did the Dark Breeds that worked for the Order who spilled out of the butcher shops and herbalist stalls on the next street down.

Why weren't any of them as tense as she was? Had the potential danger facing them all not been relayed to all Order members?

Or were they just so naïve as to believe the gods would save them all? Would take care of everything, the way a child believes its father can scare off the monsters in their closets?

Fools.

She turned slightly to make sure Nettles was still close behind, and when she couldn't find the old woman, she dropped the bags to the ground and broke into a sprint. She found Nettles one corner back—on her knees, her hands over her head, her body rocking in a manic fashion.

"Nettles!"

She tried to lift the Seer to her feet, but it was as though she had been cemented into the sidewalk. With a violent crack, Nettles's head jerked skyward, her wide eyes unblinking, her face the color of dingy snow. As Kyana tugged harder, Nettles's lips moved a mile a minute.

"Nettles! Answer me! What's going on?"

"She comes." Nettles's eyes calmed and focused on her just before she collapsed into a fetal position atop Kyana's boots.

She knelt and scooped Nettles into her arms, carefully placing the woman onto her feet and holding tight to her waist until she was sure the Seer could stand on her own. "Now?"

Nettles shook her head, her body swaying as she clung to her. "Soon. She's going to cut out my eyes if I don't read for her. Going to use them to cast a spell so she can see for herself where Cronos's ring is."

She didn't know which sentiment screamed louder in her head. *Ew* or *ow*. "Can she do that?"

The Seer struggled to swallow. The tears welling up in her fear-glazed eyes gave Kyana her answer.

"Okay. All right." She was beginning to panic herself. It took her several deep breaths to rein in her emotion and calm her speeding pulse. "Wait. Where did this vision take place? We'll make sure you don't go there."

Nettles shook her head. "I must. I've seen it. If I return home, you'll catch her."

Before or after she cut out Nettles's eyeballs?

"It happens at your house? You saw all that? Just now?"

"I did." She licked her lips. "She won't give up on her quest to find me, and I am the only Seer near Florida. She'll come for me. You must let her."

"What?"

No way would Kyana willingly put the Seer in the direct path of danger. Because of Nettles, she had discovered who'd been killing the Chosen after the breakout and had been able to catch the bastard. Nettles had clued them all in on where the key to Tartarus had been hidden, and had given her the means to save Haven before their traitor could slit her throat.

Of course, Kyana had been too late, and Haven's blood had been too tainted for purging, but that was no fault of Nettles's.

"I'm not using you as bait."

"You will because I ask it of you."

"I don't know if you know this about me, Nettles, but I don't do things *because someone asks it of me.*"

"You will. Because I bestowed such a courtesy upon you when you were begging for my help using the Charm of Nine Gods. When you so badly wanted to save the very friend you hunt now. I went against my better judgment to do as you asked, and you're too honorable not to return the favor."

Kyana raked her hand over her face in exasperation. She should have known Nettles would bring that up. Her experience with the Charm of Nine Gods and the astral projection it had induced wasn't her fondest memory. But using it had led her to where Haven had been held prisoner. Where she would have died. And Kyana would never have been able to use the charm at all if Nettles hadn't invoked it for her.

"Look, even if I was okay with what you're suggesting, it's not so easy. If I place you back in your home and wait for Haven there, she'll never come. She'll catch whiff of my scent a mile away and stay clear."

"Then turn the tables, Kyana."

"What's that supposed to mean?"

"She's been virtually untraceable for you and you suspect you know why. Use her own methods to trap her."

She wasn't even going to ask how Nettles knew any of that. It didn't matter. Nettles was one smart, crumbly cookie.

"A Cloaking Charm," Kyana said, smiling.

She damned near ruffled the old woman's hair.
She'd been so concerned about finding a way to see
through Haven's charm, that she hadn't considered
the possibility of using it against Haven as a means
of catching her.

Nettles nodded. "You have other Witch friends
who can produce one for you?"

Kyana started to shake her head, then froze. "Actually, maybe I do."

Chapter Twenty-Two

Considering all the bad things that had happened a few days ago in the Mediterranean-style tavern Spirits, it took Kyana several minutes to bolster the nerve to enter. Haven had been killed in Spirits, and Kyana had turned her into the monster she was becoming there as well.

So when the new barkeep—the previous one having been the one to kill Haven in the first place—told Kyana that Sixx wasn't there and had been spending her evenings at the Healing Circle, Kyana wasted no time dragging Nettles the hell out of there.

The Healing Circle was frequented mostly by Mystics who wore nothing but monkish clothing and took vows of poverty. Sixx, on the other hand, was dressed in leather, her black and blond hair in roughly nine million braids. She was easy enough to find amid the wandering bodies draped in burlap and tweed, even in the moonless dark that shrouded the Circle now.

Kyana dropped Nettles's bags, then plopped down beside Sixx on the low stone wall encasing the garden of herbs behind them. Sixx unfolded her legs and popped open one eye to glare before snapping it closed again.

"You broke my Zen," she muttered.

"I'll buy you a new one."

"Silas didn't tell me you were a comedian."

Kyana was sure there was *a lot* Silas hadn't told the Witch, but thought it best not to say so. She didn't want to be here. She didn't like Sixx. Not that she had any real reason to dislike her. She just . . . did.

But right now, she had to play nice so Sixx would help her.

"I have a message for you. From Silas," Kyana started, hoping her olive branch wouldn't be seen for the fake it truly was.

Nettles eased between them, brave soul, and slid her bag beneath her feet.

Sixx sighed, scooted over, and dropped her meditation stance. She wore a confused glimmer in her eye as she took in Nettles before settling her gaze on Kyana.

"If it's about him becoming Poseidon's Vessel, you're about fifteen minutes too late."

Kyana hadn't really listened when Silas introduced them, but now she heard the low, throaty whisper of Sixx's voice, and it sent a warm flow through her veins. She didn't swing that way, but she could definitely see how that kind of voice would catch a guy like Silas and hook him for a good long while. Till he got bored, at least.

Which he would. He always did.

He and Kyana had that in common.

She cleared her throat and forced a smile. One didn't bite one's enemy, then ask it for a favor. "He wants you to hang around here until the rightful Chosen is found and he can leave Olympus."

"Well isn't that just lovely?" Sixx stared up at the sky as if she thought she'd see Silas. After a minute, she turned her attention back to Kyana. "Tell him thanks, but no. We had an assignment before you rang. I'm not sitting on my ass doing nothing for who knows how long."

Seeing her opening, Kyana grabbed hold of it. "Bored?"

Sixx grinned. Not a friendly grin either. More of a sarcastic, unimpressed grin.

"I know who you are." The way her gaze traveled over Kyana, she knew she was being measured. Sixx was trying to figure out whether Silas did all the naughty things to Kyana that he'd likely done to her. She had *no* idea. "What do you really want?"

"How are you at cloaking spells or making amulets?"

This actually made Sixx laugh. "You do know I'm a Witch, right? We're practically born with the skills to make something so simple."

Oh yay. She has ego too.

Kyana didn't have a lot of time to waste. Nettles's

vision didn't give them an exact time of Haven's arrival, only that it would be before sunrise. "What do you need to do a cloaking spell?"

"Just these sexy ass hands, babe. Why?" Her gaze narrowed and she raised a perfectly tweezed black brow. "What's going down?"

Kyana ignored her question and pressed on. "How 'bout an Illusion Charm? What would you need to make me one of those?"

Sixx's brow didn't lower the slightest bit. She was intrigued. Like Kyana, she seemed more uneasy with sitting on her ass than working.

"Some precious metal. I have enough chameleon blood to do both the spell and charm."

The Illusion Charm would hide Kyana from sight, and that was simple enough. She just had to wear it around her neck. But the cloaking spell—she would have to drink a potion to make herself as concealed as possible. Apparently, the substance of choice for this particular task was going to be nasty.

Without the spell, Haven might not be able to see Kyana, but she'd sure as hell be able to smell her. Oh well. Drinking blood never turned Kyana off before.

"All right," she said, pushing to her feet. Poor Nettles looked ill. She wasn't even going to have to drink the stuff. *Wimp.* "I'll take both."

Sixx's lip twitched. To sneer or fighting a smile? Kyana couldn't tell.

"I'm sure you would. But I don't do things for free, Kyana."

Big surprise.

"What do you want?" she asked through gritted teeth.

"If I have to sit one more minute in this horribly dull place, I'm going to sacrifice myself to Zeus. I need action. Fun. And you're going to give it to me."

Being Witchless didn't seem so bad now.

"I'm not babysitting you. I'm trying to save the damned world."

Sixx's painted red lips curled into a grin. "Find another Witch then."

As she pushed past Kyana, she caught a whiff of something that froze her in place. Sixx's pheromones weren't just Witchy.

There was an underlying base of cider, of dead roses that she knew all too well.

"Holy shit," she breathed, catching Sixx's arm. "You're half Vampyre."

Chapter Twenty-Three

Why hadn't Kyana smelled it sooner? Maybe because she'd never smelled a Witch/Vampyre combo before. And to her credit, the Vampyric scent in Sixx's blood was far weaker than the Witchy one.

"Genetic. Not turned," Sixx hissed, jerking her arm from Kyana's grasp. "And could you keep it down? I'm not particularly fond of anyone knowing my business."

"What does that mean, genetic?" The only genetic Vamp Kyana had run into had been disfigured and disgusting.

"It means a great-great-great-great something-or-other was pure Vamp and had babies and generations later, voilà." Irritation fired to life in Sixx's black eyes. "I don't drink blood. Hell, I don't even eat meat. Pure vegan here, so you can stop looking at me like I'm on your to-be-hunted list, 'kay?"

Wow. Procreating Vamps. Kyana knew it was possible, but it was so rare that she'd never met another Vampyre who'd been able to have kids in the more than two hundred years that she'd been alive.

"Is everyone in your family fertile?"

Sixx stepped back, her face scrunched into a grimace. "Do you want my help or not? I might not drink blood, but I'm quick and strong and can more than hold my own if you run into trouble."

Kyana had to admit, she was less hesitant to take her up on it now that she was so intrigued. Haven made up three species: Witch, Lychen, and Vampyre. Before Kyana's goddess blood was fully developed, she made up two of those breeds: Lychen and Vampyre. Sixx made up a separate combination of the beast inside Haven: Witch and Vampyre. The odds were definitely more in Kyana's favor if she brought Sixx along.

"All right," she said. "You're in. But I need the charms and the spell pronto."

"Fine." Sixx pushed past Nettles. "I need to get to Silas's bike so I can get my bag."

"We'll wait for you at Spirits." Not that she was particularly excited about returning to the tavern, but they'd need privacy to perform the magic and they weren't going to get that here.

"Do I get to know what this is about any time soon?"

Kyana scowled. "You'll learn only what you need to know, when you need to know it. Now go. And Sixx? Hurry the hell up."

Since Kyana didn't own a watch, she wasn't sure how long it took Sixx to show up at the tavern, but it felt like an eternity when the Witch finally made her reappearance.

"I hate being kept waiting," Kyana scolded.

"Deal with it," Sixx said, tossing Kyana a charm. "Don't put that on till you're ready to use it."

Knowing better than to disobey when it came to Witchy magic, Kyana put the thing in her pocket. Sixx slipped the mate between her breasts, then pointed to the stairs.

"I can do the spell in my room. Let's go."

Waiting for Nettles to go first, Kyana paused at the bottom of the steps and glanced around the near vacant *kafenion*. The place still reeked of hookah smoke and memories of a happier time that refused to die. In the corner booth, she could still see herself sitting with Geoffrey and a very angry Ryker who'd just taken a swim with the spirits of the River Styx thanks to her. And the table where she and Haven had sat discussing the state of the world before its biggest threat had become so personal.

This had once been her second home, where she came to fulfill her need for blood with a little raki. Where she shot the shit with the barkeep Marcus before she'd killed him for murdering Haven.

"Are you coming?" Sixx's demand was whispered, but it made Kyana jump. She couldn't lose her focus. She might not be able to make up for past hurts, but she could sure as hell try to fix the future.

She followed the other two women up the stairs, past the room where she and her friends, old and new, had spent so much time trying to identify the traitor who'd been killing Chosen, and stepped into a room at the end of the hall.

An entire wardrobe covered the carpet. Kyana was pretty sure she was walking on dirty underwear as she made her way to the bed where Sixx was getting situated.

"Sure you don't want to let me in on what we're doing?"

Kyana shook her head. Sixx would find out soon enough that they might be coming face-to-face with Haven. But if Haven didn't show up, there was no reason to let Sixx in on the details.

Her gaze fell upon two curved knives lying on Sixx's pillow. "You're not going to need those."

Sixx tucked the knives into the sheaths at her waist. "They go where I go."

She knelt on the bed, smoothing the blanket under her knees, then pulled two small vials out of her cleavage. Apparently, her breasts were her pocketbooks. Kyana didn't want to know what else she kept hidden in there.

"Here. Sit." Gesturing for Kyana to settle beside her, Sixx waved a free hand at a chair in the corner. "Nettles, you can sit over there. Just remain as silent as possible."

Nettles curled her little body on the ratty chair and wrapped her arms around her knees. The poor Seer looked ready to piss herself, and if the pallor of her face meant anything, possibly faint. Kyana offered her a sympathetic look before taking her place beside Sixx. As she sat down, she couldn't help but wonder if this was a bad idea.

Her gaze dropped to the weapons at Sixx's waist. She had no reason to trust Sixx's abilities, other than Silas's brief recommendation. For all Kyana knew, she could end up with nothing more than a major headache when all this was done.

But without Sixx's magic, getting to Haven wasn't even a possibility right now. If she was going to lay a trap, she had to become undetectable. Blind faith was required, and it soured Kyana's belly that she had no choice but to place that faith in a Witch she didn't even like. A Dark Breed Witch, no less.

This could turn out very, very badly.

She cleared her throat. "What do you need me to do?"

Sixx handed her one of the vials. "Pop the cork and hold the vial to your lips but do not drink. Hold my hand, and when I squeeze yours, tilt your head back and let the contents run down your throat."

Kyana raised her brow. "Why do I have to hold it in my mouth?"

"Because if you let go of my hands to lift it to your lips, you'll no longer be in my circle. You want this to work or not?"

"Fine. Fine." She popped the cork, releasing a bitter scent into the air that was so strong, her eyes watered. How was she supposed to keep that so close to her nose while Sixx cast her spell? "What the hell's in this?"

"Other than lizard blood?" Sixx smiled. "You really don't want to know."

The Witch placed the lip of the vial between her own, leaving Kyana to wonder how she was going to cast a spell with that thing in her mouth. But rather than waste more time with questions, she mimicked her actions. The glass vial clinked against her teeth, and she tightened her lips into a thin line, gripping the thankfully light weight as tightly as possible.

Careful to keep her head down so the liquid wouldn't spill too early, she let Sixx grab her hands, noting how icy the woman's skin was. Like Kyana's. Vampyric skin.

"I could perhaps hold the vials for you both and pour them into your mouths when you signal me."

It had become so quiet in the room, Nettles's suggestion nearly caused Kyana to fling the vial out of her mouth and across the room as she snapped her head to look at the Seer.

"Yeah," she muttered around the tube. "Lesh do tha'."

"Fine." Sixx pulled the potion from her mouth. "I'm not used to spell crafting with other people. Nettles, come take them. Watch for my eyes to open. That will be your signal to pour. Kyana, keep your mouth open and your head tilted so that you're ready when she is."

Kyana nodded, grateful for the feel of the vial being slipped out from between her lips as Nettles carefully claimed possession of the potion. Sixx grabbed her hands again and shifted on the bed so that they sat Indian-style, facing each other.

"Get on with it," she said.

"Close your eyes."

She obeyed, fighting the urge to crack one eye open enough to watch Sixx, but afraid to do so in case that one act of defiance screwed up the spell. Sixx's voice filled the small room. She was pretty sure the words were some form of Gaelic. Somewhere in the foreign language, she thought she heard a reference to chameleon, but that was only a guess.

Sixx could have been summoning a camel for all Kyana could tell.

It was in that moment that warm liquid flowed into her mouth. She sputtered, nearly forgetting to keep her eyes closed, and struggled not to flail and let go of Sixx's hands. The potion tasted like taking a big gulp of freshly paved road that had just been engulfed in a wildfire. The instant Sixx dropped her hands; Kyana gripped her throat and let loose a string of coughs.

When her eyes stopped watering and her throat stopped burning, she swallowed and found her voice. "Thousands of years of Witchcraft and not a one of you can make a potion that doesn't taste like ass."

Sixx looked at her speculatively, then shrugged. "It's magic. Not fine dining."

Kyana ran her tongue around her mouth, grateful there was no lingering aftertaste. "Did it work?"

"It will work in conjunction with the amulet I gave you." Sixx eased off the bed, slung her bag over her shoulder, and waited for her to stand. "When we're ready to disappear, put the charm around your neck, grip it in your fist, and Haven will not be able to sense you."

Kyana stiffened. "I didn't say anything about Haven."

Sixx eyed her and smirked. "Not all blonds are stupid. Everyone knows who you're hunting, so it's pretty easy to figure out who, exactly, you don't want tracing *you*."

"You won't touch her," Kyana warned. "Whatever you think you know, the only thing you need to remember now is that she is *not* your prize to catch."

Sixx shrugged. "Whatever. You're the mighty Huntress. I'm sure you won't have any trouble bringing her down on your own."

Rising to her feet, Kyana inhaled deeply to find calm. She froze. "Some of my scent . . . *your* scent, is already gone."

The Witch nodded. "By the time we get downstairs, it should be completely untraceable. But you need the potion *and* the charm to make all other evidence of your presence disappear."

As Sixx had predicted, by the time they were outside, she couldn't have traced the Witch even if she'd shifted into Lychen.

"You're good," she offered reluctantly.

Sixx grinned. "I know."

They walked with Nettles nestled safely between them. After they'd traveled a couple of blocks, Kyana fingered the charm in her pocket.

"Haven makes me Illusion Charms so when I shift back and forth from Lychen, the rest of the world sees me clothed." Which, by the way, had led to one of her most embarrassing moments this century—finding out Ryker and all gods/demigods, could see through the illusion. She had been strutting around naked in front of him and hadn't realized he'd seen every bit of her for hours on end. "Why does this one need a potion to make it work?"

They turned down a side street and onto the cobblestone path that would take them to Nettles's townhouse. "Because you're using both an Illusion Charm and a cloaking spell together. If you don't use them as a pair, the Illusion Charm will wipe away the effects of the spell and vice versa. You'll be invisible but your scent will return."

Interesting. She would have to remember to ask Haven if she knew of the combination when all this was over.

"Are you sure you want to do this?" she asked Nettles. "We can take your belongings back to your house. Enough of your scent should be on them to make Haven think you're there."

Instead of answering, Nettles stubbornly lifted her chin. Sixx looked at Kyana with raised eyebrows. "She on a mission or just got a death wish?"

"Seers are an odd bunch." Of course, since Nettles was the only Seer she had ever been around, she wasn't sure if Nettles was the exception or the norm, really. "She had a vision and feels if we don't do everything as she saw it, then I won't catch Haven."

"Hmm. And did she see me in her little vision?"

"Didn't ask."

"You might have been under your Illusion Charm in my vision. You *could* have been there," Nettles said, sounding miffed.

"Okay. I'll buy that." Sixx turned back to Kyana. "What happens if we don't stop your friend?"

Not liking the *we* in that question at all, yet knowing there was no way around it, Kyana sighed. "Haven will cut out Nettles's eyeballs and find a spell that will give her the answers she wants."

"Ew."

"Ew, indeed." She quickly ran down her plan of attack. "When Haven makes her move, I'll bring her down."

"And me?"

"Protect the Seer and get her to safety if your spells don't work and Haven gets past me."

"You'd better not let it get that far. Your threats aside . . ." That smug look filled Sixx's face again. "If she comes near the Seer, it'll be the last move she makes."

Kyana spun around and pinned her with a glare. "Don't even think about laying a hand on Haven or I swear—"

"There's a bounty on her head. She's fair game

and your threats don't hold weight when it comes to the wishes of the gods."

"I *am* the gods now. Understand?"

"If you hope to catch your friend, you need to learn not to threaten those trying to help you."

She couldn't help it. She lunged for Sixx, wanting to smack the sass right out of her. But before her hand could close around Sixx's throat, the Witch began to flicker as though she stood in the middle of a hundred candles.

Then, she disappeared leaving Kyana holding nothing but air.

"Oh my," Nettles gasped, blinking as though trying to clear her vision.

"What the—" Kyana felt a tap on her shoulder, spun around, and found herself standing nose to nose with Sixx.

"Something in the genetic Vamp DNA," she said, grinning. "Cool, huh? Only lasts a couple seconds but has saved my ass more than once."

Kyana expected her to try to throw a punch, but Sixx surprised her by broadening her smile. "I'll leave your friend alone, Kyana, if you can handle her on your own. But in return, you're going to have to cool your temper. You can be badass without being a bully."

She picked up one of the bags Nettles had dropped in her moment of shock, and slung it over her shoulder before continuing down the path. Kyana contemplated popping Sixx's braids out of her head one by one, but discarded the idea. She might not like the Witch, but Sixx had piqued Kya-na's curiosity enough to make keeping her around intriguing.

Who the hell is this woman and what other tricks does she have up her sleeve?

Chapter Twenty-Four

Nettles's house was as dark and quiet as when they'd left it. There was no trace of Haven, and Kyana was hoping against hope that this meant she hadn't yet arrived. She and Sixx made quick work of turning off most of the lights while Nettles did her part and prepared for bed. This, Nettles had insisted, would be the most believable scenario for Haven to walk in on since only Dark Breeds tended to be awake at this hour.

Besides that, this was how she'd seen it in her vision, so this was how it had to go down.

When Nettles reappeared in the hall outside her bedroom, Kyana stopped her task of turning off lights. Her hand dropped to her side and she blinked in disbelief, her jaw agape as she struggled to hold back her laughter.

Despite her efforts, a snort escaped. "You actually wear that to bed?"

The Seer's pink pajamas were covered with tiny

gray mice and there were feet . . . *feet* . . . sewn in, a hood stitched into the back.

Nettles shrugged and wiggled her mousy feet. "I get cold."

When she lifted the hood and gently placed it over her spunky hair, Kyana couldn't help it. Her struggle to keep her laughter quiet made her eyes water.

"You . . . have . . . *ears!*"

Nettles pierced her with a glare that might have killed her if the old Seer had been bigger than a mouse herself.

"You just make use of your charms so I can get this over with," she grumbled.

Sixx appeared at the end of the hall, took one look at Nettles, then looked at Kyana and rolled her eyes. "Oh my gods, turn around. I have to know if you have a tail."

Sixx was just teasing of course, but Nettles turned around, and sure enough, about seven inches of pink yarn hung from her saggy little tush. Kyana was going to have to use her charm. Right now. If she didn't, Haven would hear her laughter long before she arrived. But it felt so good to laugh. So good to forget, even for half a second, what they were here to do.

She pointed to the bedroom and fought to clamp down her laughter. "You go . . . get in . . . bed. Sixx will be watching you . . . from the hallway."

Nettles shook her head so hard the ears on her pajamas came around to pop her chin. "You both should be in the room with me. I'd feel better knowing you were there even if I can't see you."

Her composure finally gathered, she gave Nettles's shoulder a pat of reassurance. "I need to have a clear view of the house so I can see Haven and make sure she's alone."

"It's going to be fine," Sixx said, wrapping her arm around Nettles's shoulder. "You lay quiet and I'll be in the corner until the psycho bitch shows."

"Watch it," Kyana scolded. "She's not to blame for what she's become."

"Just go do your thing and let me do mine."

Forcing herself not to draw the woman into another round of who-hated-whom-more, she nodded at the bed, then at Nettles. "Let's get this going before Haven realizes something is up and decides to be a no-show."

If that happened, they'd be right back in the middle of a guessing game. Haven wouldn't give up until she had the Eyes of Power. She believed Nettles could find them for her. The old Seer didn't stand a chance of avoiding Haven for long.

She made her way back through the house, shutting off more lights as she went, bathing the house in enough darkness to create the illusion needed to bring Haven out of the shadows.

She sat in the dark for what felt an eternity but in actuality was only a couple of hours. The sky outside was lightening, but only by a fraction. Gray skies instead of black loomed overhead, and it was becoming difficult not to doze off. Sixx had surprised her with her ability to stay alert. So far, she hadn't complained once about how long it was taking for them to see action. Maybe she wasn't half bad.

Or maybe Kyana was just too tired to care anymore.

Finally, a soft birdcall whistle brought her back to the stairs, where she found Sixx waving her down. The Witch pulled her charm out of her pocket. "Time to don the accessories. Your friend is on her way."

Kyana sniffed the air. Only Nettles's scent hung in the room. "How do you know?"

"The Seer said so." Sixx rubbed at her arms as if trying to massage a sudden chill from her body. "And there's a charge in the air that wasn't here two minutes ago."

She felt it too. It was as though someone had poured a static fog into the house, making every hair on her body stand at attention. "Protect the Seer. Leave Haven to me."

Sixx pulled the charm over her head and disappeared from sight. With a sigh, and a tiny prayer that this time Haven wouldn't get the upper hand, Kyana slipped her own charm over her head, moved onto the front porch, and waited.

No more than ten minutes had passed before she picked up the sound of determined footsteps coming up the deserted street. There wasn't a trace of Haven hanging in the air, but by the electricity dancing on the wind, she was close.

Bracing her hands against the railing, she watched the street. A lone cat, bathing itself on the walk, suddenly stilled. A low hissing, almost a growl, filled the night air. Slowly, the cat pushed to its feet, watching the darkness. With a screech, it shot down an alleyway, knocking over a trash can in its rush to escape.

The footfalls closed in and she found herself holding her breath. When her head started to spin, and still Haven hadn't arrived, she forced herself to pull in small breaths. When the sound of her heartbeat faded from her ears, she realized the footfalls had stopped too.

Adrenaline set fire to her blood. Her gaze darted around the yard, the darkness hiding nothing but silent houses. Had she imagined the footsteps? The feel of Haven on the wind?

She'd just about convinced herself that it had all been in her head when a sound pulled her gaze back to the door. Haven stood two feet away, her hand on the knob, her head tilted as she peered through the gaping hole in the door.

Kyana quickly played out all the options in her head. Bringing Haven down before she entered the house was her best bet. If she failed to stop her, maybe Haven would flee without going after the Seer.

Not bothering to uncloak, she threw her invisible form forward, hitting Haven square in the back. Haven let out a loud *oomph*, her eyes wide as she tried to see her attacker. Wrapping her arms around Haven, Kyana shoved her to the ground, landing on top of her, her forehead connecting to the back of Haven's skull.

Haven hissed and shimmied away, but Kyana grabbed hold of an ankle, jerking her back to the ground. As she knelt with one hand braced on the rough wooden planks of the porch, Haven's gaze darted in every direction, searching.

"Come on, Kyana," she all but sang. "You won't get the satisfaction you want if you don't fight fair."

With the fluidity only a goddess could possess, Kyana pulled the chain from her neck and launched herself forward. Her fist connected with Haven's jaw at the same time her leg swung out and knocked Haven into the porch railing behind her. Fully visible now, she straddled Haven and looked her in the eye. She didn't recognize the person staring back at her, but she had to believe that somewhere in those black depths, Haven still existed.

"I'd offer to help you, but I'm guessing you still won't accept."

Much like her eyes, Haven's laugh was cold and bitter. "Don't you think you've helped me enough?"

Guilt loosened Kyana's hold, but not enough for Haven to break free. "I can't take back what I did, but I can make it better. You don't have to be a pawn. You don't have to do these things. He can't control you if you don't let him."

Haven hissed. "Cronos's pawn now, or the Order's later. At least this way, I can embrace what you've made me."

She bucked with enough force to throw Kyana off balance and slipped out from under her.

Determined not to let Haven get away again,

Kyana quickly regained her balance and spun around. She grabbed the back of Haven's hair and snatched her to her chest. A whistle rang out above their heads and she glanced up to find Sixx leaning over Nettles's railing, a chain dangling from her fingertips.

It fell with a soft clink at Kyana's feet, and she recognized it right away. A Binding Charm like the one Silas had made in Cassadaga. As she bent to pick it up, Haven's eyes widened and her mouth fell open.

"Cheater," she said, a grin spreading across her face. She swung out, catching Kyana in the chin with her sharp nails, but Kyana knocked her head back with her elbow, securing Haven once more.

She wrapped the chain around her left wrist, looped it again into a figure eight, then slipped the other circle around Haven's right hand. The chain sealed itself closed.

The door opened behind her and Sixx stepped out, followed by a very nervous-looking Nettles.

"Am I safe?" the Seer whispered, keeping her distance from Haven.

Kyana nodded, tightening her hold around Haven's waist.

The Binding Charm Sixx had given her was completing its work, and she could feel Haven's energy draining as she slumped against Kyana's chest. Weak as a newborn, she'd give no more fight. She was safe.

Kyana hung her head and wept with gratitude.

Chapter Twenty-Five

Ryker itched like hell. It was hard to concentrate on what Zeus was trying to explain when he felt as though he were on fire. And what was that damned buzzing noise? He bent his head over his knees, the stone bench beneath his ass as cold as a glacier.

"You must focus, Ryker."

Zeus's voice was like a freight train in a tunnel. Booming, echoey, and getting on Ryker's last nerve. "It's hard to pay attention when I feel like you just forced me to eat fire ants."

Even for a demigod, having his body infused with such powerful blood made him feel like his soul was trying to ooze right out of his pores. Why hadn't Kyana warned him about this? Or Geoffrey? Hell, even Silas had undergone the same thing a few hours ago, and he hadn't said a word either. All right, so neither man liked Ryker much and the feeling was mutual, but Kyana—

He shook his head. She didn't like him much either, since he'd abandoned her.

Zeus stared down at him with disdain. "If you can't handle it now, how do you plan on surviving when the full power of my blood surges through you in seven days? Perhaps your lineage doesn't make you strong enough to handle the transformation, after all."

Ryker rose, swaying as the grass around his feet swelled and receded. "I just need a few minutes to acclimate—"

"It's been an hour!"

Zeus's roar bounced off the bronze statuary all around them. The temple grounds were deserted save for a pair of guards, but a dozen birds shot out of pear trees nearby and let out brain-impaling shrieks as they zoomed overhead.

"Show me again." His queasiness subsided and his flesh began to cool. There were still insects building a small city beneath his skin, but he could cope with that part. If Geoffrey and Silas had been able to deal with this and go straight out to do their jobs, he damned well could too.

Zeus stuck out his hand and he took it, wincing at the enormous strength behind the ancient god's squeeze. His fingers crackled under the pressure, but he steadily held the god's gaze.

"Now," Zeus said, "focus on that itch beneath your skin. Bring it to the surface so that the finest hairs on your arms sizzle with electricity."

He focused, just as he had been trying to do for

the past hour, but the itch and fire remained buried beneath his flesh. He'd never worried about being in over his head before, and he didn't like it. Staring into Zeus's icy blue eyes, Ryker let his frustration build. Frustration over not grasping Zeus's powers quickly enough. Over the stupid games he and Kyana insisted on playing with each other. Over doing everything in his power to not become like his father and fearing he was failing.

The resentment over Ares's devotion to his duty and the Order had worn away most of Ryker's desire to be a real son. Or so he'd thought. But these days, he'd been faced with very similar choices and he was too close to following in Ares's footsteps for his own liking. How could he ask Kyana to give up everything she believed about herself long enough to give him a real chance when he kept letting the Order get between what he felt for her and what he hoped she was beginning to feel for *him*?

"You're not worthy of her," Zeus declared after several agonizing seconds of silence. "She's to be the Goddess of the Hunt, and with no time to prepare herself, she is out there trying to fix what is broken. And you . . . you can't even manage the most simple of my powers."

Ryker tensed. He knew he was being goaded but that didn't stop the ire from boiling inside him.

"Shut up," he said between clenched teeth, squeezing his eyes shut to tune out Zeus's voice and concentrate.

"Ah, there it is. That weak center of yours. You

know you're not good enough for her and my words only confirm that fear. Isn't that right?"

Ryker's grip on Zeus's hand tightened and he wished with everything inside him that he could snap the god's bones in two. "Shut. Up."

"I know you've bedded her," Zeus continued as though Ryker hadn't spoken. "You know, women are my weakness. Willing. Unwilling. Buxom or lean. Tell me. Does she taste as good as she looks? Perhaps I'll sample her soon."

Ryker's blood gave a violent jolt and sent energy through his veins and into his hands. An electric charge exploded from his fingertips and Zeus was lifted off his feet and sent to his ass just a few feet away. The guards who'd been granted permission to stay on Olympus came running from their posts at the foot of the temple stairs, swords drawn.

Zeus held up his hand to keep them at bay, a large smile lighting up his face. "Your weakness seems to also give you strength. Odd, that."

Hoping Zeus's ass would be black and blue come morning, Ryker reached out and helped him to his feet.

"Hold close that feeling." Zeus patted down his robe and adjusted the staff hanging at his hip. "I won't always be there to piss you off."

His gaze drifted to the conduit. He hadn't yet entrusted it to Ryker, and wouldn't until Ryker could master a few of Zeus's most common skills. Like emitting lightning from his damned pores. Trivial things like that.

As Zeus turned away from him, however, Ryker's body warmed and tingled again, but this time, it wasn't unpleasant. "Do you . . . feel that?"

Zeus turned back, his blond eyebrows raised inquisitively. "I feel nothing but a sore tailbone." He stepped toward Ryker, his cold blue eyes warming a tad. "Describe what you're experiencing."

He couldn't name it. Couldn't figure out what exactly felt so strange, and yet so right. But the ants had stopped construction and his body was becoming all gooey and soft. "I feel like I'm dissolving into mush."

It was the best he could come up with to explain.

Zeus's smile was one of mockery. Placing his hand on Ryker's shoulder, he turned them both so they were facing the newly constructed portal to Below several yards away. "You are, I believe, experiencing what I experience every time Hera is nearby."

"Hera . . ." Zeus's wife. Ryker swallowed. "Kyana."

Zeus closed his eyes, his body swaying slightly as his grip on Ryker's arm tightened. "Yes. She is near. And it seems she has done what we all suspected she could not. She is bringing Haven home."

Confirming Zeus's words, Hermes flitted through the portal from Below, his wrinkly face beaming, giving him the appearance of a drunken Keebler Elf.

"She has done it!" he yelled. "She has captured the one who was to raise the dark god!"

A cheer rang out, startling Ryker. He looked around at the two dozen minor gods stepping out of what he'd thought had been vacant forest lands. Apparently, they'd been watching Ryker's training from a safe distance. But with Hermes's pronouncement, their hiding places were forgotten as they grouped together to talk with vivid animation.

As Hermes drifted toward Zeus, Ryker ran toward the portal, knowing Kyana would be taking Haven to the prison Below. Zeus called out after him, but he didn't slow or turn around. He had to see with his own two eyes that Kyana was okay.

"Do not leave the safety of Below!" Zeus shouted.

Ryker raised a hand to acknowledge that he'd heard, then slipped through the portal.

She probably wouldn't even want to see him, but whether she knew it or not, she needed him more right now than she'd ever admit. She'd just captured her best friend and was about to throw her in prison to face a hearing that might end with the very outcome Kyana had been trying to avoid.

He couldn't make his feet move fast enough as he sprinted down the streets of Below toward the beach and leaped over the jet black stones and geysers outside the prison. He ducked inside the musty, dark cave that held the gods' criminals and didn't stop running until he caught a glimpse of Kyana at the magically charged barrier that would hold Haven captive.

He finally stopped in the large archway and forced air into his lungs. She'd been gone only hours, but the worry that had filled every single minute had extended her absence into an eternity. He wanted to grab her. Hold her. Kiss her.

Instead, he waited.

She stood so stiff, he feared one strong wind would snap her in two. When she issued orders to the Witches and Mystics attempting to restrain the screaming captive, her voice shook. Anyone else would've guessed it was anger controlling her, but Ryker saw the trembling in her hands, heard the panic and worry in her demands.

"Ky?"

She spun around, her face blotchy, her eyes red. She'd been crying. The sight ripped through his heart and urged him forward. He waited, his breath hitching as she took one tentative step toward him. He made it easy on her and closed the distance. The minute she was within reach, she fell into his arms and pressed her face to his neck.

Kyana was so happy to see Ryker, she forgot to be angry with him. She simply held on as tightly as he'd let her and drank in the beautiful scent of sunshine emanating from his neck and hair.

"You did it, Ky," he whispered, his breath momentarily warming some of the chill that had settled into her soul.

"Tell me they're not going to kill her after everything I've done to save her."

She wasn't crying anymore, but her voice was tight with the struggle not to. He ran his fingers through her hair and kissed her temple. "She'll have a fair trial. Artemis wouldn't have sent you after her if she wasn't planning on doing everything in her power to redeem Haven."

His words didn't give her the reassurance she needed. Kyana pushed away and leaned against the wall to stare blindly at the cleansing going on behind the invisible barrier.

"It's too late to purge her. They can cleanse her to make the need to feed less urgent, but that takes months to complete. And we both know that even a nonfeeding Vampyre or Lychen is *still* a Dark Breed. I'm proof enough of that."

Gods, she ached for Haven. Ached with guilt, remorse, and empathetic pangs from the link that existed between her and her Childe. But more than that, she ached with the link that bonded them as friends. As sisters. She wanted to be cleansed like Haven, wanted to be free of the ugliness that coated every organ in her body.

"You're proof that a Dark Breed doesn't have to be condemned, Ky." He kissed her brow. "You've done far more good for the Order since joining us. Give yourself a break."

"Maybe," she sighed. "Maybe when all this is over and Haven is all right. Until then, I don't deserve a break."

The urge to weep again was overwhelming. She hung on to the thread of pride she had left and turned away in case it snapped. Ryker reached out to her again, but she stepped away and turned her attention to Haven's cell. Sixx and a Healer knelt on either side of Haven. Two sentinels at Haven's head and feet held her pinned to the ground.

"Why is she here?"

Kyana offered a weak shrug. "She helped me catch her. She'll help the Healer with the cleansing. Make sure everything's done quickly and with the least amount of pain as possible."

"You trust her?"

Shaking her head, she turned away from him to better watch the scene inside the cell. "No. But Silas seems to. He wouldn't be with her if she was complete trash."

Sixx took hands with the Healer to complete their circle and began chanting the ancient words of a calming spell. Haven's curses and promises of a very slow and very painful death screeched above their whispers.

"Where's Geoffrey? He's going to want to see her," Kyana whispered, her emotions slowly calming as the realization hit her that, whatever else happened, Haven was safe. "Maybe he can bring our Haven back. I obviously couldn't."

"I'm sure he'll come when he can."

Kyana nodded. To distract herself, she studied Ryker. He'd changed. A lot.

It had been only a few hours since she'd seen him, and already he'd taken on a few of Zeus's traits. His hair had lightened a bit, as if the rays of the sun had dipped down to run their golden fingers through it. It had grown a little longer too, now brushing the tips of his collar.

His silver eyes . . . the sight of them caught the breath in her throat for they were no longer silver but icy, cold blue. Nearly white. Like the turquoise seas of the Mediterranean tipped with ocean foam. But one thing about those eyes remained the same. The way they looked at her.

Worried. Caring. Soft. They offered her so much that she wanted to take, but for his sake, probably never would. Not until she knew without doubt that she could commit to him the way he seemed to need her to.

"I'm surprised you're not in there with her."

Pulling herself together, Kyana gave a light shrug. "Sixx asked me to leave. Apparently the sight of me makes Haven more difficult to restrain." She smiled. "I tend to bring that out in people, don't I? The anger and frustration? I think I've found my talent."

She caught a glimpse of Ryker's fangs as he returned her smile. The sight of them calmed her even more. The reminder that just because a breed had fangs didn't make them destined to do evil gave her hope that Haven could be saved. She ran her tongue over her own fangs, noting with dismay that they were virtually gone now. In a few days, they would be gone forever. So would Ryker's.

She wasn't sure how she felt about that.

Ryker traced the line of her jaw with his finger. "Your talents are many, Ky. Every day you show me a new one."

"Yeah, like what?"

Haven's screams of protest interrupted Ryker's reply.

Kyana spun, her body tense again as she rushed toward the cell. "What are you doing to her?"

Ryker grabbed her shoulder and yanked her backward as though he thought she might throw herself through the invisible bars. "Let's get some fresh air, Ky."

Because Haven might feel better if her worst enemy wasn't watching the show. That's what he'd really wanted to say, and exactly what Kyana was thinking herself.

Still, if leaving made this easier on Haven, then Kyana would walk away. Worrying wouldn't do anyone any good. No matter the outcome here, she'd set out to do what she'd needed to. She'd given Haven a fighting chance at survival. She should be celebrating.

Keeping his grip firmly on her shoulder, Ryker guided her toward the exit. They'd made it to the first step outside before she jerked away, indecision turning her muscles into knots. "I need to be here. She could have valuable information about Cronos. Something we can use to stop him. And she didn't have the trident. I still don't know where it is."

Ryker retook her hand. "When she's calm, she'll be questioned."

Remembering her own interrogation, her determination not to leave Haven doubled. "By Ares? He's too heavy-handed, too cocky. He'll never get anything out of her. I need to talk to her first. If they can cleanse her enough to get our Haven back, she'll talk to me, tell me what we need to know."

Her words didn't ring true in her own ears, but thankfully, Ryker didn't call her a liar. "Ares can be a hard-ass, but he knows what he's doing." Tilting her chin up so she had no choice but to look at him, he smiled. "And I promise, if she needs you, someone will come find us."

"But—"

"But nothing, Ky. You need to recharge. Let Ares do his job. When she's ready to talk to you, someone will come get us."

Before Kyana could find a reason to argue, he tightened his grip and led her away from the prison.

Chapter Twenty-Six

Leisurely soaks and massages weren't really Kyana's thing, but Ryker had insisted she could use a little TLC, and she wasn't in the mood to argue. The Turkish bathhouse Below was vacant of other guests, but employees waited in the corners to be called upon if needed. She had never been here before, though she'd frequented the neighboring establishment, Spirits, a million times.

Adrenaline was making it hard to think coherently anyway. She was nearly coming out of her skin with the need to do *something*. Hopefully, a massage would ease some of that out of her, because right now, the very air around her was crackling with energy she needed to exert.

She'd caught Haven before she could raise Cronos. She'd done the impossible, and while Haven's fate wasn't yet clear, Kyana was on a high.

The owner of the bathhouse—a short, bald man with rosy red skin that had likely spent far too much time being cooked to well-done by the steam—ushered them toward the row of stalls at the rear of the farthermost room and handed Kyana a bathing suit. She stepped inside the dressing room obediently, simply because her brain still wouldn't allow her to speak coherently. She was afraid if she opened her mouth, a thousand random words would tumble out in a string of sentences that would make no sense at all.

It took her longer than it should have to slip the flimsy triangles of the bikini over her breasts and secure them in place. Her hands were trembling too badly to make a success of the ties. It seemed her body hadn't yet come to terms with the idea that her duty was done. She only needed to find and return Poseidon's trident to him now, and she'd be able to focus on becoming the goddess she was supposed to be.

And yet every inch of her flesh was still ready to hunt. To fight.

Ryker was already waiting for her when she made her way out of the stall. He wore mid-calf trunks and a very nicely sculpted bare chest that made her silently praise the sport of surfing that kept him so tanned and toned. He leaned against the wall, his eyes half closed as he watched her. She felt his gaze rake over her, felt the heat of the trail that stare left behind, and quivered.

Maybe her body wasn't aching to hunt or fight. Maybe it was aching for something far more fun . . . more delicious.

More likely her sudden burst of libido stemmed

from the excitement of what she'd accomplished today. It was all she could do not to throw him down, tear his shorts off, and give her adrenaline an outlet.

"Your masseuses are ready," the manager said. Kyana jumped, her already erratic heartbeat stumbling into an all-new rhythm.

"No," she said. "No massage. Show us to the baths and excuse your employees."

Her gaze never left Ryker's, and as his stare narrowed in question, she let herself show only the faintest of smiles before turning away.

Ryker called himself every sort of fool when his feet disobeyed his brain and followed her to the baths. She'd managed to devour him with one quick stare, and his body was still trying to recover. Her intentions had been written all over her face. She wanted him. But more than that, she wanted to celebrate catching Haven and forget that she might still be sentenced to death. In other words, she wanted to use him.

So sad that he was so eager and so willing to be used.

Gods, he was a damned fool.

He stopped in the doorway, swearing he wasn't going to take another step inside. If he did, he was doomed. He was still recovering from the last time he'd made love to her.

The door shut behind the stodgy manager, leaving him alone with Kyana as she tentatively touched a toe to the steamy water. His throat went dry and he could barely find the will to swallow as he watched her reach behind her neck and untie the thin strings of her bikini. She turned, her dark eyes glimmering as she watched him.

He couldn't move. He was hard as a damned rock, but he couldn't bring himself to move and touch her as she was so blatantly begging him to. When she slid the bottoms from her hips to her ankles and daintily stepped out of them, a sharp throb pulsed in his groin.

Stark naked and stunningly gorgeous, she was offering herself to him. Again. But this time, he was going to make her ask for it. This time, if he let her use him, if they used each other, she was going to have to work for it. Even if it killed him.

"Getting in?" she asked, her voice low and much deeper than normal.

She turned away from him before he could answer, and one by one, she descended the steps into the bath, coyly glancing at him over her shoulder. She submerged herself into the water and surfaced again, steam shrouding her in a faint fog. Her black curls clung to her cheeks and neck, draped over her shoulders, and teased him by barely veiling her nipples.

"Are we playing another game?" he asked, finding the strength to push away from the door.

If he took her now, there would be no tenderness. No gentleness. It was going to be hard and fast and wild as hell, and by the gods, it was going to be earth-shattering. She'd better be damned sure she knew what she wanted before he put even one toe in that water.

"No games," she whispered, standing straighter so that the water no longer covered her bare belly.

Gods save him, he wasn't strong enough to deny her.

He'd been in love with Kyana Melek Aslan for a decade. She was his, whether she knew it or not, and he was certainly hers whether she wanted him or not. He'd seen her strength and her tenderness. He'd seen her love for her friends and her determination to right the wrongs done to them. And every bit of who she was made him want to claim her. Brand her. Mark her. Forever.

"If I touch you, I'm not going to stop," he said. His throat felt as though someone had torched it and left it to burn, turning it to rubble.

"I sincerely hope not."

The steam sucked the air from his lungs as he stepped down into the water.

Kyana watched Ryker take the steps slowly, his jaw set, his eyes dancing as he battled with himself over what she offered him. She knew he wanted her. He'd be a fool not to take it. She needed release. Needed to purge herself of all the tension that had been building inside her for days. And Ryker was the only one she wanted to lose herself in.

Only him.

That thought disturbed her immeasurably, but if she allowed herself to contemplate it further, she'd back off. And that was the last thing she wanted. All she cared about right now was walking toward her. Beautiful. Bronzed. A god and a man with the power to make her knees weak. She wanted to taste him, to feel him, and whatever that might mean to her would have to be worried about later.

"You should probably feed, Ky. Ambrosia—"

"I don't need ambrosia." She was tired of waiting. She walked toward him, wrapped her hand around his wrist and pulled him down the last step before gently pushing him to sit on the steps.

She spread his legs and moved between them, leaning in to cup his face and nuzzle his neck with what remained of her fangs.

"Then what *do* you need?"

"You." Blood rushing to all sorts of interesting places in her body, she slid her hand down his chest and let it rest between his thighs. "This."

His low growl made her purr, and when he grabbed her backside and lifted her, forcing her to straddle him, she didn't protest.

Her nipples hardened beneath his stare, and she looked up to find his gaze darkened by desire, his chest heaving slightly faster than usual. She placed her lips on the curve of his shoulder and trailed them up his neck. Ryker pulled her closer, pressing her breasts against his chest and the tip of his cock against her belly. She moaned and moved her hips slightly. Teasing. Taunting. Demanding.

Ryker gripped the back of her hair, tilted her head back, and devoured her throat.

"To hell with consequences." His words were muffled against her skin.

Kyana couldn't have agreed more.

Chapter Twenty-Seven

Kyana's kiss was deep and thorough and hotter than Tartarus. She moaned into Ryker's mouth, danced her tongue over his teeth, and lapped at the corners of his lips. He delved into the depths of her mouth, and she reached between them to cup him through his trunks, to stroke him, obviously enjoying the power her touch ignited, though it was burning Ryker from the inside out.

She panted, clinging to him as he dipped her backward and lowered his mouth to her breasts. Lifting her out of the water, he watched her muscles quiver beneath the taut skin of her abdomen as he placed her on the rim of the pool and drank in the sweet scent of her. It nearly drove him out of his mind.

"Ryker?"

The silent plea in her eyes, the way her body tensed in anticipation of his touch, had him shaking with the need to be inside her. He couldn't find his voice to answer. Instead, he dipped his head and trailed his tongue along her inner thigh, smiling when her muscles constricted beneath his touch. Her legs rolled open, offering him what he wanted, and he took it as eagerly as a god accepted a sacrifice. She tasted like warm honey and ambrosia. He traced his tongue along the soft skin between her legs, spread her folds, then gently lapped at her, drinking her.

Loving her.

Kyana arched, grabbed a fistful of Ryker's hair, and thrust her hips upward. All worries and coherent thought flittered from her mind. Her pants became gasps as his tongue plunged and retreated, slid over her clit in rhythmic circles, then plunged again.

She bucked, the pressure inside her building to an explosive climax, and when Ryker's tongue slid once more over the sensitive nub and his finger delved inside, she came.

She tugged his hair, pulling him up her body and out of the pool as she clung to him. As she struggled to remember how to breathe, his hands trailed lightly over her body, setting the simmering fires to blazing again.

Cupping his face in her palms, she lifted his head to study his eyes. She didn't want to hurt him by taking what he offered her, knowing she couldn't give him more than her body. Unfulfilled need in his blue eyes spoke to her soul, and none of the questions or concerns dancing on her tongue mattered.

"If we do this, you have to know I'm using you to forget," she whispered. It was the lie she was telling herself, and the need for him to hear it, to maybe have enough sense for both of them and pull away, made her voice it aloud.

"I know."

She read his face, saw he spoke the truth, then pulled his head down and captured his mouth before guilt could make her stop what was happening between them. She trailed her hands down his back to grip the waistband of his trunks. Smiling against his lips, she hooked her fingers in his shorts and slid them off.

His muscles trembled beneath her fingers as he sprang free, throbbing and hot against her belly. She rolled him to his back and straddled his waist, and his gaze locked on hers. Kyana struggled to read the emotions filtering in his eyes, but he masked them before she could decipher a single one.

Trailing her lips across his body, she used her teeth and tongue to taste and tease her way down him. She knelt between his legs and pressed a kiss to the tip of him. His moan was felt between her thighs in a single, painful throb.

"My turn," she whispered, lowering her head.

"Not this time."

His fingers bit into her arms as he pulled her against his chest. His lips, hot and soft, claimed hers again, his five o'clock shadow chafing her cheeks and chin as he devoured her. His fingers danced across her skin, slipping between their bodies to plunge inside her, matching the rhythm of his kisses.

Gently, he rolled them over and positioned himself between her thighs. She reached for him. With one long, slow push, he buried himself inside her. Kyana cried out at the heat of his possession. Tiny fireworks of light exploded behind her eyes as her climax stole her breath. Two strokes were all it had taken, but her satisfaction was just as short-lived. She wanted him more now than ever before.

As she spasmed around his body, her legs tightened around his waist, forcing him to plunge more deeply inside. His moan against her ear sent a tremor over her arms and legs. He held still, giving her body time to adjust to the weight of him, the feel of him, and when her spasms slowed to a steady pulse, he began to move slowly—slipping nearly out of her body before sinking into her heat again, taking her on the ascending ride all over again.

His dance drove her mad as she panted against his neck, sliding her legs down his hips, then closing them around his thighs. She pressed herself against him, her hands raking over his back and shoulders and ass in a fevered hunger of their own to discover every inch of him.

It's just a fuck. Just a good lay.
Liar!

It was more than that. He was truly inside her. Not just his body in hers, but his very essence had worked its way through her veins, consuming her, becoming one with her.

Stop! You're taking too much!

But her tongue no longer worked. No part of her body seemed to belong to her anymore. It was all Ryker's.

All for Ryker.

She squeezed her eyes shut, unable to look at the raw desire lighting his eyes from pale blue to near white. She concentrated, desperate to find some sense of control, but the more she fought, the more her body betrayed her. She found herself arching again. Screaming again. Coming again.

He drove into her over and over, sweat dripping from his brow as he rose up on his arms to stare down at her. She couldn't take anymore. She bucked, desperate to throw him off, but he was too strong. Or maybe she wasn't trying hard enough.

When she opened her mouth to demand that he stop, she heard herself whisper, "More," instead.

Thrusting her hips against his, she quickened the pace. The cry of his name on her lips was muffled by his kiss as yet another climax seized her muscles.

As his tongue dipped between her parted lips, he came, groaning into her mouth as she inhaled a bit of his soul.

Chapter Twenty-Eight

Kyana lay curled against Ryker, the frantic pace of her mind in direct contrast to the rhythm of her heartbeat. She'd had sex with him before, but this time, something between them had shifted. The usual need to bolt hadn't come, neither had the normal urge to deny anything more than a fuck had happened. The balloon of protection she'd been carrying in her chest for the last couple of centuries had popped after her last orgasm.

But try as she might, she couldn't figure out why. This time, like the others, she'd used him for the relief his body could offer hers. Relief had come, instead, to all of her.

Ryker began to lightly stroke the sensitive square of skin at the small of her back, and it hit her all at once. The difference. She'd felt, in his last kiss, the truth. He loved her. No man touched a woman as he'd touched her without love, and while Ryker had hinted at his feelings for a while now, she had always found some means to brush them off. The wall of duties and bloodlines between them had made it the simplest thing in the world to tell herself that there was nothing different between this tryst with Ryker and any of the others she'd ever had.

A liar lies to others. A fool lies to herself.

The time would come when her itch to roam would return, but she couldn't keep trying to convince herself that she was in any kind of hurry for that to happen. Why push it away when it felt so good? Nature would take its course soon enough to break them apart, but for now, she was too exhausted to do more than hold him as closely as possible.

The uncomfortable realization left her body cold. She nestled closer to Ryker, pressing her nose to his neck, breathing in the sweet, clean scent of his skin.

"When I was fifteen," she began, "my father sold me to Prince Mehmet and I thought it was the beginning of my happily ever after."

Ryker's chest stopped rising, his breath stuck somewhere between his lungs and his throat. She felt him stiffen beneath her, as though he might be afraid to so much as twitch and risk scaring her off. But now that she had started, she was determined to finish. Determined to prove to him that she was able to give a little of herself to him—perhaps not her future, but a bit of her past.

"His harem numbered more than eighty-seven women. The oldest and first wife, Azime, ruled us with a hard fist and an even more brutal tongue. But I suffered through her abuse silently. Mehmet was kind to me. He made my nights easier to bear after days of dealing with Azime. At least, for a while."

"Fifteen," Ryker whispered.

Kyana propped herself onto her elbow so she could see his face. "That's not so bad. You were there. You know women marry much later now than they used to. The youngest of his harem was only five. Of course, she was untouched, but even she knew well what being one of Mehmet's wives was going to mean for her one day."

Tracing the fine lines that defined Ryker's abdomen, she tried to summon an image of Paulina, the youngest of the harem. But no image came. Just the faint memory of blond hair and a foreign accent. British, probably. Mehmet had liked his collection of women to be eclectic. He'd had wives from fifteen different countries in his household.

When her gaze fell back to Ryker's face, she found him watching her intently. "What?"

His smile was faint as he rubbed his thumb over her chin. "That's not enough tit for my tat."

"It was plenty of tit for a little tat."

Ryker exhaled, his golden hair spreading out around his head on the cold bath tiles. "Ares came for me when I was ten."

"He told you he was your father then?"

Ryker nodded. "Tit."

"I enjoyed being Mehmet's wife until one night when we'd been married for nearly six months."

"What changed it?"

Kyana dragged her leg off his thighs and sat up. How much did she really feel like confessing? A bit at a time, and when it became too much, she'd stop. Something was better than nothing, wasn't it?

"It was the first time he raped me."

Ryker's eyes flashed, but no surprise marked his features. "The first time?"

"Yes, though not the worst by far. He saved that for the *last* rape."

He watched her and she could read on his face that he'd guessed what happened next. But it was his turn, and he was going to have to earn the rest of her nightmares.

"All right," he said, finally taking the hint of her silence. "When Ares found me, I was nearly dead in my aunt's stables. Tit."

"Bullshit. More tat."

He shook his head and closed his eyes, and Kyana swallowed back her own secrets. She'd been ready to spill it all, and he didn't seem any closer to trusting her fully than he had been two weeks ago.

"Fine." She rolled onto her knees and reached for the discarded bikini draped over the edge of the bath.

Ryker grabbed her arm and pulled her back. "I was naked and bloody. My aunt was dead. My mother was covered in blood and the whip in her hand was in two pieces. Need more?"

Her heart caught in her throat and she heard herself whisper, "Yes."

"She'd been trying to beat the evil out of me. My fangs . . . all demigods have them—a result of god blood mixing with non-god blood . . ."

Kyana knew as much. It was how the first Vampyre had been born. Something icky in Cronos's blood had caused his offspring to not only have fangs like other demigods, but also be born monstrous and bloodthirsty.

". . . the strange things I could do . . ." Ryker continued. "It was all demonic to her even though she knew better than anyone who my father was and why I was so different from the other children."

Though his eyes were closed, the pain on his face was so clear, Kyana couldn't bring herself to ask for more. Instead, she lay back down beside him and shivered.

"The last time Mehmet touched me, I was twenty. Azime had found me asleep that afternoon when I was supposed to be taking lessons with my language tutor. She beat me within an inch of my life, and that evening, when Mehmet called for me, I had no choice but to go to him even though I was in horrible pain.

"When I told Mehmet I hurt too much to let him bed me, he raped me." It was the first time in her life she'd spoken that truth aloud, and the agony of it made her dizzy. "Azime had beaten me so thoroughly, I must have had internal injuries because Mehmet's brutality nearly killed me. *Did* kill me, in fact.

"It was that night that Henry found me, taking

my last few breaths on the stairs outside the prince's chamber."

"Your Sire."

Kyana nodded. "He'd come to stay at the palace to convince Mehmet to invest in a spice trade. Henry was so adept at blending in with the human world, he never had to work to hide. Of course, Vampyre weren't such notorious myths then. Even if someone did find it odd that he was never seen during the day, they never questioned it."

"You loved him."

"Yes. He gave me life that night. And a future. Tat, Ryker. A lot of it or I'm done playing."

"Ares raped my mother and left her to die. That's why she hated me so much."

Though her heart constricted, Kyana felt herself shake her head. "Who told you that?"

"My mother. Every damned day for ten fucking years."

Kyana raised up once again. Something was wrong with what he was saying.

"Ryker, Ares isn't Zeus. He has never, in the eighty years that I've belonged to the Order of Ancients, been accused by mortal women of rape."

When Ryker opened his mouth to speak, Kyana gently placed her finger over her lips to silence him.

"The gods boast of such things. Why wouldn't Ares? Especially if such an escapade gave him a strong son like you?"

"How the hell should I know?"

He was angry now, rolling away from her to

stand. He pulled on his trunks and faced her, his brow furrowed. "It is what it is, Ky. My mother hated me for what Ares did to her, and Ares never wanted a son. He wanted a soldier."

"Then why press you to claim him as your father to the Ancients? You said that's what he wanted."

"Look at me, Kyana!" The vein in his neck bulged as he yelled down at her, and Kyana suddenly felt like a scolded child. What was meant to be a bonding moment for them had turned ugly. "*I am my father*. How can you say that I am not?"

Stumbling to her feet, Kyana fumbled with the bikini still clutched in her hands. Suddenly feeling too vulnerable in her naked state, she tugged the pieces on and faced him.

"I'm not saying that. Ares is your father," she said. "It's like he colored you with his DNA."

"Then what exactly are you implying?"

Kyana sighed, wishing she'd never started the tit for tat, wishing they could go back to the quiet of holding each other.

"I'm just saying I think you should speak to Ares. Find out his side. Maybe your mother wasn't completely honest with you."

She was actually defending Ares. The world had definitely gone crazy. But she'd spoken the truth. Of all the gods to have raped a woman, Ares was one of the few she couldn't imagine being guilty of it. If nothing else, he had too much pride to take a woman who didn't want him.

"You think my mother was a liar."

The statement wasn't a question. It was a cold, hard accusation.

If Kyana answered him now, the walls would be reconstructed between them.

"I'm just suggesting you talk to Ares. That's all." She headed to the changing rooms, her heart resuming its heavy burden in her chest.

Why did she always have to step in shit then put her foot in her mouth?

Chapter Twenty-Nine

Kyana took her time zipping up her leather pants and pulling on her boots. She sat on the small corner stool in the dressing room and was peeved to find she was still out of breath. Getting her pants on had been a trial. Her freaking legs wouldn't cooperate. It was as though they'd been sculpted out of pudding, quivering under the weight of her body like useless blobs.

The adrenaline that had spiked from catching Haven was wearing off, and her body was quivering both from exertion as well as from the need to eat and sleep. Not to mention the need to make sure she hadn't just royally screwed things up with Ryker.

Pulling up the zipper on her boot, she forced herself to stand. She'd go see Haven, make sure she was all right. Later she'd figure out what this thing between her and Ryker was evolving into and how to either walk away or fix the mess she'd made of everything. Right now, she didn't have the stomach for it.

When she exited the stall, she couldn't even meet his gaze.

She'd slept with men before. Why did it have to be different with Ryker?

"I don't want to hurt you," she heard herself say.

"I know."

She nodded, trying to convince herself that he *did* know what he was in for with her—a roller-coaster ride that didn't promise a safe exit.

"If I said anything that—"

"It's fine."

But it so wasn't. His anger was still ticking away in his jaw. She'd learned her lesson today. Never, *ever* talk bad about a man's mama. Even if instinct told her she might be a lying bitch.

Once outside, she forced herself to finally look him in the eye and didn't like the way he studied her. "I'm going to check on Haven and I need to feed and—"

"Go." Ryker silently raked his gaze over her face, his lips twisting as he seemingly argued with himself over her attempt to put distance between them, literally and figuratively. "But Kyana . . . we *will* talk about what happened here today. Before our *discussion*. You're not going to run from me forever."

She watched him go. As he vanished around the corner, she was annoyed to find that the only running she wanted to do was straight back into his arms.

* * *

Kyana took the steps two at a time and crested the top of the cavelike entrance of the prison, nodding at the two sentinels standing at their posts. She stepped past them into the alcove and found Haven lying on a blanket in the corner, well guarded and certainly not alone.

Geoffrey was with her, his lap her pillow. His Irish lilting voice carried quietly down the hall as he talked to Haven, brushing her hair back with his long, lean fingers. Even from this distance, Kyana could see the worry on his face, the pain in his eyes.

Careful not to make a sound, she slowly backed out of the cave and dropped onto the steps outside. Haven was safe and comforted. That was all that mattered. Interrupting them felt wrong, and truthfully, if anyone was going to get through to Haven, it was Geoffrey. Better to leave them in private.

Besides, there wasn't anything else she could offer Haven until the purging was complete and it was time for her trial. Kyana should return to Beyond, find Ares, and see if anyone had managed to locate the trident yet.

A sudden hand on her shoulder jerked her from her thoughts. She looked up to find Ryker standing over her wearing a worried expression.

"How is she?"

"Are you stalking me now?" she asked, a bit peeved to think he might never have left her at all.

"Yes." There was no apology in his tone, and she

couldn't force herself to appear more than miffed. In truth, she was glad he'd shown up. Walking away from Haven and leaving her to her fate was not going to be easy. Even if she was with Geoffrey.

Her gaze strayed back into the cave to peer through the darkness, and she swallowed a knot of sadness. She could barely make out her friends' shadowed forms, yet this could potentially be the last time she saw Haven.

"When will they hold the trial?" she asked.

"Day after tomorrow. It will take at least that long for the cleansing and purging to be complete."

She nodded. Two days wasn't so bad. It left her with a bit of time to try to sway the jury on Haven's behalf. After all, Kyana was supposed to have been sentenced to die and she'd been spared. That meant there was hope for Haven too, didn't it?

She closed her eyes. She needed rest, but where would she go? Now that she'd seen Haven again, she knew she wasn't ready to return to Artemis's temple. And her own home in St. Augustine was cold and empty without Haven. Her gaze trailed up Ryker's legs, his belly, and finally settled on his eyes.

"Ryker," she said.

"Hmm?"

"Can you forget that I said anything about your mother and take me somewhere?"

He looked at her with a bit of suspicion. "Are you going to pick another fight?"

"I wasn't—" Kyana sighed. "No. I won't."

He held out his hand and she took it, letting him pull her to her feet. "Where am I taking you?"

"Somewhere I can rest and eat in peace. Where no one will bother me for answers I'm not ready or able to give."

He wrapped his arm around her and she felt like half of a pair as they made their way back down the streets. It made her uncomfortable even as she found it soothing. The only pair she'd ever truly belonged to was the Kyana and Haven duo.

Could she ever let herself become part of another? Part of the one Ryker offered? She was really sick to death of stressing about it. Maybe she should just play it out and see what happened. He was a big boy. He knew the risks.

As they walked, she finally managed to dig up her voice to say, "Thank you."

"For what?" he asked, turning them onto a side street that faced the beach.

She couldn't help but smile. "Letting me use you."

"Don't kid yourself. I used you too."

"I know."

He squeezed her shoulder and as they turned left onto the beach, she realized where he was taking her. His home. She could see the rooftop from here. The closest she'd been to his place was using a shower he'd installed on the outside of his bungalow, which had led to their first sexual encounter. He'd never invited her any closer, and she'd never asked.

That he was bringing her here now was a warning she didn't care to listen to. Step inside his home and the bond got that much stronger. See a glimpse of the man inside the cool blue eyes and rock-hard abs.

She couldn't bring herself to protest.

"Your house, huh?"

"I've seen yours, I think it's time I show you mine."

"Ya know, when people say that, they're not usually talking about houses."

He chuckled. "Yeah, but we've already played that game. We can play it again later, if you like. A good night's sleep, no stress. Just me, you, a little beachside barbecue."

It sounded like heaven.

"You know," she said, "if I stay the night I'm going to hate myself in the morning."

Ryker shrugged, the hint of a smile creasing the corners of his mouth. "That's okay. If you stay the night, I'll probably hate you in the morning too. But that's a chance I'm willing to take."

Chapter Thirty

Ryker led Kyana onto the wide deck at the back of his house where the sea breeze caressed her face, lifting her hair and blowing it about wildly. Thank Zeus the waters Below hadn't been affected yet by the trident's disappearance. Here, the smell was still fresh and salty.

She eased onto a bed-sized swing on the farthest side of the deck, testing her weight with a slight bounce, then swung her legs up and lay down on her side, propping herself onto her elbow so she could watch him prepare dinner.

"I think I'm beginning to see why you like the beach so much. This is kind of nice."

He grinned and lifted the hood of a stainless steel grill parked on the other side of the deck. It was such a human appliance; seeing it here in a magical realm, being used by a god, was surreal.

"The sea is the most unforgiving place in the world," he said. "If you don't handle it just right, you die."

"And you like a good challenge?"

He eyed her, and she had her answer. If he didn't like a good challenge, he would have given up on *her* a long time ago.

She sat up and walked over to the railing to stare out at the sea. "We're not as different as you'd like to believe, I think."

"You mean as *you'd* like to believe. I've always seen the common ground between us."

"And what's that?"

"Pretty much everything. You just haven't figured that out yet." He turned back to the grill. There was a click, and then the scent and low hum of propane igniting as he pulled a tray of kabobs from the tiny fridge under the sink.

She liked the way the wind caught beneath his shirt and puffed it out, occasionally revealing a strip of belly or back. The hiss of meat hitting heat produced a cloud of the best-smelling smoke Kyana had ever caught whiff of. He was dropping small beads of ambrosia onto each piece of chicken, steak, tomato, pepper, and onion. The pink liquid instantly disappeared inside each morsel, absorbed and ready to do its work.

"I can't believe they're letting you stay away from Olympus for so long." Technically, even Kyana was supposed to have returned hours ago. She was surprised no one was coming to drag her back.

"They'll deal. Besides, you caught Haven so the major danger has passed."

The mention of Haven soured her stomach, and

she quickly searched for a new topic. "Learn anything cool yet?"

He grinned, flashing his pearly whites and making her breath hitch. "Look up."

She obeyed without question and watched as the dark blue sky lit up with a single lightning bolt that flashed directly overhead. The bolt zipped through a cloud, and she squinted to make sure she was seeing what she thought she was seeing.

"Is it . . . Is it *spelling your name*?"

"Pretty cool, huh?"

"Yeah," she said. It reminded her of the flare gun she used to gain access into the fort Above. It was charged to spell the name of its user, so that if it was stolen, the culprit could not disguise his identity. "But not very useful, is it?"

"That? Nah, but the skill itself is. It's supposed to be used to call the other Olympians together at Zeus's temple."

Kyana raised her brow. "They're not like, going to come racing here now, are they?"

"They would if we were on Olympus. But here, no. Only those Below can see it."

She snickered. "Bet the humans on the beach are pretty freaked out right about now."

"You didn't hear?" He lifted the lid again and turned the kabobs. Kyana's stomach growled and she all but drooled as the smell was released from its prison.

"Hear what?"

"The humans were taken Above this afternoon.

Most are headed to military bases around the state, but some were sent out to start rebuilding. Construction workers, people with skills that are actually useful right now."

Forgetting the pleasant aroma of dinner and the lighthearted intent of the evening, she felt her eyes practically bulge out of her head. "What? Why? Just because Haven is Below doesn't mean we've got all the Dark Breeds."

How could the gods be so stupid? And since, technically, she was one of them now, why hadn't she been in on their decision?

"The people who'll be working the streets are going to be well guarded. There's at least one member of the Order guarding each group of humans. They have to start rebuilding their world sometime, Kyana, and we're never going to quarantine all Dark Breed. That's impossible."

As soon as she opened her mouth to protest, Ryker popped a piece of chicken into it. She sputtered, the meat burning her tongue, but it took only a second before she began to chew and forgot what she'd been objecting to.

"Good?" he asked, grinning.

She nodded, swallowed, and went right back to her tirade. "We've got to come up with a better way to keep humans safe. Even if Cronos never comes back—"

"He won't."

"Whatever. Like you said, Dark Breed have been causing trouble since the beginning of time."

"I agree." He pulled the kabobs off the grill and set them on a platter between the swing and the couch. They sat, each plucking a skewer from the plate, and began to munch while they talked. "Geoffrey and I are going to talk to the Ancients tomorrow. We think we might have an idea."

"Oh?"

He shrugged, studying her as though to judge whether she'd be happy with what he was about to say. This made Kyana uneasy. She shifted, waited, chewed.

"We're considering a treaty."

A piece of onion flew out of her mouth. "With Dark Breed?"

"If we can find a way for humans and Dark Breed to coexist, the Order can focus on more important things than tracing impudent shits like Leeches, who are, for the most part, completely harmless. Witches and Mystics can come out of the closet and practice in the open . . . Imagine the benefits of having them work with humans."

Kyana couldn't even begin to wrap her brain around what he was suggesting. "Right, and what are the benefits of allowing Vampyre and Lychen to coexist with the animals they prey upon?"

"You know better than anyone that they don't have to be predators to survive." Ryker chewed the last tomato on his skewer and grabbed another from the plate. "They can learn to find other ways to feed. Hell, most have been doing that anyway. The Lychen and Vamps who've lived Above all these years have been subsidizing their diets with animals and blood banks for centuries just like you have. They know if there's a rash of killings that we come hunting. They don't want that any more than we do."

"So we stop hunting them altogether?"

Geoffrey, especially, should know better. He was, or had been, a full-blooded Vamp. Weaning him off humans had been even more difficult than weaning Kyana.

"Not altogether. Some will want to join the Order if given the chance. They'll be weaned under supervision, just as you were. Others will be given a choice—continue being hunted, or enjoy their lives by signing a treaty."

"You expect those who've lived and hunted in the dark to follow our law just because they signed their name on a piece of paper?"

Ryker gave her a look that suggested she might possibly be a little bit stupid. "Whoever signs it will be blood-linked with a group of tracers. Those tracers will be able to find the ones who sign under them any time, any place. They'll know the minute they have broken the laws of the treaty, and they will be found and dealt with."

Kyana's face must have shown her disbelief because Ryker's took on an expression of irritation. "We don't have all the kinks worked out yet. But at least our way, most Dark Breed will be unable to hide."

"Kinda like human pedophiles," she muttered. "That doesn't stop them from preying on children either."

Ryker sighed. "This was supposed to be a relaxing evening."

"Since when did you and Geoffrey become bosom buddies, anyway?" she grumbled.

"We're not. We just find ourselves in the same boat at the moment."

"And Silas is in that boat too, I guess? What does he think about all this?"

"All he cares about is passing on Poseidon's power to the right Chosen and getting back to his meaningless life." He tossed the empty skewer down and leaned back, folding his arms over his chest. "What were you thinking, sleeping with him? He's . . . Why would you . . ."

"What makes you think I slept with him?"

Ryker's scowl deepened. "He told me. Several times."

"It was a long time ago."

"Six months isn't *a long time ago*. When he could talk again, he told me you were the best he ever had."

"What do you mean, *when he could talk again*?"

He shrugged and made his way over to her swing to drop beside her.

"You're jealous."

"Shouldn't I be?"

Kyana reached up and cupped Ryker's jaw, forcing him to look at her. "If it helps, *he* isn't the best *I've* ever had. Judging by how you know your way around my body, I'm guessing you were no virgin before me either. Virgins aren't that good at screwing."

That thought soured her mood. She'd never pictured Ryker screwing someone else, and she suddenly had the urge to do real violence to someone.

"Don't say that." Ryker pulled her into him and she laid her head on his shoulder.

"Don't say what?"

"That I screwed you. I didn't screw you."

She liked the way the words sounded on his lips. She liked the naughty little tingle they set off inside her. She rubbed his thigh and nuzzled his neck with her nose.

"Why not?"

"Because it cheapens whatever this is between us. I'm not Silas. I don't want to be—what did he call it?—I don't want to be a booty call."

She rose onto her knees, sending the swing into motion, and straddled him, locking her gaze on his. "What exactly *do* you want, Ryker?"

He kissed her nose, her cheek, her lips before pulling away. "Whatever you're willing to give me tonight. Tomorrow, I'll want more."

"And the day after that?" She slipped her shirt over her head and reached behind her back to unfasten her bra, loving the way his gaze dropped and his tongue flicked across his lips.

Her bare breasts in his face, he cupped one. "Hmm . . . what?"

"I said, what about the day after tomorrow? What will you want then?"

He tightened his arms around her back. "Everything, Ky. I'll want everything."

Chapter Thirty-One

As the sun peeked out of the orangey sky outside Ryker's bedroom on the morning of Haven's trial, Kyana strolled naked to the window and watched it rise. He came up behind her, wrapping his arms around her hips as he pressed his groin against the small of her back. He was ready again, and as much as she wanted to turn around and wrap her legs around him, she couldn't. Now that Haven's cleansing had been going on for nearly two full days, her trial could take place at any moment.

Kyana had spent more than a day wrapped up with Ryker in his bed, trying to stop thinking about what was to come and desperate not to go crazy in the meantime. But the time for play was over. Reality had stepped back up to take its place in her world, and she was going to greet it with the biggest damned sword she could find.

"Can I borrow your shower?" she asked, turning in his arms to offer a kiss to his stubbled chin.

"So long as you don't mind company."

"We don't have time for that." She nudged him gently away, but the image of Ryker slippery with soap and water made her naughty regions ache. "I'd never have guessed you would be so insatiable."

"Only for you."

Though she'd never admit it, she liked the way he looked at her at times like this. As if she was the center of his universe—the princess he was meant to save from the dragon. She didn't often enjoy being a damsel in distress for any knight, but she'd be lying if she said she didn't wish, for one moment, that it was as easy and simple as a fairy tale.

"I know you're preoccupied with what's going on with Haven, but don't get so lost in it that you forget other crucial matters. Like tonight."

"What's tonight? National orgasm festival?" she teased, knowing precisely what he was referring to but not wanting to go there.

Ryker wouldn't take a hint if she'd wrapped it in a bow and covered it with naked Nymphs.

He took her face in his hands, his expression serious and solemn. "You're going to have to go to Artemis soon. She's going to need to prepare you for what's coming at sunset."

She blinked. "Prepare me? We've already completed the ceremony. I thought it was just a waiting game now for my old powers to die out completely and hers to take over."

The sympathy shining in his eyes conjured a big cloud of dread over her head.

"It is, but Artemis can help ease the transformation like Hades and Poseidon did for Geoff and Silas. Like Zeus will for me when my seven days are up. You saw what Silas went through before Poseidon arrived to assist with his change. I don't want you to go through that too."

Damned right, she'd seen what Silas had gone through. The convulsions that had overtaken him, the eerie stillness that had passed as though he'd died for an instant before Poseidon's blood had revived him. She'd been hoping that experience was solely for Vessels, not Chosen.

She swallowed and worked her way out of his arms to head to the shower. She didn't want Ryker to see the fear she knew was in her eyes. She wasn't afraid of pain or of becoming a goddess. She was afraid of losing the powers she'd known for two hundred years. Afraid of changing and becoming someone else. A stranger.

"You okay?"

She paused at the bathroom door and without looking back, said, "I will be. I always am."

Geoffrey stood outside Haven's cell and watched her dark silhouette rock with frantic motion in the corner. He didn't trust her. Not by a long shot. But by the gods, when the sentinels told him she was begging to see him again, he hadn't been able to stay away. He'd come to her just after she'd been brought in, and she hadn't seemed to recognize him. It had broken his heart, devastated him to see her like that. The chance to see her normal just one more time before her trial had brought him back here now.

No matter what Haven had become, he couldn't simply stop caring for her just because her fate had taken a wonky course.

"Geoffrey?" Her voice seared through the last of his defenses, and he took another tentative step forward.

"Lass," he heard himself say. "What have you done to yourself?"

Her shadow shifted, grew larger as it crawled toward the invisible barrier separating them. Then he was looking down into green eyes that had once been blue, but had now mingled with the yellow that came from the Dark Breed inside her. "You came."

The way she drew out the word *came* sent a chill over his arms. There was a serpentine quality to the way she spoke, as though she still hadn't become accustomed to maneuvering her tongue around her new fangs.

"What do you want, lass?" He knelt, staring at her through the sporadic blue flashes of energy that held her prisoner. "What can I do to fix you?"

He could do nothing, he knew, but damn, he wished he could.

She dug her nails into the earthy wall and clawed her way to her feet, swaying a little as she faced him. "They purged me, Geoff. I'm going to be better soon. I feel it already."

The hope in her voice tightened his chest. Kyana hadn't been fighting all this time for nothing. Perhaps all hope for Haven wasn't lost . . .

"Sit with me, Geoff. Please?" She fell to her knees in a heap and began to sob, peering up at him through filthy hair and dirt-smudged skin. "Hold me until they come for me. I'm too frightened to be alone."

"I can't do that, love. The purging is too fresh. You're still a risk—"

"Please, Geoff. His voice. I hear it . . . everywhere."

He froze in his intent for retreat. If he turned his back on her now, he'd be the worst sort of asshole. Just because she'd been purged of Cronos's possession didn't mean he couldn't find another way to make her crazy.

"You have a key," she whispered. "All the gods do. You could open the cell to come in and lock it again. I wouldn't be a danger . . . I just want to be held."

He didn't turn around. He couldn't. If he looked at her now, he'd weaken.

"I'm so scared, Geoffrey."

"Blimey." He pressed his palm to the wall and squeezed his eyes closed. "Haven, love, you're killing me. I can't open that gate. You're too—"

"All right," she whispered. "It's okay. I . . . understand."

His heart in his throat, Geoffrey closed his eyes to block out the image of the pain in hers. "I'm sorry—"

"You look different," she said, her voice hiccupping. "Still beautiful, but different."

She lifted a hand as though to touch him, but as it neared the barrier, she withdrew it. "There's silver in your hair. Just above your ears. A trait of Hades? I never met him, you know."

"Haven—"

"It's okay, Geoff," she repeated. "I just didn't want to be alone. But I'm a big girl. I'll be fine."

He truly was a damned idjit. He was actually considering ways of going to her safely. He was a god now. Above such things as love when duty was supposed to reign over everything. But turning his back on Haven at this moment felt wrong. If he walked away and didn't offer her whatever comfort he could before her trial and possible execution, he'd never forgive himself for abandoning her.

"Guard!" he bellowed, slipping the five-pointed key from his robe.

A sentinel appeared, and Geoff handed him the key. "I don't want this back until I've exited and the gate's been locked again. Understand?"

The sentinel gave a nervous glance at Haven and nodded.

"Open the gate and lock me inside."

"My lord—"

He cut off the sentinel's protest with a sharp, reprimanding glare. "Do it."

And with obvious reluctance, the sentinel obeyed and Geoffrey stepped inside.

Chapter Thirty-Two

Kyana tugged Ryker's robe around her and stepped out of the bathroom, relieved to find his bedroom empty. She strode through the glass doors and onto the bedroom deck, her thoughts so chaotic, she wasn't sure how to piece them together. Her own changes. Haven's fate. Ryker. When had her life become so damned complicated?

She leaned against the rail, letting the salty sea breeze soothe the skin Ryker had made so sensitive with his stubbled face. Her arms and legs were tender, her breasts throbbing. His stamina as a lover was unrivaled in her experience—every touch intentional, every kiss deliberate. Being with him was perfect, was *right*.

But knowing that didn't make her fears go away. She'd been worried about growing bored and leaving *him*, when truthfully, the real fear came with that situation turning the other way. She'd protected her heart for so long. Was she willing to risk breaking it for maybes and might bes?

That was something else she'd have to contemplate later. Today, she had to focus on her other worries. Namely, Haven.

Haven was likely to go to her grave today, the very thought of which made Kyana so ill she wanted to crawl back into bed and stay there. Aside from the possibility of losing her best friend, Haven would take the location of the trident with her.

Without that trident, the world's waters were dying a slow, painful death. Even Below, where the sea was only a mirror of the Earth's, the turquoise surface was beginning to look as though it had been dusted with soot, when just yesterday it had been clear and beautiful and untouched. Would Silas be strong enough to right the problems, even if he did get the trident back?

Feeling the prickling sting of someone staring at her, Kyana glanced over her shoulder to find Ryker leaning against the glass door frame behind her. He was studying her with those intense blue eyes, and she shivered under the thick robe.

"Feel better?" he asked, a slow smile crinkling his mouth.

Her stomach and legs turned to goo as she remembered how those lips felt on certain very tender places of her body.

"A little," she breathed, closing her mind to the memories. Turning back to stare at the horizon, she shivered as her cold, wet hair settled against her cheeks. Ryker leaned beside her at the railing and tucked a stray curl behind her ear.

After several minutes of staring into space, he said, "Worried about today?"

As far as questions went, it was a dumb one. "What do you think?"

"I think I'll be at your side. Through everything that hits us today."

She smiled despite herself. Doubts aside, she liked hearing that. Liked knowing she didn't have to go through any of this alone. "Thanks. But nothing's hitting us today. It's all going to hit Haven."

The worries that had weighed on her all night finally spilled off her tongue in a rambling mess. "I'm still worried, Ryker. Whether Haven is locked up or not, we still have to consider Cronos a threat. She can't be the only being in the world that can raise him. We don't know what he is capable of because he's the only god who's died and tried to come back. We don't know what connections he has to you now, or to Geoffrey, or to any of his original children. He *is* Zeus, Poseidon, and Hades, all wrapped up in one scary-as-hell package."

"Stop worrying." Ryker sighed and pulled her into his arms. "I'm not supposed to tell you— anyone—but the ring, Zeus's staff, and Hades's amulet . . . they're all safely tucked away in the Underworld. Even if Cronos came after one of us, he wouldn't be able to touch the remaining Eyes of Power. Zeus made sure they were locked up tight, and since no one can cross into the Underworld without Hermes or Geoff, they're safe."

She pushed away so she could look up at him.

"And if you need them? How are any of you going to be strong enough to fight Cronos without the conduits?"

He shrugged. "Geoff gives them back to us."

Kyana took a deep breath, blessed relief filling her for one blissful moment before shattering into a million pieces that tore at her insides. "You . . . there's no way Haven can know they're in the Underworld, is there?"

"I don't see how she—"

"Cronos. Could Cronos know?"

"Kyana, you said yourself there's no way to know what Cronos is capable of. But what does it matter. Even if he knows, he can't cross into the Underworld."

"Unless he uses Geoff. What if Cronos finds some other way to get to them now that Haven's been purged?"

"You can't seriously think Geoff would be that stupid. I'm not his biggest fan but—"

"But nothing. We just need to make sure he stays the hell away from her."

"Ky, stop. She's purged. Whether Geoff stays away from her or not right now won't matter."

Kyana wasn't so sure. She hadn't seen Haven since the purging had been complete. How could they even be sure it had worked? "Okay," she said. "All right. But I want to see her. I want to make sure the purging worked. If I see that it has, I'll stop worrying that we put Cronos's Vessel so close to the damned things he wanted all along."

"If it will make you feel better, fine. But don't work yourself up over this, Ky. Don't make trouble where there isn't any."

She glared at him and tugged the tie of the robe tighter at her waist. "If the conduits are in Geoffrey's domain and Cronos knows that, what exactly do you think he'll try to do, Ryker? He's already tried to kill me several times through Haven. Why would Geoffrey be any different?"

The stone-faced glare he'd been directing at her chipped away. "You think he's in danger?"

"I think he might be if he gets too close. She was weak while she was being purged and a threat to no one. But what if it didn't work? She could be susceptible to Cronos again."

She walked back inside Ryker's bedroom, where the scent of their cardio Olympics still hung heavy in the air. She tossed off her robe and searched the room for her clothes. "Have you talked to Geoffrey since Haven's capture?"

"No, I've been a little distracted." His gaze fell to her bare breasts but she didn't move to cover them.

"There are still several hours before the trial. I want to make sure the sentinels know to keep Geoff out of the prison until then. Hermes too. If Cronos has a backup plan, we have to be prepared."

"Now?"

She pulled her white T-shirt over her head and rolled her eyes. "No. Later when it's too late to do anything. I'm going to instruct the sentinels and then I'm going to Haven and she's not leaving my sight until her trial is over. I will not let Cronos touch her again."

She found her pants, put them on, then dug her boots out from under Ryker's bed.

As she headed to the front door, she paused to glance over her shoulder and saw him tugging on his jeans and snatching a shirt from his dresser before he chased after her. He stopped in the hall to slide on his shoes before he finally made it to her side.

"We can't stray too far from Olympus. If you're not near Artemis at sunset—"

"I know. The pain, the agony, blah blah blah. As long as my change doesn't prevent me from standing up for Haven at her trial—"

"Haven's trial is set for midnight. I think they wanted to give you time for the change so you could attend as Artemis."

"We'll be back well before it's time to find Artie."

"Fine," he grumbled. "Let's go."

Kyana followed him over the sand dunes until the streets of Below finally came into view, silence hanging between them as they made their way to the large boulders outside the prison.

When they reached the cell at the end of the long hall, she froze. Blinked. Blinked again in desperate hope that her eyes were deceiving her.

"No," she whispered, her knees giving a slight tremble, forcing her to grip the wall for support.

Haven wasn't in her cell.

Chapter Thirty-Three

Ryker watched Kyana's face turn ghostly pale even as his own gut twisted with a sickening wave of disbelief. The barrier to Haven's prison wasn't sealed, and there was no sign of her anywhere. A sentinel lay facedown in a pool of blood, a key to the cell in his hand, and as he craned his neck to look more deeply into the prison, he could see more bodies filling the eerily quiet halls. At least a half-dozen guards had been posted to guard Haven. It seemed each of them had died doing his job.

What the hell had Haven done?

He snatched the key from the sentinel at his feet. "It's Geoffrey's," he said, rubbing the emblem of Hades that had been etched into the front of the five-pointed key.

Kyana had been right to worry. Geoffrey had been here, and had obviously not left of his own free will.

"No." Kyana's whisper of denial was barely

audible. She was frighteningly stoic as she stood in the middle of Haven's empty cell, her mouth slightly parted, her eyes wide and unblinking.

"Ky?" He bellowed her name, gaining her attention. "Snap the hell out of it. Cronos has got Haven, and she's got Geoff."

"I. Know." Her face became a sculpture of porcelain, white and without expression. Her gaze fell to the dead guards and she shook her head. "I won't be able to save her now. Not after this."

"Stop it. You haven't given up on her yet." Ryker stood and grabbed her by the shoulders giving her a brisk shake. "You still believe Cronos is inside her making her do all this, Ky. If you don't, then yes, she is a goner and there's not a damned thing you'll be able to do about it."

Kyana blinked, seeming to come out of her stupor. "Of course I believe that! This isn't her fault! But the Order will want to punish *someone* and I don't see them putting Cronos on trial. Do you?"

"You have to link with Haven."

She jerked her head toward him, her eyes damp, but her cheeks dry. "I can't just fall asleep here, Ryker."

He trailed his fingers lightly up her arms. "I know you're worried about them, but you have to try. The fastest way to find Haven and make sure Geoff is all right is to link with her. Maybe we can get you a potion to make you sleep."

"Are you kidding me? You're *not* going to knock me out unless there's no other option. What if something happens and I'm helpless? What if Geoffrey needs my help and I let him die because I can't pull myself out of the potion's effects?"

She rubbed the back of her neck, looking pretty damned close to falling apart. "I'm turning into Artemis tonight, Ryker. Even if you put me under, my Vampyric powers have waned so much, I'm not sure I can link to Haven anymore. I can feel it, the difference. I'm already changing."

Forcing himself to remain calm for her sake, he closed his eyes and nodded. "I'll send someone to find Hermes. Make sure Geoffrey isn't in the Underworld. Maybe Hermes will know when he left. We can see what sort of time has passed since Haven broke out of here."

Though he didn't want to leave Kyana, he made his way through the tunnels of the prison system looking for any survivors. Since the breakout, there hadn't been much use of the massive cave system and most of the sentinels had been reassigned to more useful tasks. On the lower floors of the prison, a few guards were going about their duties, standing stoically outside the cells of the less dangerous prisoners. Because of the depth of the tunnel system, none of them had heard a single noise of alarm from the upper floor. Well trained, they showed no outward emotion over the news of their fallen brethren, but Ryker knew well enough that the moment he left them, their rants would begin. They would want justice for their brothers and sisters. They just weren't fool enough to show as much to a god.

"Find Hermes," he said to the startled guard closest to him. "Tell him to find me immediately."

"We don't have time to send a messenger for another messenger." Kyana appeared behind Ryker, her face so pale it all but glowed in the shadows.

Ryker shot the sentinel a commanding glare, and the guard disappeared, brushing by Kyana to do Ryker's bidding.

"What choice do we have?" His loose grip on his calm façade snapped. "We can't enter the Underworld to see if Geoffrey ever even left it, and I don't know where to begin looking for Hermes. That wasn't part of my damned lessons."

He took a deep breath. If he was ready to blow a proverbial gasket, he couldn't imagine what this had done to Kyana. Haven was loose, which most likely meant Cronos hadn't given up. If she was with Geoffrey, she'd have access to the Underworld without any alarm bells being raised.

She wouldn't need Geoffrey alive to gain access to the Underworld. They would only need his blood. His body.

Ryker's gaze fell on Kyana, and he wondered if she'd put the pieces together yet. That there might no longer be a Geoffrey to save at all.

It took only a matter of minutes for Hermes to appear in the prison antechamber. Kyana had no idea how the sentinel had tracked down the god so quickly, but was happy as hell that he had. The minute she'd seen that Haven was gone, her heart had sunk. Not just for Haven but for what her escape could mean for Geoffrey.

She had to find him, and if the messenger god had taken even a second longer, she would have had to figure out another way to locate them. Though, she was pretty sure she knew where Haven would have taken Geoff.

She'd wanted to get her hands on the Eyes of Power, and they were within Geoffrey's domain. The only way she and Ryker could get there to stop Haven was through Hermes. It was the reason she'd waited as long as she had.

"If you wish to see me," Hermes started, his beady eyes shimmering in the underground structure, "you need only use your mind, new Zeus. Not a blasted sentinel whose feet move too slowly. Poor soul. Not sure when he'll figure out that I've already come and gone."

"I need to know where Geoffrey is—the new Hades," Ryker demanded.

"We know where he is," Kyana whispered. To Hermes, she said, "We need you to get us into his realm."

Hermes scowled. "I spoke with Geoffrey in the Underworld last eve. I can attempt to deliver a message if you wish, but even if he hasn't left his realm, it's going to take time. However, taking you there? I'm afraid I cannot."

"You will," Kyana demanded.

Hermes shook his head, his winged helm clinking against the wall. "It's not that I won't, new goddess. I cannot. Geoffrey can escort others into his domain. My permission is for me alone. The minute you try to step inside without him or his consent, you will set off alarms and immediately be incapacitated. The new security is airtight since the breakout."

Kyana's chest squeezed so painfully, she was almost grateful for the sudden burst of life it brought. There had to be some way in.

"Even if Cronos, through Haven, took Geoff, she wouldn't be able to drag him all the way through the Underworld. And she can't know exactly where the Eyes of Power are, so it will take time for her to find them. If she used Geoff to gain entrance, she would have left him shortly after."

And probably killed him, but Kyana refused to think on that.

"We'll get her, Ky."

She nodded; the dull throb at the base of her neck was rising to a crescendo. "Damned right we will. There hasn't been enough time for Haven to have escaped the Underworld with the Eyes of Power."

"I'll get a head start," Hermes said. "I know where the conduits are hidden. I'll see if they're still safe."

When Hermes disappeared, Kyana moved to follow his path out of the prison but Ryker held her back. "Ky . . ."

"What?"

"You need to prepare yourself for what we might find."

She shook her head, tears burning and begging to break free but she refused to let them. "No. She didn't kill him, Ryker. I won't believe that."

"But if she did?"

She swallowed, unable to hold back the tears any longer. "Then it won't matter whether or not I'll have to kill her, because when Haven is free of this mess and knows she murdered Geoffrey, she won't want to live at all."

Chapter Thirty-Four

I know Haven's strong now," Ryker said as he and Kyana sprinted toward the cave that traveled to the Underworld. "But she's not been in possession of her strengths long enough to get the upper hand on Geoff. He has god-strengths that not even her mixes can match."

"Maybe she took him by surprise or maybe Cronos is nearly whole inside her. If it's Cronos"—which Kyana fervently believed the case to be—"then we don't *know* the limits of her strength. Teflon girl, remember?"

She cringed at the memory of Haven's body, untouched, impacting the Humvee and rendering it useless. No species alive was that sturdy. Fully risen or not, Cronos was far stronger than any of them had expected.

They started down the snaking staircase that led to the River Styx, and Kyana caught a glimpse of Ryker's shadow on the wall behind hers. He was raking his hands through his hair, his frustration mirroring hers. "None of this makes any sense. Sixx did the cleansing ceremony and a binding spell. Cronos shouldn't be able to possess Haven anymore."

"Maybe she wasn't really purged. Would a binding spell work if he were in possession of her at the time?"

"Shit," was Ryker's reply. "She won't get her hands on the Eyes of Power," he said as they stepped onto the shores of the river. "Geoff will never betray the Order. Not even for Haven."

"That's what I'm worried about."

If Geoffrey didn't cooperate . . . there was no telling what Cronos was capable of doing to make him regret it.

"Ky—" The pain in Ryker's voice pulled Kyana's attention to him. She stopped, several feet away from Charon's ferry, and rushed back to Ryker's side. The color had faded from his face, leaving his skin a ghostly greenish hue. She grabbed his arm and helped him sit on the cool sand.

"What's wrong?"

"It feels like my skull's about to be ripped apart," he whispered, his hand cradling his head. "The booming sounds like a . . ."

She grabbed his shoulder and gave it a hard shake. "Ryker, talk to me."

He eased to his feet and took her hand. "We have to keep moving. Shit. *Shit!*"

"Ryker, what's going on?" The frantic pitch of her voice called Charon's attention to them. Ryker dragged her toward the ferry, making her stumble as she fought to find her footing.

"Hermes was calling Zeus, but I think I just made my first interception."

She jogged to keep up with him, wanting answers but too afraid to ask.

When she moved to step onto the ferry, Ryker leaped onto the wooden planks ahead of her, placed his hands on Charon's shoulders, and bowed his head. "I give you my speed, Charon. Speed our journey through the swiftness of the gods."

The ferry jerked into motion, rocking and swaying as it glided over the lapping waves of the normally calm water. What was usually a slow drift across the river had become a speedboat jaunt and Kyana had to hang on to the side rails to keep from toppling into the spirit-infested waters around them.

Her stomach pitched so violently that she dropped to her knees and braced herself as they crashed around the bend to slip into a narrow tunnel. The path hit a fork in the river that took them away from the Fates' cave and toward the Underworld, where the scenery changed to a lush, forestlike environment.

Finally, the pitching in her belly calmed enough to allow coherent thought. The only thing that would bring this much concern to Zeus, and in turn to Ryker, was if yet another brother had been hurt or . . .

"What did you see, Ryker?" Her voice was quiet,

but demanding enough to force him to face her, his hands never leaving their guide's shoulder.

Through the ice blue of his eyes, she could see the anger and fear dwelling inside. "Geoffrey has been found."

Kyana stepped off the ferry and followed Ryker into a copse of trees outside the entrance to the Underworld. Her boots felt as though they'd been woven with steel—heavy and burdensome with each step she took. Her heart constricted with worry over what they might find when they arrived at their destination. Ryker had been given a glimpse of something via Hermes. He'd seen blood, the entrance to the Underworld, and Geoffrey. That was all they knew, and the not knowing was worse than anything else.

She glanced up at Ryker's stone-cold face, watched him squint as he tried to peer into the trees. She followed his gaze until she saw Hermes standing guard over a form that she instantly recognized. Pulling away, she sprinted past Hermes, and finally collapsed at Geoffrey's side.

He was pale. Paler even than he'd been as a Vamp. Blood pooled beneath his head and shoulders, darkening the fine sand to near black. His breaths were shallow, but he was alive.

Gently, Kyana lifted his head and cradled it in her lap. Guilt weighed heavily on her heart, but she pushed aside the blame she'd carried for a week now. This wasn't her fault. It wasn't even Haven's.

It was a hundred percent Cronos's. Kyana ached to rip him apart, limb by limb. He'd hurt Haven. He'd hurt innocents. Now he'd hurt Geoff. There wasn't a spell powerful enough in this world to keep him safe from all she planned to do to him if he was fool enough to let himself be raised.

But as much as it pained her to acknowledge it, she knew she couldn't let it come to that. Dead, Cronos was a powerful enemy. Alive . . . she couldn't take the risk to find out exactly how powerful he could be.

However, there was only one way to stop Cronos. He was going to ride Haven's body through this ordeal until he'd killed her—unless Kyana killed her first and put an end to it a lot sooner than Cronos planned. The thought made Kyana sick to her stomach, but she had no choice. The buck stopped right fucking here, and stopping Cronos meant killing Haven . . .

Kyana was the only one who could do it. This was the reason she'd been spared. The reason she'd been sent to search for Haven.

The time had come to kill her best friend.

"I'm sorry."

Geoffrey's whispered words pulled her from the disturbing path her thoughts had taken. She stroked his black, blood-encrusted hair from his brow and forced a smile.

"The Healers will be here soon," she promised, unsure how she was able to speak when it felt as though a dam had been constructed in her throat.

"Once they have you fixed up, we'll talk about what happened. Can you stand? Walk?"

He shook his head. "She cast a paralysis spell on me before knocking me on the noggin. From the manly bits down I'm as impotent as Ryker."

Her chest opened up and she could breathe again. If he was back to harassing Ryker, he was going to live. Seeming to sense that the mood had lightened, Ryker squatted beside them and glared.

"Care to set him straight on that, Ky?"

She blinked. "Not really."

Geoffrey's smile at that was broad and child-like. Then just as quickly, it vanished and his face turned somber again. He gripped Kyana's hand with surprising strength. "Don't give up on her, lass. The possession is too strong for her to fight."

"We'll talk when you're healed."

His hand squeezed hers until her bones crackled with the pressure. "I watched him take over her will. Watched her change. She's not responsible."

"I know." But that didn't change what had to be done. Tears blurred her vision. She blinked rapidly trying to hold them off.

"She's not as strong as you. Don't forget that."

"You love her." The accusation spilled from her mouth before she could bottle it.

He sat up, gripping his head, but the gesture was proof he was going to be all right. Thank Zeus.

His eyes softened and they glazed over with tears she knew he'd never spill. "Am I that read-able?"

"To me? In every way." She placed a kiss on his brow and sighed. Somewhere in the cave in front of her, Haven had disappeared in her hunt for the Eyes of Power. There was a job to be done, and since Geoffrey seemed to be on the road to recovery, she was going to have to leave him in order to do it. "How did she get in if you're out here?"

He showed her his bloody palm. "This. She fed enough that my blood in her will open whatever gates Hades and I put in place."

Kyana swallowed, disgusted at the images his confession brought forth.

"She may not be as emotionally strong as you, lass, but physically . . . the moment her cell opened, I didn't stand a chance."

"I fought her. I won. I don't intend to lose this time either."

"Aye. I saw her when you brought her in, remember? Nay, Kyana. This Haven isn't the same as that one, even. It was like she was made of steel."

Teflon girl.

"I've seen it." And she hadn't been able to fight Haven in that state either.

"Then you know. Be careful. Don't underestimate her. Don't underestimate *Cronos.*"

"I won't. There's still time. She doesn't have the trident, so even if she gets her hands on the other Eyes—"

"Aye, she does have it. It was here, hidden in the trees. If Poseidon hadn't been so injured he would have felt how close it was, but I suspect that's likely why she injured him in the first place. Cronos wouldn't have wanted any of us dead unless he was alive to soak the power from us first. Injuring Poseidon just meant tracking the trident would be more difficult."

"How the hell was it here?" But as soon as she asked the question, she answered it. "The attack on Beyond. She was left Below for hours. She must have put it here then . . ."

Kyana gripped her head in her hands, feeling like every kind of ass as she realized how well they'd all been played. "She let me catch her, Geoff. Maybe she wanted Nettles, maybe she didn't. Regardless, she wanted to get caught. Wanted a way to stay Below where she'd be close to . . . you." The prison sat right smack in the center of Below, only a few blocks from the cave that led directly to the Underworld. What a conniving bastard Cronos was. "We made it possible for her to get her hands on *you*. That's exactly what she wanted. She played me like a damned poker game—wait. Silas is Poseidon now. Shouldn't he have sensed the trident was so near?"

"He's never put his hands on it before. Even if he felt something, Silas wouldn't know what it was." Geoff closed his eyes and took a deep breath. She could read all over his face that he thought she was right. "I'm so sorry. This . . . was about me. About getting to me so she could get to those conduits. I'm a fucking idjit."

He craned his neck, revealing two puncture

wounds on his jugular. "Drink, lass. If you're to enter the Underworld, you'll be needing my blood since I can't escort you."

She opened her mouth to protest but quickly shut it again. He was right. If she was going into that cave, there was no other way. And now more than ever, she wanted to get her hands on Haven. But whether it was to save her or kill her, Kyana couldn't tell anymore.

She tongued her teeth, frustrated to feel her fangs gone. Tonight she would become a goddess, but right now she needed the trademark of her Dark Breed lineage and they were gone.

"I can't," she admitted.

He nodded, understanding as he too had been stripped of his fangs the moment he'd replaced Hades.

"There'll be no need for that," a Healer said, scooting to Geoffrey's other side. "He'll be good as new as soon as we can get to work on him. He'll be able to escort you."

The confidence on the woman's face relieved the tension in Kyana's shoulders. At least one thing had gone her way today. She could be thankful for that much.

As promised, Geoffrey was up on his feet again ten minutes later, though his color was still ghostly pale.

He shooed the Healers on their way and faced Hermes. "Have you checked on the Eyes of Power?"

He sighed and shook his head. "It's as we feared."

"She has them?" she guessed. "How could she have possibly gotten to them so quickly?"

The Underworld was massive, a realm unto itself. Haven would have had to know precisely where to go through the mazelike tunnels and stairways.

"More than likely, Cronos had somehow known where we'd placed them all," Geoff said, taking a sip from the skin of water the Healer held out to him.

"That's it, then," Kyana said. "She has all the tools she needs to raise Cronos."

Except one.

Her blood turned to ice water, chilling her from the inside out.

She scanned the copse of trees and the shores along the River Styx. Haven would still need to get Cronos's bones, and only two people could take her there. One was safely tucked away on Olympus. The other . . . had disappeared from her side.

Chapter Thirty-Five

When the Healers had arrived to tend Geoffrey, the chaos gave Haven the perfect opportunity to snatch Ryker like he was nothing more than a two-year-old kid. Her unnatural strength hadn't even belonged to her Dark Breed halves. It had belonged to Cronos.

But whatever Illusion Charm she'd placed on them both to get them through the streets undetected still hung over them like a small bubble making the outside world oblivious to his plight.

"You'll either do what's asked of you or you will die. The choice is yours."

"Easy decision," Ryker managed. "Kill me if you can."

The Binding Charm Haven had shackled around his neck, after she'd thrown a muting spell on him, cut into his skin with each breath and made talking difficult.

As much as the woman standing before him looked like Haven, he knew it wasn't. Her dark eyes and menacing smile belonged to Cronos. And the disdain in Ryker's voice was aimed solely at *him*.

Haven's laughter, much like her strength, her voice, and her eyes, wasn't her own. "Then I'll kill you and make your father port me to my destination."

She gripped Ryker's hair and dragged him forward. He managed to get his feet beneath him and pull them to a stop. His strength dissipated with each passing second the Binding Charm remained around his neck, but he fought against Haven's attempts to carry out her possessed orders.

It wouldn't take long for Ky to figure out that he was missing and come looking for him. If he could just last that long . . . or at least outlast the Binding Charm, maybe he'd get out of this alive.

"Ares will never give you what you want."

Haven tugged again. "Perhaps he will be more cooperative if it's the only way to save his son."

Ryker would have laughed if he could have. "I hope you have a backup plan. Protecting the Order, keeping the human world safe, and ensuring Cronos's sorry ass never walks again are more important than an estranged son."

"We'll see about that."

Haven prodded him through a small backstreet that led around the far side of the prison cave where she'd been held captive. A thatch of trees walled the easternmost side of the structure, changing the scenery from beach to mountain as though they'd stepped into a strange painting. It was a spot for worshipping, meant to appear secluded from the rest of Below.

As Haven pushed Ryker through the trees, he found himself staring down the side of the cliffs, his toes precariously close to the edge.

She caught him by the collar and yanked him backward as the wind shoved him toward a very painful death. Thankfully, he was thrown to his knees. It was easier to balance like this. Easier not to sway on his feet at the horrifyingly high fall he'd been faced with.

He craned his neck, watching the wildness in Haven's eyes. It was hard to believe the mall-rat Barbie-doll Witch who refused to so much as say the word *shit* was hiding beneath the maniacal gaze staring down at him now.

"If I port you—if I give you what you want, someday when this is all over, you won't be able to live with yourself."

She laughed, quietly at first, until it crept to the crescendo of a chest-bouncing cackle. "As if I care. You could throw this Vessel off this cliff right now, and I would prevent her from breaking into a million pieces."

It was the first time he'd heard Cronos speak through Haven as though they were separate entities. Cronos was definitely growing stronger, and that didn't bode well for how today would turn out.

"Look at her. She has already tried to stop me from using her. And failed."

Thrusting out her arms, she shoved beneath his

nose white skin that was marred by ugly red scars raking from palm to elbow. Dozens of slashes, horizontal and vertical. She lifted her filthy dress, baring her belly, and revealed a puckered wound between her ribs.

"Even piercing her heart with silver didn't work," she said. "I will not let her go."

A new hope lit up inside Ryker. Haven wanted out. Wanted death. She hated what she'd become so much, she'd rather die than live with it. It was a good sign, a sign that somewhere under all this, she'd retained some of the Haven Kyana knew and loved.

"On your own you don't stand a chance, Haven," he said, hoping he could break through whatever hold Cronos had over her. "But if you help me, I can banish Cronos forever. He'll never be able to hurt you again. I swear it."

"You think she'd choose to let you take her in? To let you exile her to that desolate island as I once was? She wouldn't. She'd never allow herself to become food for my children the way her boyfriend was."

Her ex-boyfriend had been delivered a cruel fate for his crimes of murdering Chosen, it was true. He'd deserved no less than to be fed to the pure Vampyre on the penal isle. But Haven was different. Or at least she could be if she just took his offer for help. And he believed Cronos was wrong. Haven was good enough to accept that punishment if it was given to her. But none of this was her fault. She wouldn't get sent anywhere if he had any say in the matter. Cronos, however, was going straight to Tartarus . . . as soon as Ryker could get the damned Binding Charm off.

He struggled to his feet. "Haven! Haven, if you can hear me . . . don't stop fighting this prick. You have me and Ky and Geoff fighting for you out here, but I need you to fight even harder *in* there!"

She scratched at her throat. Her black eyes flickered to green and the stoniness left her face. "I don't have Geoff anymore. He's . . . I killed—"

Haven was back! He had to hang on to her, had to convince *her* to hang on to herself. "No he's not. You didn't. Didn't you see him? When you grabbed me? The Healers were tending him. He's fine, Haven."

"He said I'd killed him."

Right. She hadn't seen that Geoff was okay because it had really been Cronos at the scene, not her. Ryker slowly reached out to her, but she stepped out of his reach.

"Geoff is going to be fine. Give me your hand and I'll take you to him."

Haven shook her head. Her tears fell faster. Her hands trembled. He watched her battle to hold on to her soul. And in the blink of an eye, the young woman slipped back into nothingness as the black, soulless eyes filled her watchful stare once again.

Cronos was back.

"You think you can save her with a few kind words." Haven swung and hit Ryker in the jaw. He staggered but managed to keep his feet. "I'm done with the games. You either help her complete her mission or I'll torture you until you do."

"Give it your best shot," Ryker spat. "I won't grant her access to your bones."

"You think because you carry the blood of my son that you can beat me? It didn't save Hades."

"You didn't kill him and you won't kill me either." He swayed on his feet. If he didn't reach Haven soon, have her unleash him, the Binding Charm would kill him without Cronos's help, Zeus's blood or no. With each passing second, it was draining him of his power, draining him of his life force. He had to get it off. Had to find a way to fight back.

"You're weak," he said. "And when I get this collar off, I'm going to that island, all right, but it will be to grind your fucking bones into ashes."

Through Haven, Cronos struck Ryker four times in the ribs in rapid succession. Ryker stumbled, crashing to his knees. The Binding Charm intensified the pain of the beating, but he hid behind a mask of outrage.

"I wouldn't count on that." Haven's body leaned forward and whispered, "Your father might not go against the Order to save you, but will you be able to do the same when it's Kyana's life on the line?" She tightened her fist in the binding collar and grinned. "I don't think so."

The thought of Cronos hurting Kyana sent a fire through his belly that made it difficult to tamp down his anger.

"Kyana can hold her own," Ryker choked out in a harsh whisper. If he flew off the handle now, he'd do something rash and get himself tossed off the damned cliff. "She doesn't want to kill Haven, but if it's the only way to stop you, she's prepared to do it."

"Oh, if that were true, she would have done it already." Ryker was jerked to his feet like a rag doll. "Draw your circle or I will test how immortal you've become."

"Unbind me and I'll show you." Ryker shook his head in an attempt to clear the blood from his eyes. His head pounded, his body ached in every imaginable muscle and some unimaginable ones too.

He struggled to hold on to his strength, to stall Haven and Cronos long enough for Kyana to find them. "Come on, Haven. Fight it, damn you. You're stronger than this piece of shit."

"You can't have her." Cronos's evil cackle sent birds scattering. "There's only one option here. Port her and I'll save your life."

It took several failed attempts, but Ryker finally managed to get on his feet. He stared at Haven, not seeing the small blond, but the monster hiding within her. "I'll see you in Hell first."

"Have it your way."

Chapter Thirty-Six

Kyana raced through Below looking for some sign of Ryker even though her gut told her she wouldn't find him there. Not alone anyway. Haven might have all four pieces of the Eyes of Power, but she still needed Cronos's bones to complete the resurrection ceremony. Ryker was one of only two who could port her to that island where the bones had lain for so long. It didn't matter what threats they used; he would never let Haven get within spitting distance of Cronos's corpse.

Which meant she'd kill him when he refused.

As Kyana knelt beside several droplets of blood, fear tripped over itself, causing her hands to tremble. Whatever spells Haven had cast to snatch Ryker so deftly, she hadn't, thankfully, used a Scent Removing Charm. Not even the infusion of Zeus's blood had caused the scent of sunshine and ocean to change. However, hanging in the air like a storm cloud were the base pheromones of Haven *and* Cronos.

Maybe Haven wanted Kyana to follow. Maybe deep down . . .

Frantic, she followed their trail, determined to get to Ryker before it was too late. He would never unleash evil onto the world. Never port Haven and allow her to raise Cronos. He'd rather die than hurt the humans he valued so much.

She couldn't let that happen.

She raced along the path to the cliffs. Footsteps pounded behind her, but guessing they belonged to Geoffrey, she didn't turn. When she entered a wide clearing on the cliff's edge, she froze. Haven had Ryker on his knees. Even from this distance, she could see the blood and bruises. As Haven's fist came down on Ryker's jaw, Kyana flinched for him. It took all her willpower not to leap into action and keep hold of what little calm she'd retained. Being hasty could cost Ryker his life, and his life had become too valuable for her to risk.

That revelation tore at her chest until a faint sob escaped her. She cupped her hand over her mouth and ducked behind the trees, her mind spinning with ways to pull him away from that cliff before she made her move.

As she watched Haven strike him again, Kyana couldn't comprehend why he wasn't defending himself, or why he hadn't sent Haven flying over the cliff's edge, ending Cronos's attempts to regain power once and for all.

What the hell are you doing? she wanted to shout at him, but her voice refused to cooperate. Thankfully, though, her feet were no longer immobile. If she revealed herself slowly, she might distract Haven enough for Ryker to make a move. She closed the distance, stopping only when Haven pulled Ryker to his feet and shoved him closer to the cliff's edge.

"Take one more step and I'll let him fall."

The sound of rocks breaking free from their precarious hold kept Kyana rooted.

"Kill him, Cronos, and you'll never get what you want." She shifted half a step closer. "If he goes over, I'll make damned sure Haven goes with him. There'll be no one to bring you back."

She looked at Ryker. His face was so swollen that he was barely recognizable. It was then that she saw the binding cuffs linked around Haven's wrist and Ryker's throat. That was why he wasn't fighting back. He was under her spell.

His crisp, clear, ice blue eyes penetrated the pulp that had become his face, eyes that spoke words his battered lips couldn't form. He slowly lifted his hand to grip the Binding Charm around his neck. Though he pulled with enough force to make the muscles in his arms bulge, the necklace refused to release him. His gaze shifted from Kyana, to Haven, to the cliff, then back to Kyana.

Her heart stopped. He was prepared to sacrifice himself to stop this. She couldn't let him do it. Kyana kept her gaze on Ryker, but spoke to Haven. "I'm sorry I let that bastard get his hands on you."

Haven turned to glare at her, giving her the opportunity she'd been waiting for. She threw herself at Ryker. The instant she collided with his back, she jerked sideways, forcing them away from the edge and into Haven, knocking her on her ass. Their breaths escaped in a whoosh of agony. Then Haven shoved Ryker aside and scrambled to her feet.

Before Kyana could regain her breath or find a way to free Ryker from the bond that was killing him, Haven's foot connected with her ribs, sending her careening toward nothingness.

She dug her hands into the rocky soil, her nails ripping in an attempt to find a handhold. She slipped over the edge before finding a root that would support her weight. Grasping the thorny vein with bloody fingers, she pulled herself up to find Haven standing over her. The maniac inside Haven laughed and ground her heel into Kyana's hand.

Biting back a cry of pain, she searched for another safe place to grab. Her gaze dropped. Nothing but a mist of sea foam and jagged rocks lay beneath her. Even as a goddess, she'd never survive the fall.

"Make your circle . . ." As Haven spoke to Ryker, she knelt in front of Kyana and gripped her throat. Her long nails bit into the flesh sending tiny rivers of blood snaking down Kyana's neck. ". . . or I will kill her."

Her bloodied hands made finding a secure grip difficult, but Kyana held on for dear life, thorns puncturing her palms and poking at her bones.

She visualized snatching Haven by the hair and tossing her over her shoulder and down the cliff. But if she acted on that impulse, she'd go down too, and while she wasn't afraid to die, she knew her responsibilities wouldn't allow for direct suicide.

The stone on the charm around Ryker's neck pulsed bloodred. If he didn't get it off soon, it would kill him. She stared at him, blocking out all thoughts of fears and pain until it was just the two of them on that rocky cliff.

The only thing keeping Kyana from careening down the mountain now was Haven's vicious hold on her throat.

"Don't do . . . it," she managed to squeak out. "Don't . . . port her."

She could read the determination in his eyes. He'd rather die than risk Haven completing the ceremony that would bring pure evil down on them all, but he was struggling with the sight of her life in jeopardy.

She caught his gaze, pleaded with him silently as Haven swung Kyana's body up and over the ledge, throwing her with a hard thud onto the dirt beside Ryker.

"You didn't kill me," Kyana sputtered in surprise, her throat aching and raw.

"If I kill you, he definitely won't port us, will he? Now"—Haven turned her attention to Ryker—"port me, you dumb prick."

Kyana made a big ordeal about struggling to her feet so Haven wouldn't hear her whispered plea to

Ryker as she rose. "Don't do it. I'll figure something out, I just need time."

There was so much doubt in his eyes, she worried he wasn't going to listen.

His gaze locked with hers, then shifted frantically; the hint of a nod at something to her left had her tossing a glance over her shoulder. No one was there.

She turned back to face Haven. "I will stop you."

"You had your chance and you blew it. All this is on your head, Huntress. The next time we meet, you'll die."

"You'd better hope she can't raise you, Cronos, because once you're corporeal again, there's nothing stopping me from ripping your fucking head off."

Ryker was drawing a circle in the sand, his mouth moving as the inaudible words were said that would take them from here. "No, stop!"

But he'd finished his circle. Haven stepped forward and placed her hand on his shoulder. A vortex slowly formed in front of him. He held out his hands as if offering prayer to the swirling light that gradually consumed them.

Just as Kyana sprung off her toes and leaped through the air toward them, a hand grabbed hers. But rather than hold her back, the body propelled her forward. Her hand contacted Ryker's thigh and she had only a second to turn her head and see who her uninvited guest was before she was being yanked through the painfully bright wormhole.

Ares.

Chapter Thirty-Seven

The instant they dropped out of the vortex and onto the sandy beach, Ares laced his fingers with Kyana's and pulled her to her feet. Her blindness only increased the panic crushing her ribs, but until Ryker spoke the words to release her, she'd see no light. The need to stay with him, to protect him, warred with the need to throttle him. What had he been thinking?

He'd just condemned them to Hell on Earth—if they even survived to see another sunrise. The Vampyre here were deadly to gods, and while Ryker hadn't changed into Zeus completely yet and Kyana hadn't yet fully become Artemis, Ryker was still a demigod, and Ares was still Ares. The monsters who resided here were the firstborn Vampyre—created when Cronos shared his blood with the other exiled, and with them bore the first Vampyric children. That pure evil was deadly near the pure auras of the gods. It drained them, sucked

the life right out of them just by being too close—
with the exception, it seemed, of Cronos.

She had to get Ryker and Ares off this island
before sunset and those sons of bitches came out
to hunt.

Hindered by her blindness, she felt herself being
carried away from the crashing waves of the beach
while Ryker and Haven were still recovering.

"Hush," Ares demanded, releasing her. "She
doesn't know we've come with them yet."

She craned her neck skyward and wished with
desperation that she could see how low the sun
was. Sunset would be upon them shortly. They had
to get moving.

"Why the hell did you let him port?"

Ares crouched behind her and covered her
mouth with his hand, stifling the curse she wanted
to scream.

He pressed his mouth close to her ear. "To save
his life. I can port us off now. We just needed
time—"

"*Libero.*" Ryker's voice sounded weak, like he
was a million miles away, but he was close enough
to return her sight, and with it, her determination
to reach his side. She fought against Ares, but he
held her tight.

"If you want to save my son, you have to trust
me. This is the only way."

Ares's whispered breath was hot against her
ear, but it calmed her momentarily—or at least,
it gave her back her ability to reason. She didn't

want to put her faith in someone who hated her and despised his own son, but her choices were limited.

The second he released her, she scrambled to her knees to peer through the underbrush at the empty beach. "Where are they?"

Ares pointed toward a path about a dozen yards away before grabbing her hand and pulling her to her feet. "Let's go. We have to get my son . . . before I'm unable to port us out of here."

The weakness in his voice, the way he grabbed his chest as though he was having a heart attack, frightened her. Wherever the Vampyre were sleeping, they were near enough to taint Ares already. This was going to be very, very bad.

She couldn't stand the prick, but she needed his port to get the hell out of here. There was no way they'd survive twenty-four hours for Ryker's ability to return. Even Kyana, unaffected by the Vampyre thus far, wouldn't be able to last once . . . Oh gods, she was doomed to change at sunset. They *really* had no time to waste.

She couldn't afford to tote a huge, hulking god with her in his current state. Moving as quickly as she could, she dragged Ares back to the beach, hoping the salty air would help ease his pain. Thankfully, the closer to the water they got, the easier Ares seemed to breathe.

He dropped to his knees. "Thank you," he mumbled.

"I'm going to find Ryker. Bring him back here."

She pointed her finger at him. "Stay put and don't die," she ordered.

He looked like he was going to argue, but suddenly gripped his chest again and peered up at her with a panicked expression. "Hurry."

She left him and sprinted down the path toward the center of the island. It didn't take her long to reach the clearing they'd used as base camp when they'd first found this place a week ago. Crouching, she scanned the clearing.

She listened for any sounds of Ryker or Haven, but only deafening silence greeted her. Raising her head, she sniffed the air, almost crying out with relief when she detected the faint hint of Ryker on the breeze.

Watchful of each step, she worked her way toward the far side of the camp. When she reached the overgrown trail leading to the cave that had become Cronos's grave, she heard the faint sound of a twig snapping. Spinning, she prepared to lunge at Haven, only to find herself staring into Ryker's icy blue eyes. He was bound to a large palm tree, his head immobile, his chin lifted upward at an uncomfortable-looking angle from where Haven had secured him in place with the Binding Charm. His face was pale, his eyes glassy and empty. But he was breathing.

"Thank the gods," she whispered, rushing to his side.

His forehead was bloody. A deep wound gushed from below his hairline like a crack in a perfect foundation. She snatched at the chain around his neck and slipped her dagger from her boot.

The weapon passed straight through the strands, but before the rope could fall away, they reentwined, holding him in place. Kyana knelt in front of him and shook his shoulders.

"Ryker? Ryker, I don't know what to do."

His eyes fluttered closed and partially opened again. He tried to lift his head from the trunk of the tree, but the combination of the beating he'd taken, the binding spells, and the creatures on the island were taking their toll. His head jerked back toward the tree trunk and she thought his eyes were rolling back in his head, but as she leaned closer to shake him awake, she saw he wasn't losing consciousness.

He was staring at something overhead.

Her gaze followed his to the object dangling above him. Tied to a thick branch swung a cracked vial of ambrosia. She watched in horror as one undiluted pink droplet oozed out of the crack and plopped on Ryker's head. He let out a muffled roar as steam escaped the bloody wound on his brow and spread it open even further.

"That sadistic bastard!"

She struggled not to panic as she tried to yank the vial down, but like the bonds holding Ryker, it wouldn't tear free with physical strength alone. "Tell me how to get you out of here!"

His horribly swollen lips moved, but all she heard was the rush of his exhale. She leaned forward, placing her ear as close to his battered face as she dared.

"Damn it, Ryker. *You* say it! If you know the words that will release you, then say them!"

"Can't . . . be . . . me . . ."

She understood. He couldn't set himself free of a spell that was cast on him. Someone else had to do it. *She* had to do it.

He began whispering a little more clearly, but it still took three tries before Kyana could piece the garbled sounds together to form a coherent word.

Before she could repeat it, another pink drop fell, splattered on his head, and Ryker convulsed. This time his eyes really were rolling back in his head, and if she didn't hurry he wouldn't be awake to help her.

"Slacciare?" she whispered, silently praying she pronounced it correctly.

Much to her relief, the golden strands fell away from his chest to rest loosely at his waist, and the vial of ambrosia clattered to the ground, shattering at their feet. Kyana hopped out of the way, dodging the splatter and pulling Ryker with her.

When the liquid settled, she grabbed hold of the chains hanging from him and tossed them aside. Without the pressure of the binds, Ryker began to sway on his feet. She barely managed to catch him before his face crashed brutally into the ground.

"I'm going to get you back to the beach. I need you to try not to make any noise."

She slipped his arm around her shoulder with

one hand, grabbed the waistband of his pants in the other, and hoisted him to his feet. Every muscle in his body stiffened in protest, but he didn't make a sound.

"We have to hurry," she panted, walking as fast as she could back the way she'd come.

She didn't know how he stayed on his feet, with them tripping their way through the jungle like a drunken pair of elephants, but thankfully, he managed. She considered carrying him, but if he could get to safety on his own, she wouldn't have to use the strength she needed to reserve for confronting Haven.

As they approached the sand, Ares rushed to her side. Effortlessly, he lifted Ryker and carried him to the water's edge, setting him gently in the sand just out of reach of the surf. He paused long enough to brush Ryker's hair from his bloodied face before shifting to draw his circle in the sand.

"We have to get out of here," he said. "Now."

Kyana stepped out of reach of his porting circle. She couldn't leave. Not yet. She wiped the beads of sweat from her forehead and pulled in huge gulps of air. "I know where Haven's going. Take care of him. I'll be back as quickly as I can."

He looked at Ryker, then back to Kyana. "There's no time."

Darkness was less than an hour away, but if she hurried, she still had time before the creatures came out of their hole in the ground.

And if she was damned lucky, time to stop

Haven from completing the ceremony that would raise Cronos.

"I have to stop her."

Ares looked at Ryker, then back to Kyana. "If it means leaving you here to die in order to save his life, I will."

"Give me an hour. If you can." Not caring that Ares watched her, she brushed her lips lightly across Ryker's. "If I'm not back by sunset, leave without me."

Chapter Thirty-Eight

The deeper Kyana traveled into the forest, the harder it was to tell the time through the thick canopy of branches overhead. Haven had bought her a watch years ago, but it lay dusty on her dresser at home, even the soft tick-tick too much technology for Kyana to handle. Now, a little pain would've been worth knowing exactly how much time she had before darkness fell, exactly how much time until the pure Vampyre were released upon them all.

Exactly how much time before Artemis's blood finally overtook her own and she no longer knew how to work her own body.

Normally, her Vampyric senses told her such things, but it seemed she didn't have much Vampyre in her blood anymore.

She summoned Artemis's powers now, one of the few she'd managed to tap into: speed. Like the wind, she flew through the trees—branches and leaves nothing more than a blur as she wound around their trunks and over rocky obstacles in her path. Like the last time she'd been here, the eerie silence chilled her bones.

No birds. No ants. Nothing.

All life on this island had been exterminated long ago, leaving the pure Vampyre trapped with nothing to feed upon. They too were in danger of extinction, and the minute they smelled their living, breathing, uninvited guests, their hunger would make them unstoppable.

When the ground became a muddied quagmire, she leaped skyward, grabbed hold of a branch, and began swinging her way in monkey-bar fashion across the trail, deeper and deeper into the woods.

Farther and farther from her port out of here.

She had to push her fear to the back of her mind, lest it consume her fully. One second's panic could cause one second's hesitation. She didn't have that kind of time to waste.

The cave she was looking for sat smack in the middle of a deep copse of trees. There was enough darkness here to allow the Vampyre to come out and play if they dared, but the tunnel system where they dwelled was a good distance away. Chances were, they'd stay put until any threat of sun exposure was over.

At least she hoped.

She swung herself onto the top of the cave, her body pumping with adrenaline, and took a moment to survey her surroundings. Face tilted, she sniffed the air. She caught Haven's scent and scanned the ground where footprints had flattened the grass outside the cave. Stooping, she slid her dagger from her boot once again, and took a deep breath.

Pressing her palms to the hot rock under her feet, she pushed, throwing herself to the ground, where she landed directly in front of the entrance.

It was scarier going inside this time—now that she knew what lived on this island. Being oblivious had its perks that way. But at least this time, she was prepared. All senses on high alert.

As she ducked her head and stepped inside, she told herself it was all going to be okay. They'd all get off this island alive and Cronos would no longer be a threat.

She was such a damned liar.

The rancid air of the cave cloaked her, encasing her as if it was a physical force trying to keep her from entering. She took shallow breaths and wished she still held on to the Vampyric side of herself that didn't require air. The choking weight of evil caused her steps to falter in the darkness, but she pushed on to the farthest corner of the cave where Cronos's bones had lain for thousands of years.

Determined not to alert Haven to her presence, Kyana carefully stepped over pebbles and loose dirt. A strange warmth spread over her, like giant hands grabbing her around the waist and lifting her over the rubble.

She was almost positive if she looked down at the moist earth, not even her footprints would be visible. Another trait of Artie's, perhaps?

As she approached the final bend, she paused. Listening. Waiting. Trying to determine where Haven was and if she had completed the ceremony she'd come here to perform. Soft whimpers whispered over the rocky, muddy walls to settle around her ears. She craned her neck to listen, heard a sob, then pressed herself deeper into the shadows when she saw movement at the end of the tunnel.

Why would Haven be crying? Was she fighting against Cronos? Refusing to do his bidding anymore? Coherent enough to fight him?

Kyana stepped into the open and was immediately punched in the face with enough force to send her flying backward several feet before landing harshly on her ass.

"Hello, Kyana."

Though Haven's lips moved, the voice wasn't her own. But this was good news. He was still inside Haven, which meant he hadn't yet returned to his own body. There was still time to stop the resurrection.

Not bothering to wipe the blood from her mouth, Kyana sprang to her feet. "This ends. Right now."

"Oh, you're right about that." Haven closed the distance, slowly circling, testing her. Waiting for the moment to strike.

She had an infinitesimal wave of doubt settle over her. Cronos, through Haven, might be able to kill her. But, if she was meant to die, then she'd make damned sure her last act was to take Haven with her and leave Cronos to rot for the rest of eternity.

"Haven, please," she whispered. "Don't make me do this."

Haven bared her fangs and hissed.

She wanted to reach out to her best friend, to make one last attempt to get her to stop this madness. But deep inside, she knew it would do no good. Cronos was buried so deeply within Haven's body and mind, she'd never be able to claw her way free. Not now, when Cronos's body was so close and his dream of resurrection so near to realization. He'd never let loose his hold on her.

The only way to stop Cronos was to stop Haven, and as much as it was going to devastate her to do it, Kyana was going to have to kill her best friend.

With a growl, Haven charged at her. They collided with enough force to make the loose pebbles on the cave floor skitter. Kyana slammed her fist upward into Haven's kidney, stunning her long enough for Kyana to flip Haven behind her. By the time Haven recovered, Kyana was on her feet again.

Anger, hatred, and regret fed her like ambrosia. She stood her ground, letting Haven come to her. When Haven launched herself at her, she caught Haven by the throat. With a roar, she flung her away, but Haven wouldn't stay down. She just kept coming and coming, again and again, until her assaults became weaker and weaker.

Kyana steeled herself each time Haven rose to her feet, and each time Haven charged, she reached into her gut, into her determination as Artemis had told her to do, and flung Haven backward.

The tactic was working. Haven was spending all her strength and the frustration was muddling her ability to strategize.

"I expected more from you, Cronos," Kyana said, trying to keep her own breathing even so he'd catch no glimpse of her own growing fatigue.

Something in her belly was aching, likely from one of Haven's misguided blows. Whatever it was, it was stealing her breath with each passing second.

Haven's mouth opened and her throat visibly constricted with the desire to speak, but no words escaped. She lowered her head and stooped slightly, and Kyana prepared to be charged by a lunatic bull.

Nothing happened.

"Haven?"

Haven just stood there, limp, like a hanged corpse whose feet were firmly planted on the ground. She could make out Haven's black eyes peering upward at her through her long hair, but other than the slight sway of her body, she did nothing.

Kyana would have preferred another attack. This was simply chilling. Eerie.

She was torn between stepping forward to check on her friend and stepping backward for her own safety. The minute Haven's feet drifted off the ground and she began to hover, Kyana followed her instincts and took a retreating step, her back pressing to the muddy wall.

"What the—"

Haven's body spun; her head was thrown backward. Her arms reached out, grabbing at air. One leg bent, the other pointed its toes toward the earth. It was the form of the crucified, and the horrifying scream that exploded from Haven's mouth sent Kyana's hands over her ears in a desperate attempt to keep her own head from exploding.

Rocks jumped in place overhead before crashing around her. She lifted her hands from her ears to her head, protecting her skull from the fist-sized stones pelting her shoulders and arms.

Whatever was happening, it was coming from inside Haven. If Kyana didn't stop it, they were going to be buried alive.

Keeping one arm up to protect her head, she bent and ran at Haven. But instead of knocking her out of thin air, Haven caught her by the throat and threw her. It was no little toss. Kyana whipped across the room at the speed of light, her body folding in on itself as she crashed against the wall and crumpled to the ground.

Stunned, it took her a moment to orient herself. She picked herself up, her arm hanging limply at her side. Her shoulder had dislocated from the impact and she was forced to crush it back into its socket.

The sound of bone on bone churned her stomach, and the pain made her ill, but she didn't dare look away from Haven, who was spinning again. Her body glowed, shimmering, lighting up the dark cave.

One glimpse into her eyes had been a mistake, for she saw in there not a monster, but a friend. Black eyes had turned yellow, her pasty pallor now once again golden tan.

"Let her go, Cronos!" Kyana screamed. "Take me! Use *me*!"

As Haven's head moved to look at her, the pleading in their depths broke Kyana's heart and ripped through her soul.

"Kill me," Haven whispered.

"No! Haven, fight him!"

She rushed at her friend once again, this time grabbing Haven by the ankles and tugging with all her Vampyric, Lychen, goddess strength to bring her back to the ground.

Haven wouldn't budge. She remained suspended like a puppet, tears streaming down her face.

"Kill me."

The desperation in Haven's face nearly destroyed Kyana. She didn't realize she was crying too until she heard the tears in her own voice.

"I can't. Haven, please. Help me. I can't do this. Fight him."

Laughter caused a new quake and before she could steady her stance, Haven's body fell into her arms.

They tumbled to the ground in a heap, and as she struggled to free herself from the weight of Haven's body, a glimmer in the corner of the cave caught her eye.

"Shit. No. No, no, no, no, no!"

Haven turned, her eyes wide, her face soaked with tears. As she set her gaze upon the horror, she grabbed Kyana by the arm and yanked her up before shoving her toward the exit.

"Run!"

But Kyana couldn't move.

Cronos's bones were radiating an eerie neon aura.

The laughter around them grew louder and louder, deafening Haven's pleas for Kyana to run. Greens and golds sparkled like jewels as the fragments of his body inched toward one another. Leg and arm bones attached themselves to the torso. The torso and neck attached to the head. Fingers moved. Knees bent.

Cronos was rising.

Chapter Thirty-Nine

Her gaze not daring to stray from Cronos's bones, Kyana grabbed the daggers she'd lost with Haven's first punch. The skeleton continued to piece itself back together—tiny bones slithering across the rock-strewn floor like stony worms. In horror, she watched as muscles materialized and tendons stitched themselves into place.

"You have to get out of here," Haven pleaded.

She couldn't look away. Morbid fascination held her attention as the body before her slowly rebuilt, repaired itself, became whole again.

"Kyana. Get out of here!"

She snapped out of her temporary hypnosis. Haven wore a frantic expression, her body half leaning toward the exit, half leaning toward Kyana.

When she turned her attention back to the bones . . . they were gone. All of them. There wasn't a single trace of Cronos anywhere around the abandoned Eyes of Power.

"What the hell?" She turned in a small circle, keeping Haven at her back. "Where did they go?"

The ground began to vibrate until the sound was deafening. The cave was closing in on itself.

"He's rising, Kyana! We have to run!"

"Sonofabitch!"

Cronos intended to make his tomb become theirs. Kyana snatched up the Eyes of Power, grabbed Haven's hand, and charged to the exit.

She tossed Haven up and through the opening, but when she attempted to follow, pain ripped through her body, so intense, so mind numbing, that it doubled her over. She fell to her knees and wrapped her arms around her belly. Her vision blurred. Her entire body shook so hard her teeth rattled.

"Give me your hand."

She managed to tilt her head in the direction of the distant voice, and forced herself to see through the pain.

"Give me your hand, damn it! Let me help you."

Somehow, she found the strength to lift her arm. To wrap her fingers around Haven's wrist. Haven pulled her to her feet, then slowly through the opening. They'd barely managed to extract themselves before the rocks collapsed, sealing the cave completely.

Kyana lay on her back. Her stomach felt like it was trying to eat itself. Bile rose in her throat. Had this been Ryker's fear? Was this why he'd been adamant about her staying Beyond and near Artemis?

Prying one eye open, she stared at the sky. Darkness was upon them.

Her transition had begun.

"Oh no, oh no, oh no."

Haven's fear-filled whisper pulled Kyana's attention from the sky. The color had drained from Haven's face. Her lips moved, but nothing more than *no* escaped.

"What is it?"

Haven pointed toward the canopy of trees in the distance. They were coming alive, swaying with some hidden force she couldn't see or feel. "They're coming."

As Kyana cursed Cronos, she kicked at the rock-sealed opening, wishing now that they'd stayed inside. It would offer them some protection against the creatures hunting in the darkness. But Ryker and Ares were on the beach. They had nowhere to hide. Ares could port them out, but if there was any life left in Ryker, she knew he'd die at the hands of these creatures before he left her.

She wouldn't let her pain prevent her from getting them off this island.

Using Haven as a crutch, she managed to stand. How did she hope to outrun these things when she could barely breathe?

"We're going to run," she said, inhaling as deeply as she could to summon strength from agony. "Don't stop. Don't look back. Don't think about what's chasing us. When you hear the surf, start screaming for Ares to start his circle. Do you understand?"

"What are you going to do?"

Try like hell to keep up. But in case that didn't happen, she had to know the others were safe. "Just do as I say, damn it!"

She shoved Haven to get her moving. Keeping her gaze locked on Haven's back, she stumbled along behind her as fast as she could, clutching the Eyes of Power against her chest. Her Vampyric speed was deserting her. Her goddess speed was lost in the lava boiling in her belly and spilling into her legs.

Trees popped from the ground like cannon fire. Branches crashed around them like thunder. The very air hung with the oppressed odor of death. Even without seeing them, she knew the creatures were almost upon them.

She tripped over a gnarled tree root and dropped Zeus's staff. When she stooped to retrieve it, another sharp pain seized her neck and electrified her brain.

"Ares!" Kyana yelled, hoping the faint sound she heard was the ocean and not her blood whooshing in her ears. "Get us outta here!"

"Ky?" Her name, carried faintly on the wind by Ryker's voice, had never sounded more beautiful. "Hurry!"

"Gogogogo," she chanted, both to prod Haven to move faster and to her feet to keep moving forward. The pain in her gut was spreading into her chest. Every breath was like inhaling razor blades. Only the sheer will not to be ripped apart by those hunting them helped her see beyond the agony.

Hard, packed earth gave way to the soft, sugary sand of the coast and she almost wept with joy. They'd made it. Her knees gave out and she went down hard, the Eyes of Power rolling beneath her body as she struggled to keep them near.

Haven skidded to a stop and turned back.

"Get to Ryker," Kyana screamed. "Make sure they get out of here."

For a split second, Haven looked like she might ignore the demand, but the Dark Breed broke through the underbrush and dropped from the trees, cutting off any hope Kyana might have had of escape.

The last thing she heard before the creatures closed in on her was the sound of Ryker bellowing her name.

Chapter Forty

Ryker couldn't pull his gaze off the spot where Kyana went down. The pure Vampyre spilled onto the beach behind her, their numbers so great that their stark white bodies illuminated the moonless night. Their hisses and growls, combined with the leathery scraping of their wings, blocked out the sound of the waves crashing on the beach and muffled Ares's demands that Ryker stay back.

If he didn't act fast, the creatures would be upon Kyana's fallen body in mere moments. He concentrated all his energy inward. His body warmed and his eyesight became sharper as the power within him took over.

He held his hands out before him, prepared to stop Haven despite Kyana's wishes, but one look into Haven's frightened face told him she was once again their friend.

Shifting his energies, he focused his mind and knocked the three beasts closest to her back into the jungle, giving her time to reach his side. It was all he could do. Going to her, getting closer to the domain of the pure evil emerging from the trees would kill him.

Get up, Ky. Get the hell up!

But she wasn't moving.

He shoved Haven toward Ares. "Draw your circle. I have to get Kyana, and you better be ready when I get back."

"If you go after her, you're dead," Ares said.

"She needs help. I'm not leaving her."

He waved his hands, causing several more Vampyre to go flying backward as he slowly inched his way forward. "Just be ready to port when I return."

"Those things will kill you too," Haven said.

He didn't want to look at her. She was standing here, safe, while Kyana was lying helpless in the sand. He wanted them to change places . . . *now.*

As he inched forward, his chest tightened with each millimeter he traveled. The sheer number of the Vampyre was staggering. For every three he sent flying, ten more charged at them. He doubted he could make his way to where Kyana's body lay and back to Ares before the nearness of the creatures alone killed him, but he had to try.

The fear on Haven's face vanished. The tears stopped. She pushed to her feet, and before either man could react, pulled Ares's sword from the sheath at his waist and ran past Ryker.

"What are you doing?" he roared.

"I'm the only one who can get close enough to

help her," Haven said, already out of Ryker's reach. "Stay here!"

Like hell. If anything happened to Haven now, Kyana would kick his ass when all this was over. He followed slowly behind Haven, mentally pushing back a few Dark Breeds at a time, giving him room to move farther and farther as Haven pushed on toward Kyana's unmoving body.

Each step became more difficult. Each breath more labored. The pain in his chest threatened to cripple him, but he didn't stop.

He made it another three feet when he heard Haven scream. Shifting, he saw the Vampyre surround her, stepping between her and Kyana. Why weren't they attacking Ky? She was vulnerable. A sitting duck and easy prey. Yet they ignored her completely, even seeming to purposely avoid going near her body.

He moved toward Haven as quickly as his body would allow, his gaze catching a glimpse of the Eyes of Power lying beside Ky's body.

That was why they weren't touching her. She was protected by the conduits.

Haven screamed again, thrusting Ares's sword upward as a pair of leathery wings wrapped around her. He pushed the creature backward with his mind, but the Vampyre dragged Haven back with it.

As Ryker approached, the one holding Haven bared its teeth. Its hiss of warning was like a rancid punch in the chest. He didn't give himself time to consider what touching that thing would do to him. Turning his focus inward, he gritted his teeth against the electric charges suddenly humming through his blood. He fed it, focused on it until it surfaced to his skin.

Then, reaching out and with both hands, he gripped the Vampyre's head and released the power. The monstrous face began to smoke. It opened its enormous mouth to let out a piercing scream just before its head went up in flames.

Ryker's fingers burned, and he lifted his hands overhead and shot off the lingering magic before it could incinerate *him*. Around him, a bubble of light exploded as three waves of electricity burst from his hands and destroyed the beasts approaching from all sides.

It only managed to clear about five feet of space around them, but it was enough room to extract Haven from the suffocating wings still bound around her face from the headless corpse.

When she was safe, Ryker collapsed onto his back, blackness clouding his mind like an impenetrable fog. The nearness of the Vamps was too much, stealing every second heartbeat and making it hard to remember that he was supposed to be running. Saving Haven and himself.

Saving Ky.

"Get the hell up!" Haven screamed at him, grabbing him by the collar and dragging him into a sitting position. "I can't carry you both back!"

He blinked, desperate to clear his vision, then

wished he hadn't. His gaze was locked on the woods. So many Vampyre spilled onto the beach that they blocked the jungle from view. There was no way he could use his powers to keep that many Dark Breed off them.

He struggled to stand, fought to breathe. He heard Ares shouting his name, and knew even the God of War could not fight back this enemy.

Thunder rumbled overhead and lightning flickered out of the sky. Three bolts smacked the forest not fifty feet away, felling a copse of trees to his right. Another bolt punctured the sky and pierced the heart of a palm ahead of him, unearthing the tree so that it landed with a loud boom and crashed into the brush at its roots. Then, like pearls on a broken necklace, the forest began to pop. One tree after the next, exploding from the inside out, raining leaves and bark down upon the beach.

Ryker lifted his arm to protect his head, searching for the source of the chaos. Had Cronos fully risen? Was he doing this?

"Get down!" he yelled, forcing his own body back to the sand.

What the fuck was going on?

Belly-crawling his way behind a small dune, he squeezed his eyes shut to protect them from the debris. He had to get to Kyana. But each time he moved, another tree was uprooted, was suddenly on the beach or in the ocean.

Then, everything was quiet. Not even the sound of the Vampyre broke the silence.

Ryker opened his eyes and lifted himself to peer over the top of the dune. The creatures stood close enough that he could smell them, but he and Haven no longer held their undivided attention. One of the larger beasts turned to stare into the distance. The others seemed to watch it, waiting to see what it would do.

The brewing storm continued to build, turning the crisp coral and blue sunset to charcoal gray. Ryker squinted against the flying sand to see what held the Vampyres' attention. When his gaze finally found the source of the commotion, he forgot how to breathe.

He blinked twice to make sure he wasn't imagining things. The weight lifted from his chest and he found himself smiling.

Kyana.

She was standing where she'd fallen, wind whipping her hair about her face. The goddess aura lit her eyes, spilling forward to make her skin glow as she hovered an inch off the sand. Artemis's powers were filling her, and Ryker swore he saw a black fog waft away from her body, the remnants of the Half-Breed she'd been for the last two hundred years leaving her forever.

The golden aura continued to pulse until her body could no longer contain it and it seeped outward to surround her. His mesmerized paralysis broke as a loud, eerie howl shattered the calm. As one, Vampyre charged toward them again.

Kyana moved so quickly, she appeared to float

even higher above the sand. Shocked, he couldn't take his gaze off her. He'd never seen anyone move so fast.

She stopped in front of him and raised her hands heavenward. She gripped Zeus's staff—*his* staff—in both hands, and thrust it skyward. The storm intensified. Lightning crackled so fast and so loud, he couldn't tell when one bolt ended and another began. The hum of electricity caused the hair on his arms to stand on end. The wind and rain pummeled him, and still he couldn't take his eyes off Kyana.

The glow around her swelled, pulsing from the tip of the conduit she wielded like a pro. Her lips moved, but her words were lost in the wind. She opened her eyes and held the staff in front of her. Lightning flashed from the jeweled tip, nearly blinding him. The pulsing energy changed to bright white light, and it was then that Ryker understood.

It wasn't light she was summoning. It was the sun.

Cursing, Ryker pivoted and ran like mad toward Haven, fighting every aching organ in his body to grab her by the arm and take her safely away.

"No!" Haven screamed. "Don't leave her!"

"If those rays touch you, you're dead!" He shoved her toward Ares, who had returned to making his circle, then once more faced the beach.

The rays of sunlight lit up the area around them like a golden bubble, just inches from turning

Haven into fireplace debris. The staff shook violently in Kyana's hands, but she held tight, turning slowly, aiming the deadly rays at the circling enemy.

As Ryker ran for her, hundreds of Dark Breeds burst, combusted, died. Ashes fell atop the sand like a gray blanket. Not a single body part was left behind. The filth filled his nostrils, clogged his throat, coated his hair and skin as he ran. The pain easing, the need to get to Kyana, to make sure she was safe, was all he cared about.

The Vampyre that were still able fled back into the jungle, removing the last bits of constriction in Ryker's chest. He stumbled when the weight of their evil left him, crashing into the sand and rolling back to his feet.

Standing again, he found Kyana an inch away, a smile making her face glow more radiantly than the sun she'd created as she lowered the conduit and thrust it toward him.

"I believe this belongs to you."

He took it from her, wincing as the heat from the staff made his skin sizzle. He might carry Zeus's blood, but because his transformation wasn't yet complete, he couldn't wield it as Kyana had. He tucked it under his arm, letting his shirt provide a barrier and leaving his hands free to support her as she leaned heavily against him. All her strength, all her power had been expended in her one show of glory. Heat was radiating off her body like steam.

He had no idea what to say. He was stupefied,

in awe, totally impressed, and couldn't find one single word to say that wouldn't make him sound like a moron.

"Can we get off this damned beach now?" she asked. " 'Cause I don't think I can do that again."

Smiling, he wrapped his arm around her shoulder, pulled her to him, and kissed her. It was neither the time nor the place, but damn it, he'd come so close to losing her. Thought, in fact, that he had. Who the hell cared if Ares was watching? She was alive and felt so good pressed against him that he didn't want to ever let her go.

Reluctantly, he let her slide away, let logic back into his own mind and led them back to where Ares stood on the shore. Kyana hadn't destroyed all the Vampyre here. Once the magically conjured sunlight disappeared again, they would return, hungrier than before.

"Get us home, Ares," he said, stepping back so Kyana could stand within reach of the god for the port home.

She stepped forward and held out the other Eyes of Power to Ares.

He shook his head and stepped backward. "Goddess. I can't think of anyone better charged with taking these home safely than you."

Chapter Forty-One

Kyana studied the group around her, her body feeling foreign and tingly and all wrong. What she'd just done had astounded her, and yet she certainly didn't feel as though she deserved the looks of awe directed at her now.

She'd nearly died back there, and when her hands had reached for Zeus's staff, they hadn't felt like her own. It hadn't been her mind conjuring ancient words she'd somehow understood. It had been Artemis. The goddess's powers belonged to Kyana now, and she wasn't quite sure how she felt about that. It was like waking up and finding you'd stepped into your mother's skin, her life. Familiar, yet so damned wrong.

"Stop staring at me," she muttered. Ryker and Haven quickly returned their attention to Ares and his porting circle.

She wanted off this island more than she wanted air, but she had to tell them . . . had to confess that their pride in her was misplaced. She'd failed.

Haven was safe, true, but Cronos had risen. Some-where on this island, the most evil and powerful of all gods was being reborn.

She wrapped Hades's amulet around her neck and tucked the trident under her arm. Wherever Cronos was, he had his ring back, and there was nothing she could do about that now. The damage had been done.

"He . . . disappeared with the ring."

Ares froze, his circle forgotten. "He has risen?"

"I raised him. I didn't want to . . ." Haven whis-pered. "As long as he has that ring, he cannot be stopped."

Ares looked as though he wanted to drown Haven.

Kyana might have too, if she hadn't seen for her-self how horribly Cronos had already made her suffer.

She couldn't think about this anymore. Couldn't strategize or contemplate. All she wanted to do was sleep and breathe and figure out how to be who she'd become and mourn the person she no longer was.

"Please," she whispered to Ares. "Get us off this island."

Ryker took her hand and they waited for Ares to finish creating his port. She felt him stroke the backs of her fingers and closed her eyes. His touch was so comforting and warm that it was hard to remember she was freezing all the way to her marrow.

"Cronos can't get off the island without a port,

Ky. Remember? Risen or not, he couldn't escape it then, and he can't escape it now. Our main priority is returning the amulet and the trident to their rightful owners. Once Geoff, Silas, and I can tend our duties as we're meant to, the human world can begin real reconstruction."

Ares gave them a look that told them the time for talking was over. Now, he'd need silence to finish the port, and soon, they'd be back in St. Augustine, away from this hellhole, and they'd have to explain everything that had gone wrong here today.

"You okay?" Ryker whispered in her ear.

"Hush. You'll make him steer us off course."

He smiled and squeezed her waist. Together, they each stepped inside the circle and placed their hands on Ares's shoulders just seconds before the vortex opened and sucked them in.

The blindness that kept her eyeballs from bursting from their sockets was different this time. Colors so bright she could make out the reds and blues and greens rushing past her even though she couldn't open her eyes. They seemed to be trying to pull her hand away from Ares. Only Ryker's fingers tightly laced with hers kept her from panicking and giving in to the hypnotic pull. Yank yank, pull pull. She'd never felt this resistance before.

The flashes of light slowed and they fell down, down, down. Cold water washed over her, dragging her under and stealing her breath. Someone grabbed hold of her hair and pulled her back to the surface.

"Libero."

Kyana blinked against the salt burning her eyes as she took in their landing strip with exhausted exasperation. She turned to glare to Ryker. "I knew you were going to send Ares off course! We're in the middle of the damned ocean."

"We're not in the middle," Ares said, spitting out a mouthful of seawater. He pointed behind Kyana. "Lighthouse is a couple dozen yards that way."

He wasn't about to get off that easy. *"Ryker* never dropped us in the middle of the ocean."

By the time they climbed the slippery rocks of the jetty, Kyana had almost forgotten about the odd sensation of the lights trying to pull her out of the vortex. She shivered against the wind and looked out over the vastness of the sea. Something felt out of place, but though her eyes had no trouble penetrating the darkness, she couldn't detect anything that might explain away the odd sensations.

"You all right?"

Chalking it up to her emotions being stuck in overdrive, she nodded. "Yep. Wet, tired, and cold. Just peachy."

She refused to allow the weight of what was to come settle around her shoulders. There'd be time to worry about that later.

She turned to Ares who was gripping Haven's arm tightly enough that bruises were already forming on her pale skin. Her gaze slowly met Haven's, and she felt a wash of gratitude that they'd both made it out alive. Scarred, for sure—no one could

endure all that Haven had and not be touched brutally. But she was alive. Deep down, Kyana hadn't
been sure that outcome would have been possible.

"Haven—" she started.

"Kyana." Haven made no apology for her interruption. "No more games. I won't fight against the
punishment I deserve, don't worry."

Her face was ashen, and Kyana wished she
knew how to comfort her. Despite that it had been
Cronos holding the reins on Haven, she'd still be
forced to stand trial. The Order couldn't be certain
when the possession had first occurred, and there
were dead Mystics who deserved justice. If Haven
had killed them of her own accord, she would
be punished. Severely. There was nothing Kyana
could do to prevent that.

She looked at Ares. "Take her. Gently." To Haven,
she added, "We'll speak once I've talked to the Ancients. They need to know all that happened here
today. That Cronos . . . is alive."

When Ares led Haven away, Ryker pulled Kyana
into his arms. "What about me? What can I do for
you?"

She smiled against his chest, though what she
really wanted to do was weep. "You're finally going
to get to give me that piggyback ride."

Chapter Forty-Two

Kyana stood on the grounds of Artemis's temple, *her* temple now, and studied the crowd that had begun to gather just minutes after their return. She hadn't had time to eat, sleep, or even think, and already the Order of Ancients was demanding that their new Goddess of the Hunt tell them of the past few days' events.

Artie stood on her left, Ryker on her right. Occasionally, his fingers brushed her hand in a not-so-casual gesture. He'd refused to leave her side for even a minute. He wanted to discuss the things that had happened on the island, the things that would happen to Haven now that they'd brought her home, but Kyana had refused. She wasn't ready. She had a duty to see to, and she intended to train like hell until she was capable of seeing it through.

She had, however, been given one moment of brilliance—a loophole much like the one that had gotten Ryker out of becoming Ares's Chosen. The

Order had declared Haven would be tried after her final cleansing . . . but they hadn't said when the cleansing had to occur.

If she could offer her friend nothing else, maybe, at least, she could offer Haven *time*.

She owed Haven that much.

Since their return less than an hour ago, they had talked at great length about Cronos. Kyana had hoped that the possession would give Haven an insight on where he'd go, what he intended to do first now that he'd been returned to a corporeal state.

Haven couldn't tell her anything she didn't already know. He wanted revenge. He wanted his sons to suffer and die. He wanted to get off that island and resume what he considered his rightful place on Zeus's throne.

And he'd use anyone, destroy everything, to see those things happen.

Mostly, however, Haven had talked about her twin sister, Hope. How her sister's spirit had never left her since the possessions began. That Hope had forced her to hold on to the tattered shreds of her humanity. It had nearly broken Kyana's heart to hear Haven cry over losing her sister for the second time. Especially now that Kyana knew what it felt like to lose someone she considered a sister herself.

But never in all their talk had they approached the topic of what was to become of their friendship. No, it hadn't been Haven who'd done all those horrible things. But Kyana had hunted her, and they'd tried to kill each other. It was a little difficult to simply hug out the tension that had come between them.

It was Kyana's greatest hope that one day . . . hopefully soon . . . they might become sisters again. But first, there was healing to be done. On both sides.

"It's your duty as the new Goddess of the Hunt to release your prisoner to the guard." Artemis's whispered words pulled Kyana from her thoughts.

Her gaze fell once again on Haven, who knelt before them on the temple lawn, awaiting news of her sentencing. Ryker's fingers drew a tiny circle at the small of Kyana's back. She leaned into him for half a second before gathering her resolve and taking a step forward.

"You will go willingly and quietly with the guard and will remain imprisoned until you're tried for the murder of the Healers in charge of your care at the time of your Turning," she said, every word an effort as she tried to sound as authoritative and sure of herself as Artemis might have. "The Order has agreed that you will not be held accountable for the offenses that took place after Cronos's possession of you."

Haven held Kyana's gaze. There was no malice, no anger in her eyes. Just understanding and acceptance. "Yes, Goddess. It's more mercy than I dese—"

"A trial will be scheduled for the day following

your purging and cleansing to contain the beast that now lives within you. The beast . . . I created in you." She prayed Haven could read the apology in her eyes. She couldn't show such weakness now, in front of the Order, but hopefully Haven knew her well enough to hear the regret in her words when no one else would be able to detect it.

"Yes, Goddess," Haven said.

"But as the goddess charged with your apprehension," Kyana continued, "it is my will that you be given adequate time between the purging and the cleansing. You've been through an ordeal, and it's too risky to cast so much magic on you at once."

She had no idea if that was even true, but when no one called her out for it, she pressed on. "You'll be purged immediately so that whatever fresh blood you've consumed over the last few days is completely removed from your body. It will help tame the beasts so that the cleansing will be easier to bear."

The cleansing would be brutally painful if it was anything like Kyana's had been. It was the equivalent of rehab. While the purging rid the body of blood already ingested, the cleansing was a slow, torturous process that would eventually soothe the need to feed at all. The urges to kill and to prey on the weak would eventually slip away until they were nothing more than horrible memories.

"You will be given a month's respite before the cleansing begins."

The collective gasps from the spectators rolled over the mountain like an avalanche. The purging would take a few days; however, the cleansing could take weeks or months depending on how quickly Haven mastered the ability to control the breeds inside her. Add to that the month Kyana had just given between the two events, and that should leave plenty of time for a miracle to happen and for Haven to find some way to redeem herself within the eyes of the Order of Ancients.

"You can't be serious."

The voice came from the foot of the temple steps and Kyana craned her neck to peer over the crowd to find its owner. Athena glared up at her, her dark eyes flashing with menace.

"You have something you wish to say, Athena?"

"Yes." She stepped forward. "I do. You give this creature leniency because she was your friend. I know you're new at this, Kyana, but we do not play favorites within the Order. Rules are rules—"

Kyana held up her hand to shut the goddess up. "And this was *my* hunt. Not yours. Not Zeus's. *Mine*. Is it not my right to determine the days and times of the trials I'm to hold, just as it would have been Artemis's were this her criminal?"

"Yes, but—"

"Then I have only done what was within my rights to do. There will be no favoritism at the time of her trial. I merely determined *when* the trial would be." She lowered her voice and hardened her stare. "Now back the hell off."

Athena jerked her head as though she'd been slapped, and Kyana was pretty sure she'd just made her first real enemy on Olympus now that Ares no longer despised her.

"Very well," Athena muttered. "As I'm to sit in on her trial, I'll make certain you keep to your word and she is justly punished."

"You do that. In the meantime, go home." Kyana raised her arms toward the crowd. "All of you. Go home."

Two members of Ares's Elite Guard stepped forward and seized Haven by the arm. Ares stepped in front of them and they dropped their hands, relinquishing Haven to him.

"I shall see to it that your wishes are carried out personally." He bowed, then took Haven's arm lightly in his hand. He turned, and with several members of his Elite Guard following discreetly in his wake, left to take Haven to her new home.

"Are you ever going to stop being a mystery?" Ryker asked, his breath whispering against her ear. "You're never going to give up on her, are you?"

"No more than she'd give up on me. I can't save her, but I can give her time to try and save herself."

"I wasn't sure you'd be able to keep your promise." Artemis linked her arm with Kyana's and led her inside the temple. "I'm impressed."

"What promise?"

Artemis smiled. "The promise you made to save Haven. To protect the gods."

She swallowed, easing out of Artie's grip. "I didn't stop Cronos. He still has his ring. His followers. He's going to come after his sons."

Ryker pressed a calming kiss to her forehead and pulled her into his arms. "He can't get off that island, Ky. Not without a port from me or Ares."

She hugged him briefly before stepping back and admitting her deepest fear. "I'm not sure I'm the person meant to finish this mission if he does show up."

Artie's dark brows rose. "You're going to quit now?"

She shrugged, not liking the burn of regret in her belly. "I don't . . . I don't know how . . ."

"Training, Kyana," Artemis said. "You've yet to begin. But once you've mastered what it means to be the Goddess of the Hunt, you'll not doubt yourself any longer."

Ryker forced her to look up at him. "You have to stop hating yourself. It's going to fester, rot away the goodness in you. Hate is what feeds Cronos. Don't become like him."

She sighed. It was good advice, but she wasn't sure she could follow it. There was only one way to forgive Haven, and in turn herself. She was going to have to find Cronos.

And kill him again.

But how did one go up against the most powerful god in the world and win?

Ryker gave her another light kiss before leaving the temple to follow after Ares. He'd make sure Haven was settled as a favor to her. But as he walked away, an emptiness filled her, making her ache to follow him, to ask him to stay with her for the night.

"You know, you're only what you think you are if you choose to believe it," Artemis said.

Kyana blinked. "Huh?"

Artemis's laugh lit up her eyes the way Kyana imagined a mother's might when cast upon her daughter. "This belief you have that you'll never lose your Vampyric sensibility to remain unattached to others . . . it's only true if you make it so. You've attached yourself to Haven. To Geoffrey even. I see the way you look at our new Zeus, and Kyana, it *is* all right to want a future with him."

She shrugged, uncomfortable with the topic but determined not to show it. "I don't know what you're talking about."

"All right, then. But I see no harm in the temples of Zeus and Artemis becoming one, if both parties choose it to be so. Just because I was a virginal goddess does not mean you have to be." Artemis placed a hand on Kyana's shoulder and gave it a light squeeze. "An eternity is a very long time to be lonely, Kyana. Trust me. I speak from experience. An even longer time to pine after the one who owns your heart."

"No one owns my heart but me."

This time, it was Artie who shrugged. "So long as that's how you choose it to be and it's not what you believe you deserve. You're not Vampyre anymore, Kyana. Do not be afraid to explore what that might mean."

And with that, she walked back outside, leaving Kyana standing alone in the vast, empty temple. She stared blankly into space, her heart pounding in her chest. Part of her wanted to tear off after Ryker, but fear held her in place.

Could she abandon a lifetime's worth of beliefs and trust Ryker with who she really was and what she really wanted? And if she chose to take the next step, what exactly did that mean?

"You look ill." Ryker's voice was suddenly in her ear again, and she looked to her left to see him smiling down at her. "Artemis said you wanted to talk to me before I questioned Haven?"

From the main entrance, Artemis turned and gave a friendly wave.

Traitor.

"She lied," Kyana muttered. "Go on. I'm all right."

He eyed her with suspicion. "You don't look all right." He nuzzled her neck. "Stay at my temple tonight? Or, if you prefer, I can stay at yours. I know a hundred ways to make you *all right* again."

She opened her mouth to say no, but Artie mentally scolded her.

"Mine," she heard herself say. "We stay at mine."

It wasn't a commitment of forever, but it was one hell of a huge first step.

Ryker grinned, kissed the back of her hand, then headed back outside, where Ares was waiting for him to finish their escort of Haven.

Her heart thudded in her chest as she watched him go, and she couldn't help but feel a tremor of excitement over the possibilities of what the night might bring.

She let her gaze linger on Haven's escort, her heart suddenly so full that it left no room for fear and worry. But as Haven and her guards disappeared, another sight grabbed Kyana's attention, and she had to blink to make sure she was truly seeing what she thought she was.

A ghostly little girl followed behind the procession, her body transparent, but her eyes sparkling blue. The child stopped, looking over her shoulder at Kyana. After several seconds, she smiled a big toothy grin, offered a friendly wave, and skipped off after Haven.

Kyana felt her face break into a grin worthy of a true goddess. "You're wrong, Haven," she whispered. "She's not gone. She'll always be right there with you."

"Who will be with her, Goddess?" someone asked from nearby.

Kyana didn't turn away. "Hope. Hope will always be with her."

As she mumbled the words, her mind's eye brought forth images of the things that gave her hope. Ryker and Geoff. Even Silas, slutty Sixx, Nettles, Ares, and her minions, Farrel and Crag. Artemis. Perhaps even Haven again one day. Friends. They were her family now.

It didn't matter that she didn't know how to end

Cronos's miserable existence for good this time. Even though she'd failed once, and might again before they saw this through, her family would still be standing by her side, ready to help her every step of the way. Ready to die beside her if it came to that.

A calming warmth settled around her as the realization struck her. She *did* know how to go against the toughest god in the world *and* she knew how to beat him.

With family.

With hope.

That night, Kyana waited for Ryker in her bed, her body warm and drowsy from an overindulgence of much needed ambrosia, while her nerves twitched in anticipation. In the hours since retiring to her chamber, Artemis's words had plagued her until finally, now, she knew what needed to be done.

She wasn't Vampyre anymore. Who was to say that she had to behave like one?

When her door creaked open, she propped herself up on her elbow and smiled at the man who had entered her world with far less subtlety than he entered her room now. He'd more or less crashed into her life. Unasked for. Unwanted.

My how things have changed.

"I thought you might be asleep by now," he said, tugging his shirt over his head and easing onto the bed beside her.

Kyana rolled over, pressing her chest to his as

she lay atop him and forced him to meet her gaze. Thanks to his godly blood, the bruises on his battered face had faded to a faint yellowish-green. The swelling had completely disappeared. Only the ambrosia-inflicted wound on his forehead remained red and raw-looking, made her grimace over the pain he'd endured at Haven's hand.

She pressed her lips gently to the wound. "I might break your heart," she said.

He shrugged. "I could just as easily break yours."

She swallowed. "I don't know if I'm okay with that."

Something flickered in his eyes as he watched her and traced his thumb over her lips. "What? Breaking mine or yours?"

"Either." She sighed and laid her head against his chest. "I'm afraid it's not me you want, Ryker. I'm afraid it's this crazy notion you have of me. I'm terribly flawed, you know. Proud and stubborn—"

"I hadn't noticed."

She poked him in the rib. "I'm serious. I won't change."

He took her head gently in his hands and lifted her gaze to his. "I hope not."

Swallowing down that stubborn pride she'd been speaking of, she tried to find the truth in his eyes. She found them smiling up at her with a slight twinkle. For now, her flaws were all right, just as she was able to bear his. Overthinking, duty-bound, morally righteous though they might be. But one day . . . one day they might get tiresome and one of them might not choose to stay anymore.

What then?

"Does it make you happy?" he asked. "To have me here?"

She nodded.

"I love you, Ky. I've loved you for ten years. Can you deal with that?"

Her heart was racing and the urge to flee from his arms was nearly overwhelming. But this time, she wasn't going to listen to her head. She was going to listen to her heart.

"I can't promise you forever. I can't even promise you all of me," she said, kissing his cheek, his nose, his mouth.

"I know."

"And you're okay with that?"

His lips thinned and his expression turned solemn. Kyana ran her hands through his hair, brushing the golden strands off his face so she could better see him.

"If you can look at me now and tell me your feelings for me are strong and have potential, then yes, I'm okay with that. But Ky, I don't just want you in my bed. We can't give this a shot if you keep closing me out."

She sighed, content as he gently rubbed the small of her back, his arousal waking her from her drowsy state. He was right, and she'd been trying. Little by little, she was becoming more of herself around him.

"I'll try," she conceded, nuzzling his neck. "But Ryker . . . tit for tat."

"Deal."

"This," she said, as he slid his hands down her back to cup her ass and his *tat* strained against her belly, "is about to get really interesting."

Next month, don't miss these exciting new love stories only from Avon Books

All Things Wicked by Karina Cooper

After Caleb Leigh betrayed their coven, Juliet knew she'd never forgive him, no matter what they once meant to each other. Caleb can't hide from the demons of his past, but he will stop at nothing to fulfill a promise he made long ago: protect Juliet, no matter the cost.

A Town Called Valentine by Emma Cane

When Emily Murphy returns to her mother's hometown in the Colorado Mountains looking for a fresh start, a steamy encounter with handsome rancher Nate Thalberg is not exactly the new beginning she had in mind.

A Devil Named Desire by Terri Garey

Hope will do anything to find her missing sister, even make a deal with the Devil. Archangel Gabriel will stop at nothing to keep an ancient promise, even become mortal. With the fate of the world hanging in the balance, Hope and Gabriel learn that desire can be a devil that's impossible to control.

A Secret In Her Kiss by Anna Randol

A near brush with death convinces Mari Sinclair it's time to end her career as a British spy. But when her superiors send in Major Bennett Prestwood to see that she completes her final mission, passion and desire change all the rules.

978-0-06-184132-3

978-0-06-202719-1

978-0-06-206932-0

978-0-06-204515-7

978-0-06-207998-5

978-0-06-178209-1

At Avon Books, we know your passion for romance—once you finish one of our novels, you find yourself wanting more.

May we tempt you with . . .

- **Excerpts** from our upcoming releases.

- Entertaining **extras**, including authors' personal photo albums and book lists.

- Behind-the-scenes **scoop** on your favorite characters and series.

- **Sweepstakes** for the chance to win free books, romantic getaways, and other fun prizes.

- Writing **tips** from our authors and editors.

- **Blog** with our authors and find out why they love to write romance.

- **Exclusive content** that's not contained within the pages of our novels.

Join us at
www.avonbooks.com

AVON
An Imprint of HarperCollins*Publishers*
www.avonromance.com

Available wherever books are sold or please call 1-800-331-3761 to order.

FTH 0708